HAPPINESS IS A
WARM GUN

THE "INSPIRED BY" SERIES
OF ANTHOLOGIES EDITED BY
JOSH PACHTER

The Beat of Black Wings:
Crime Fiction Inspired by the Songs of Joni Mitchell

The Great Filling Station Holdup:
Crime Fiction Inspired by the Songs of Jimmy Buffett

Only the Good Die Young:
Crime Fiction Inspired by the Songs of Billy Joel

Monkey Business:
Crime Fiction Inspired by the Films of the Marx Brothers

Paranoia Blues:
Crime Fiction Inspired by the Songs of Paul Simon

Happiness is a Warm Gun:
Crime Fiction Inspired by the Songs of The Beatles

JOSH PACHTER, EDITOR

HAPPINESS IS A WARM GUN

Crime Fiction Inspired by the Songs of The Beatles

Down & Out Books
3959 Van Dyke Road, Suite 265
Lutz, FL 33558
DownAndOutBooks.com

The characters and events in this book are fictitious. Any similarity to real persons, living or dead, is coincidental and not intended by the author.

Cover design by Margo Nauert

ISBN: 1-64396-340-6
ISBN-13: 978-1-64396-340-2

TABLE OF CONTENTS

Introduction

It was sixty years ago today—give or take a bit—that the Beatles exploded onto the scene with the 1964 release of their first studio albums, *Introducing...The Beatles* on Vee-Jay Records and *Meet the Beatles!* on Capitol. By the time *Let It Be*, their final studio recording, came out in 1970, less than a decade later, the Fab Four were international superstars, and I'm sure I don't need to tell you that each of them went on to have successful solo careers.

Both collectively and individually, the lives and work of the Beatles have been thoroughly—some might say exhaustively—explored. There've been dozens of film and television documentaries, more than two *thousand* books, and many, many thousands of newspaper and magazine articles.

Want to know what Paul McCartney eats for breakfast? London's *Telegraph* addressed that subject in 2021. Curious about the events leading up to John Lennon's murder? Read Kenneth Womack's *John Lennon 1980: The Last Days in the Life*. Interested in what his family and friends had to say about George Harrison? Martin Scorsese's got you covered with his 2011 film, *Living in the Material World*. Need more info about Ringo Starr? There've been multiple biographies—plus Ringo's own *Another Day in the Life*. Like to test yourself on Beatles trivia? The 'Zon offers paperback quiz books by Peggy Allport, Skylar Emery, Mike Freze, Steven Miller, Dale Raynes, and others—not to mention the special Beatles edition of Trivial Pursuit. And then there's Mark Lewisohn, who's made a career of writing and lecturing about the lads from Liverpool.

So do you really need yet *another* Beatle book competing for your attention?

I hope to be able to convince you that the answer to that question is, in fact, "Yes(terday)!"

In the Swinging 'Sixties, the Fab Four influenced not only popular music but also film (think *A Hard Day's Night* and *Help!*), hairstyles (think Beatle cuts), fashion (think Carnaby Street), and art (think Peter Max). So why not give John, Paul, George, and Ringo an opportunity to influence crime fiction, as well?

As with my previous "inspired by" anthologies—*The Beat of Black Wings: Crime Fiction Inspired by the Songs of Joni Mitchell* (Untreed Reads, 2020), *The Great Filling Station Holdup: Crime Fiction Inspired by the Songs of Jimmy Buffett* (Down & Out Books, 2021), *Only the Good Die Young: Crime Fiction Inspired by the Songs of Billy Joel* (Untreed Reads, 2021), *Monkey Business: Crime Fiction Inspired by the Films of the Marx Brothers* (Untreed Reads, 2021), and *Paranoia Blues: Crime Fiction Inspired by the Songs of Paul Simon* (Down & Out Books, 2022)—readers of crime fiction will find plenty to enjoy in these pages: murders, robberies, kidnappings, a cornucopia of crime in all its permutations and combinations.

Meanwhile, Beatle fans will enjoy teasing out the connections between the stories and the songs that inspired them. And as an extra treat, many of the stories are chock-full of Easter eggs—hidden treasures that nonfans are likely to miss but that'll give the sharp-eyed Beatleologist a chuckle upon discovery.

As I approached this project, the first question I had to wrestle with was which albums to include. I settled on the seventeen U.S. studio releases, from *Introducing...The Beatles* through *Let It Be.*

Think about that: seventeen albums in a span of seven years—actually, just under six and a half years. And then think about this: six of those seventeen albums came out in '64 and another three in '65...so more than half of the Beatles' U.S. recordings were released within a two-year period of truly astounding productivity.

Limiting my contributors' choices to the studio albums, by the way, meant that some terrific songs that didn't appear on any of those records—"Paperback Writer," "Lady Madonna," "Hey Jude," "You Know My Name (Look Up My Number)," and others—were unfortunately not up for consideration. I'm not happy about that, but I had to draw the line *somewhere.*

Speaking of contributors, I began by inviting a number of U.K. authors whose work I admire: Paul Charles (who in addition to his fiction is also the author of *The Beatles Encyclopedia*), Martin Edwards, Vaseem Khan, Tom Mead, Christine Poulson, and Marilyn Todd.

Second, I reached out to a select few of my closest friends in the crime-fiction community—Michael Bracken, David Dean, John Floyd, Rob Lopresti—not just because they're my friends, but because this is the *Beatles,* for heaven's sake, and I know that Michael, David, John, and Rob can be counted on to produce top-quality, award-worthy fiction, practically at the drop of a hat.

Third, you'll also find in this collection stories by John Copenhaver (a very talented novelist who doesn't often write short fiction) and Kal Smagh (who's been writing a series of self-published novels inspired by the Beatles).

Fourth, in all of my anthologies I like to include at least a couple of authors who are either new to writing fiction or at least new to writing *crime* fiction, and for this book I've scored what I consider to be two real coups. First, award-winning crime-fiction bloggers Kristopher Zgorski (of BOLO Books) and Dru Ann Love (of Dru's Book Musings)—both of whom have frequently collaborated on how-to-work-with-a-book-blogger panels at conventions including Malice Domestic and Bouchercon—agreed at my invitation to try their hand for the first time ever at writing fiction of their own, taking as their inspiration the song "Ticket to Ride" from the *Help!* album. And second, nonfiction writer and academic Anjili Babbar presents here her own fiction debut with what I hope you'll agree is a powerful take on "Hey Bulldog" from *Yellow Submarine.*

Finally, readers familiar with my previous "inspired by" books may remember that I wrote the title story myself for each of them. I didn't do so this time, though. Why not?

Well, I originally planned to. But after I'd assigned albums to sixteen other writers, I got an email from Martin Edwards in England. He'd mentioned the project to Kate Ellis, and she was very interested in participating. Was there a chance, Martin asked, that I might have room for her?

I didn't—but I loved the idea of getting Kate involved, so I decided to step aside and let her take over "Happiness Is a Warm Gun."

Later, though, the author who'd accepted the challenge of writing a story inspired by "She Loves You" from *The Beatles' Second Album* wound up turning in a piece that was way too long to be included. We talked about trimming it down, but ultimately agreed that the story was simply too plot-rich to make that possible. That left the book short one story, and with my deadline looming I took up the slack myself and used "I Call Your Name" from the same album as my inspiration.

So, that's the slate of contributors, and you can learn more about them by reading their biographies at the back of this volume. I hope you'll be so please, pleased by their stories that you'll be motivated to seek out more work by those with whom you're not already familiar.

Okay, enough introductory chitchat. It's time now to roll up for the mystery tour and dive into the seventeen stories in *Happiness is a Warm Gun*!

Josh Pachter
Midlothian, Virginia
April 30, 2023

Introducing...The Beatles

Released January 1964

"I Saw Her Standing There"

"Misery"
"Anna (Go to Him)"
"Chains"
"Boys"
"Love Me Do"
"P.S. I Love You"
"Baby, It's You"
"Do You Want to Know a Secret"
"A Taste of Honey"
"There's a Place"
"Twist and Shout"

"Anna (Go to Him)" is by Arthur Alexander.
"Chains" is by Gerry Goffin and Carole King.
"Boys" is by Luther Dixon and Wes Farrell.
"Baby, It's You" is by Burt Bacharach, Mack David,
and Luther Dixon.
"A Taste of Honey" is by Ric Marlow and Bobby Scott.
"Twist and Shout" is by Phil Medley and Bert Russell.
All other songs are by John Lennon and Paul McCartney.

I Saw Her Standing There
Robert Lopresti

When I first saw her, she pissed me off. We were alone on the roof, but she was standing where I needed to be, on the edge, looking across the valley.

Then she turned, and I damn near forgot why I was there. She was porn-star gorgeous and still in her teens.

I headed toward her, like there was no place else in the world to go.

The Knowles home was part of the spell, I guess. It was practically a castle: the edge of the roof had turrets and alternating high-low walls, like in the Robin Hood movies. The flat part was like a patio in the sky, lit by colored lights on poles.

Anything would look magic up there, but *she* would have stopped my heart at the DMV.

She looked up as I reached her, and I saw hazel eyes, my favorite. She smiled.

"Hi," I said.

"Hi, yourself." She frowned, wrinkling her forehead adorably. "Have we met?"

"No, but I'm looking forward to it."

She laughed. "I'm Nicola."

"My name's Fred."

What an idiot. I obviously had to use a phony name, but Fred? *I could have been River. Or Storm. Something cool.*

"How do you know Lindsay?" she asked.

Lindsay. *That* wasn't a bad name. Better than Fred, for God's sake.

"Friend of a friend. I know a guy at his school."

"Oh, yeah?" She gave me a new look. Anyone at Lindsay Knowles's school would have rich parents. "Cool."

"How about you?"

"Oh." She smiled and shrugged. "Some boy invited a friend of mine, and she dragged me along. I don't know where she's gone."

Probably with the boy. There were lots of bedrooms in the mansion, and some must be in use by now.

Lindsay Knowles, world-class spoiled brat, had started planning this party as soon as his parents decided on a second honeymoon in Bermuda. At eighteen, he'd already been to court twice, for DUI and malicious mischief. Considering how rich mommy and daddy were, he must have gotten away with a shitload of other stuff before his luck ran out.

It was sure to be a wild party, but that wasn't why I was here.

Music started playing, Billie Eilish. The hidden speakers were the best money could buy.

"Do you want to dance?"

Nicola grinned. "Sure. But up here, okay? There's a mob scene inside."

That suited me for more reasons than one.

My God, she could move. She was wearing these tight low-rider jeans, and when she swung her hips I thought I'd lose my mind.

We kept going till David Bowie came on. Then Nicola made a face. "I can't stand these cobwebby golden oldies."

I like Bowie but didn't argue. "How old are you, anyway?"

"Seventeen."

Wow. Barely legal, if you know what I mean.

But that was crazy thinking. I would never see her again—

and if I did, I'd be in deep shit.

"How old are *you*?"

"Eighteen." I was actually twenty-two, but this party was for high schoolers. And my brother Mike says I'll still get carded when I'm collecting Social Security.

That's why I was here.

"You can get in without drawing attention," Mike had told me. "Otherwise, I wouldn't let you near this."

"Don't be a mother hen." We were in the apartment we shared, though he paid most of the rent. "I'm an adult."

"Yeah, but you're a screwup."

"Not fair."

"Says the only shoplifter in history to get caught by a blind woman."

"Missus Klein isn't blind. She just has bad eyes."

"Not bad enough. And that time I sent you to deliver some cash, you traded it for magic beans."

"Don't be a smartass." I had gotten mugged.

"My ass is smarter than you are, Jeremy." Mike swigged beer. "But the guys agree we need your baby face."

"The guys" were Mike's partners. Epstein was the brains, Jackson the muscle. Neither was a member of my fan club. They were coming over to plan the heist, which is why Mike was explaining things, "so you don't stick your sneaker in your mouth as usual."

"You're a riot."

"You know who the Algernons are?"

Of course I knew. They were famous husband-and-wife tech geniuses, now retired to Lester Heights, one county over.

"Well, they ain't home. Gone on a spiritual adventure to India or someplace. There's nobody in their palace except security guards."

"Whoa. I've seen videos of their joint. It's like a museum."

11

"Bingo. Now get this. The night guard isn't happy. He spends the afternoons in bars griping about how bored he is."

"Bored? They've got a swimming pool and a home theater and God knows what."

Mike nodded. "But if he gets caught bringing in ladies, he'll be out on his ass."

"How does that help us?"

My brother grinned. "What he hates most is Martha."

"Who's she?"

"A bitch. Literally. The Algernons have an English sheepdog. Old and incontinent."

"What's that mean?"

"She shits everywhere. And Rocky—that's the guard—has to clean up after her, which is not in his job description. Martha can't hold it overnight, so when she starts whining, he has to let her out in the backyard and stay there to protect her from, I don't know, coyotes or something."

"That sucks," I said. "But *how* does it help us?"

Mike grinned again. "Rocky says the Algernons skimped on the alarm system. When he turns it off to open the back door, it's off all over the freaking mansion."

Nicola and me danced until something by Death Cab for Cutie came on. "Another song my mother would know," she complained. "Where can we get a drink?"

"There's beer down a flight. Be right back." I was supposed to stay on the roof, but I figured I had time for a quick beer run.

I wanted to bring up a whole cooler, but it was too heavy. I spied a jock passing by.

"Hey, little help here."

Together, we lugged it up to the roof.

"Whoa," he said. "I didn't know this was up here. Cool!"

He hustled away as I handed Nicola a beer.

"Now you've done it," she said.

12

I SAW HER STANDING THERE

"What do you mean?"

"He'll bring the whole football team. We won't have any privacy."

In my head, Mike yelled: *You're not on the hill to hook up, fool. You're the lookout.*

The problem for Mike and his friends was how to know when Rocky let the dog out. The Algernons' backyard was half the size of a football field, surrounded by brick walls and trees—no way to see in—and their outdoor lights stayed on all night. Plus, the bitch didn't bark, so that was no help.

"There's no place to watch from," Mike had said.

"You can't do it from the road?"

"There are cops nearby, guarding the billionaires. Park for five minutes, and they'll be on your ass. No, the only place to see in is from the Knowles mansion. And that brat of theirs is gonna party while mama and daddy are away."

All I had to do, Mike said, was take an Uber there, convince the bouncer I was part of the prep-school crowd, and stay on the roof until Rocky loosed the mutt. Then I'd text the boys, and they'd go in.

"What if the Algernons' door is locked?"

"Of course it's locked, genius. But Epstein can get through with a bump key, once the alarm is off."

"What if the guard hears you?"

"He'll be out back with poochie. First thing he'll know about it, we'll have him tied up and blindfolded."

"Great. And how do I get away?"

"We'll text you when we're leaving. Just walk up the street and wait for us." Mike shrugged. "So simple even *you* can't screw it up."

"What are you looking at?" Nicola asked.

13

I sipped beer. "The view. It's fantastic." Mike was right: I could look straight down into the Algernons' brightly lit yard.

"Rich people, huh?" She shook her head. "It's not enough they own everything; they need the prettiest views of whatever they *don't* own. Do you know whose mansion that is?"

I almost told her, but she might ask: *how do you know that?*

"Nope. All billionaires look alike to me."

She laughed. It made me dizzy.

The speakers started playing "Let's Go to Hell" by Tai Verdes.

"I love this one!"

We danced. Damn, she was good.

When the song ended, there were a dozen more people on the roof. I hadn't even noticed them arriving.

"They found us," Nicola said.

"No more privacy."

She frowned and turned away. "I think I've got all the privacy I need, thanks."

What happened? Had I screwed up somehow?

"Hey, you wanna dance?" It was a tall Goth with a ponytail and half a dozen piercings. I couldn't imagine he was her type, but Nicola smiled.

"Sure!"

Maybe she just liked weirdos.

The valley was still empty. Wasn't that damned sheepdog ever going to need a piss?

"Come on, Martha," I muttered.

"'Scuse me?"

Another girl had come up to me, a pretty blonde with a gap between her front teeth.

"Just talking to myself. You can listen if you want."

"Will you say anything interesting?"

"How would I know?" I looked at her empty hands. "Can I get you a beer?"

She nodded.

I headed over to the cooler and snagged two bottles. Turning around, I saw Nicola dancing with the Goth.

I almost dropped the beers. Something in the way she looked, dancing with him....

The blonde just sort of faded away, and when the song ended Nicola patted the Goth on the chest and walked back to the roof's edge. I headed over there and saw the blonde giving me the finger.

I handed Nicola a bottle. "Who's your new friend?"

She laughed. "Some punk who thinks his daddy's money makes him special. His pick-up line? 'We should get matching tattoos.'"

"Gross."

"You don't think that's a good idea for a first date?" She did a little spin and tapped her chest. "Maybe a blackbird right here?"

"It wouldn't be as pretty as what it covers."

"Aw, you're sweet." She looked down at the beer in her hand. "Speaking of sweet, I need something nonalcoholic. Do they have Cokes?"

"I saw some in the home theater, or whatever they call that mausoleum one flight down. Be right back."

While I hustled through the packed hallway, I was trying to figure out how to see Nicola again. Like tomorrow.

I had to hip-check a chunky redhead for the last two Cokes. She flipped me the bird, making it two girls in an hour. But who cared? Nicola liked me.

When I got back to the roof, she was thumbing her phone. I felt a ridiculous burst of jealousy.

"Giving Goth boy another chance?"

She laughed. "Christ, no. I just got a text from Wendy."

"Who's that?"

"The girl I came with. She's off with some new dude, the slut."

"Hopefully not to get a tattoo."

"She's got full sleeves. Oh, I love this song."

It was "Tell Me" by Hunter Hayes. A slow one.

She put her arms around my neck, and we started. I bumped into someone and was shocked, because I had forgotten anyone else was there.

"Something on your mind?" Nicola asked.

"Yeah. But it's too crowded for it."

"Maybe later."

That got my blood pumping. I looked away, trying to calm down, and—

The Algernons' back door was wide open.

I pushed Nicola away and hurried to the wall. There was a man with a dog in the backyard. Martha had finally heard Mother Nature's call.

"Shit."

"What's wrong?"

"I gotta send a text."

"Who to?"

"Doesn't matter." How long had Rocky and the pooch been there? How long since I'd last looked in that direction?

I texted Mike: *Now.*

The reply came back instantly: *K.*

Nicola stepped in front of me, but I stayed focused on the scene below. Mike and his pals were three blocks east, the closest they could park without being hassled by cops. Now they had to race over and get through the locked front door before Rocky came back inside and reset the alarm.

"What's going on?" Nicola looked from me to the mansion and back. "What's happening?"

"Just wondering who's out there. Is that a dog?"

"Sure is. What's he doing out in the middle of the night?"

I almost said, *she's a she.*

"Out for a pee, I guess."

Nicola laughed. "Well, duh. I should have thought of that. Let's dance."

16

What the hell. There was nothing more I could do for the guys.

She moved free as a bird, all rhythmic and smooth.

Two more songs, and I saw the doors were shut again. Rocky must have taken the dog back in.

By now Epstein would be through the lock, and the guys would have Rocky tied up. The plan was they'd be out in ten minutes, max.

Another slow dance. I clung to Nicola like a drowning man.

"You've got great moves," she said.

"I think I love you."

She pushed away, eyes and mouth wide. "That's not funny, Fred."

"No joke." I shook my head. "Look, I know it's crazy, but I've never felt—"

"Wait. Just wait." She was checking her phone.

"Who is it?"

"Wendy again. Romeo's getting freaky, and she wants me to pick her up."

I checked my phone. Mike should have texted me by now.

I sent: *OK?*

"What is it?"

Come on, Mike.

"Fred?" She looked from me to the mansion. "What are you up to?"

"I have to get down there."

Her eyes were wide. "Something *is* going on. What are you mixed up in?"

I put my phone away. Then I pulled it out again. "I need an Uber. Look, Nicola, I wish I could stay and get to know you, but I have to go."

She shook her head. "It's Saturday night. Sunday morning. It'll take an hour to get a ride out here. I'll take you."

"I can't ask you to leave."

"I have to pick up Wendy, remember? But she can wait.

17

Sounds like Romeo is too drunk to do much harm. You've got yourself a driver."

And she slipped away through the dancers. I followed her.

This was crazy. I imagined talking to my grandchildren someday.

Grandpa, tell us about your first date.

I took your Nana to a home invasion.

But I had to find out what had happened to the guys, and short of jumping off the roof and running through the valley there was no other way to get there.

Her car was a silver Audi. We climbed in, and she started the engine.

"Why are you so desperate to go to that house?"

"It's better you don't know."

"Oh, shit." She slammed into gear. "I didn't peg you for a bad boy, Fred. Why do I always pick 'em?"

"I'm not bad."

"Yeah? What's going *on* in that house you've been spying on all night?" She took a corner way too fast. "Lemme guess. You're watching terrorists for the FBI."

"Take it easy. You don't want to—"

"What? Attract cops? Maybe that's what I *should* do. Drive straight to the police."

I was beginning to panic. "You can't do that."

"No?" She turned and glared at me.

Watch the road!

"What'll you do if I try? Hurt me?"

"No. Never."

Nicola turned onto the Algernons' street.

"I believe you, Fred. Not about loving me, and not about being bad—"

"I swear! I meant every word!"

"—but I don't think you'd hurt me." She turned up the driveway. "Now let's see what kind of shitstorm you've fallen into."

Mike's car was there. So was a dark blue van. The guys must have stolen it to carry stuff.

Nicola climbed out and I followed. I was wondering how to explain this to Mike. Who brings a date to a robbery, for God's sake?

The front door was high above street level, up a set of steps like in a courthouse on a cop show. A scary thought.

"Door's open," Nicola said.

"Wait." I grabbed her arm. "We can't just walk in there."

She shook me off. "Watch me."

She ran up the steps. I followed.

There was a big man just inside, and he wasn't one of Mike's friends. The gun in his hand made him look like a freaking giant.

He did a doubletake. "Sadie? Who's the brat?"

She let the Hulk step between us. "He was their lookout, Dan. I had to bring him, 'cause he was gawking like the yard was full of strippers. People were beginning to notice."

My jaw was hanging. "What the hell—?"

Dan hit me in the gut. "Shut up, Honey Pie." He looked back at Nicola, who he had called Sadie. "If you had to, you had to. Do the honors."

I lay on my stomach, trying to breathe. She climbed on top, grabbed my hands, and tied them together with something he'd given her.

"On your feet, Freddy."

I couldn't breathe to talk.

Dan did most of the shoving as they took me through a long hallway into a room bigger than the assembly hall at my high school.

There was another guy there, built like a football player, all in black, also carrying a gun.

"Sadie!" He held out his arms and she—whatever her name was—rushed into them. He grabbed her ass with his free hand.

"How's it going, Martin?" she asked.

"Aces. The van is nearly full. Desmond's emptying the safe.

Thanks for warning us about the amateurs. They strolled right in."

He waved a hand at four men lying against the wall. They were hog-tied, with duct tape across their mouths.

Mike, Jackson, and Epstein stared back at me. They weren't happy. The fourth guy was a stranger; the security guard, I guessed. Now I heard a dog scratching on a door down the hall. Martha was in a bad mood, too.

Nicola pulled away from the football player and turned to me. "You're a great dancer, Freddy, but not much of a spy."

"You bitch."

She put on a mock frown. "Is that any way to talk to the woman you love?"

She gave me a quick peck on the lips, then covered my mouth with duct tape.

Two more men came in, carrying a painting half the size of a billboard.

"Careful with that," Martin said. "The insurance company will pay a shitload for it."

"Safe's empty," one said, "and the cameras are dead. What'll we do with the B Team?"

The football player looked at Mike and the others. Then he looked at me.

It hit me: we might not get out of this alive. Why leave witnesses?

I am such a loser.

"Put the boy toy with the others for now."

Nicola/Sadie grinned at me. "You know my name, sweetheartSweetheart. Two of them, in fact. Gimme a call sometime."

Martin laughed.

She reached toward me, and I lunged. My arms were pinned behind my back, but I slammed into her and she tumbled.

Her boyfriend yelled, but I slipped past him and ran for my life.

If I could get away, free myself, I could at least call the cops. We'd get arrested but stay alive.

I passed the front door.

One of the thugs was backing out of the van. I jogged to the left to dodge him.

Ever try to run down a flight of stone steps with your hands tied behind your back?

Flying.

Crashing.

It was the hardest fall I ever took. A streak of white fire shot down my left shin, like Jose Ramirez had swung on it with a baseball bat.

I blacked out for a second. *Open your eyes now.* I did, and the stars were spinning overhead. I felt a wave of nausea.

Then the pain in my leg said hello. My jeans were torn, and I saw blood leaking and bone sticking out. A compound fracture. It hurt like a kick in the balls.

I lay back and watched the bright stars shine. Nicola's friends hustled by.

She stood over me, examining my leg with mild curiosity.

"Wow, Fred, that's quite a booboo." She turned away. "Looks like it'll be a while before you dance again."

She was wrong about that. I should have known better than to trust her, but I'd learned my lesson. From now on, I'll never dance with another girl.

Meet The Beatles!

Released January 1964

"I Want to Hold Your Hand"
"I Saw Her Standing There"
"This Boy"
"It Won't Be Long"
"All I've Got to Do"
"All My Loving"
"Don't Bother Me"
"Little Child"
"Till There Was You"
"Hold Me Tight"
"I Wanna Be Your Man"
"Not a Second Time"

"Don't Bother Me" is by George Harrison.
"Till There Was You" is by Meredith Willson.
All other songs are by John Lennon and Paul McCartney.

Don't Bother Me
Kal Smagh

November 12, 2022
Miami, Florida

When I checked my news feed, the first headline read: *Van der Veen's Vote Decides Deauville's Doom.*

zfather, the city councilman who'd cast the swing vote that would bring the old hotel down within the next twenty-four hours.

Weather permitting.

Outside, a siren blared, a mournful wail. Its rise and fall made the hair on the back of my neck stand up.

"It won't be long now," Dad said. "Tomorrow's D-Day." We were standing in his designer home of muted greige. It smelled of roses in here, while outside an epic storm brewed, the sky a hushed metal dome. "That's D for Demolition, dummy."

"I get it," I said. "I'm not as dumb as you think."

He cleared his throat. "After they canned her, your *oma* was arrested trying to break into the damn place. Eight times, she tried! She'd roll over in her grave if she knew I was the one who finally brought the old wreck down."

I looked at the brown urn on the mantle, the one that held her ashes. "You had her cremated," I said. "She doesn't have a grave."

His eyes narrowed, and I could feel another insult coming on. That was how my father kept control, a tactic of his political life that bled into his personal relationships.

"It's an expression, Craig. If you'd gone to college, you'd know that." His eyes studied me derisively. "And maybe you'd wear better clothes. And not have a kid half your age."

That one stung.

My grandmother—my *oma*, born in The Netherlands—was an enigma. She'd been in the Dutch Resistance during World War II, was taken prisoner and carted off to a German labor camp, where she worked as the commandant's maid. According to Dad, the commandant lived well in a house adorned with artworks the Nazis had looted from their rightful owners. When the war ended, he managed to escape, and no one knew where he wound up or what happened to him. Oma made her way to Florida, became a maid at the Deauville, and was later fired for stealing from the hotel's wealthy guests.

The way my father told the story, they let her go the week after the Beatles' famous visit, and she couldn't find another job. Hotel managers talk.

"Did you ever ask her why she kept trespassing?"

"I never cared. We fought about it, and I admit I got pretty nasty. Told her she was a lunatic, a miserable Nazi whore. After that, she never said another word about it, just muttered to herself in Dutch."

"Saying what?"

"Stupid things. *Was het verleden schoon met nieuwe lucht.* Some bullshit about washing the past with fresh air."

"Anything else?"

"I remember her saying *val me niet lastig, jongen.* 'Don't bother me, boy.' I don't think she liked me very much. She was crazy about you, though, for some damn reason. Then she got run over in 1990. She was sixty-five."

* * *

I have only a few memories of my grandmother.

Once, when I was a little kid, we saw a man walking a dog, and she said it looked like the German Shepherds she'd seen in the war. Another time, she told me there were twelve wooden steps leading up to the big house where she'd worked in the camp.

Little things like that stuck in my head.

She was killed crossing the street. The driver was a tourist, an older guy—he had to have been eighty if he was a day. Said he didn't know the area. Now her death was part of our broken family history.

Dad was right: he was her son and she loved him, but she didn't really *like* him. She called him a "goody-goody boy."

I remember her telling me, "Craigie, sometimes it's okay to be a bad boy. Every day there is fresh air that washes away the bad. Don't forget that."

That was thirty years ago. I still think of it, every now and then.

The trailer I share with my daughter Shiloh shook in the wind. I was only seventeen when she was born—the same age she is now. Her mother was fifteen and is long out of the picture.

"He's happy the Deauville's coming down," I told her.

"Why?"

I shrugged. "Purges his demons, I guess."

"You mean from your *oma*?"

I nodded. "I think that's why he went into politics in the first place, to dispel the family shame. Or cover it in rubble."

Shiloh said, "We should go look at it."

"The Deauville? It's a dilapidated shell."

"I think you need to take a look, Dad."

"Why?"

Her arm went around my shoulder. "For closure."

I laughed. "I don't need closure. Until there was you, kiddo, I wandered aimlessly through my life. All I've got to do now is give you a better father than the one I had."

She shook her head. "You're walking in your *oma*'s shadow, just like him, and you won't even acknowledge it."

I hated that she had me pegged like that.

"Come on," she added, crossing the worn linoleum to our cramped avocado kitchenette. "Let's check out what the good life used to look like."

"What do you know about the good life?" I dropped onto our shabby sofa. "And what's so special about the Deauville, anyway?"

"Your *oma* got arrested there, and your dad hates it."

She never called him Opa, or even Grandpa.

In the end, we drove down to 67th and Collins under a leaden sky of swirling clouds and helicoptering palm fronds. A crowd was lined up outside the hotel like an undulating snake. We had to park blocks away and walk back, Shiloh's hands on her hair in a futile effort to keep it from tangling.

A chain-link fence threaded with long strips of green canvas surrounded the perimeter, and security guards in gray uniforms patrolled the street to keep out protesters shouting, "Save the Deauville!"

The decision makers couldn't hear them, of course. They were in their open-floor-plan McMansions, sipping cocktails and eating canapes.

Once upon a time, the glitterati had vacationed in that sagging old relic, and my *oma* was just a nobody. The land-of-plenty thing had never worked out for her. Later, she became what the police would have referred to as a public nuisance. They probably asked her to leave nicely at first, then later more sternly.

A part of me needed to know why the Deauville had affected Oma so deeply—and why she'd tried so hard to break in, again and again, in the weeks after the Beatles left.

***

Shiloh was better at the internet than I was, her fingers faster on the keyboard. "The five-hundred-and-thirty-eight-room hotel," she read aloud from the screen of the library's computer—I couldn't afford to give her one of her own—"was built in 1957 and occupies nearly four acres of prime oceanfront real estate. Stretching for several city blocks, the resort...blah, blah, blah...okay, check this out: rooms 1211, 1215, and 1218."

"The Beatles' rooms?"

"Looks like it. How old was Oma in 1964?"

"She was born in '25, so, um, thirty-nine?"

I felt a sudden wave of nausea at the thought of Oma in the war. She would have been seventeen in 1942, Shiloh's age.

"What are you thinking?" my daughter demanded.

"Nothing."

She turned back to the screen. "It says here they met Cassius Clay."

"I thought he'd changed his name by then."

"Like I care? Hey, look, they used to have a sign with a star over the 'i' in Deauville. Cute." She clicked on a video, and our conversation faded into unspoken tension at our crumbling family legacy.

Three hours later, back in our darkened trailer, Shiloh was in bed after a mostly silent supper and I was dressed in black and clicking a flashlight on and off, trying to talk myself out of the insane plan I had cooked up for the Deauville's final night.

She appeared at my door, fully dressed. "I'm going with you, Dad."

I glanced up soberly. "Nope."

"I'd rather be arrested with you than sit alone here worrying."

"If you come with me, who'll bail me out when I get arrested?"

We argued back and forth, but she finally wore me down.

"At least stick this in your backpack," I said, giving up, and handed her a heavy monkey wrench for just-in-case.

Diagonal rods of rain pelted the deserted Miami streets. Once again, I parked blocks away—this time to make sure no surveillance cameras would record the plate number of the heap I drove. Streetlights flickered around us, and Shiloh held onto my arm as we leaned into the wind.

"Look out for cops," I said.

She replied, but her words were carried away in a gust of wind.

By the time we climbed the fence and ducked under the *porte cochère* that had welcomed Sinatra, Louis Armstrong, JFK, and so many other famous people, we were soaked.

"After Ed Sullivan in New York," Shiloh panted, "the Beatles went to Washington and played a sold-out show. Then they came here and stayed for eight days."

"Shiloh, this is crazy. We should turn around and—"

"Stop, Dad." Her jaw jutted out. "We won't get another chance after tonight."

She was right. I wanted to hold her hand—more to reassure *myself* than her—but she wasn't a little child anymore. It wouldn't be long before she was more of an adult than I was.

The glass doors weren't locked, and we went into the darkened lobby.

"The Beatles did a promo with Muhammad Ali here," Shiloh said, her voice echoing in the huge open space. "Before the name change."

"I thought you didn't care."

"I changed my mind." She put a hand over my flashlight, and I clicked it off. "Someone's here," she said, her voice barely audible over the raging wind outside.

In the distance, a white beam bounced off a wall. I grabbed

Shiloh's arm and pulled her up the lobby stairs to the landing. We crouched down and struggled to calm our breathing. The light disappeared, and we let a full minute pass. There was something on the floor beside me, and I felt for it and picked it up. It was, for some reason, an old discarded shoe. In the dim light that filtered up from below, I saw that it was brown. I wondered whose it was.

"Who was that?" Shiloh whispered.

"Security guard."

We moved on into a dim ballroom, where broken windows admitted blasts of wind. I pointed at the dilapidated wooden stage. "Lots of history there," I said. "The Beatles, the Rat Pack—"

"The *Rat* Pack?"

"Look it up. Frank Sinatra, Sammy Davis Junior, Dean Martin—"

The ballroom door opened, and a flashlight poked through the crack. I pulled Shiloh to the floor. The light panned across the room, then vanished, and the door closed with a *whump*.

"Up the fire stairs," I said. "To Oma's floor."

The empty building shook with wind. We climbed as quickly as we could without making unnecessary noise, not sure whether the security guards were bothering with the upper stories.

By the time we got to twelve, my lungs were tight, my thighs burning.

The fire door opened with a mournful creak.

I was lightheaded. This was where my *oma* had worked—until she was fired. Why had they let her go? What did they think she had stolen? And what had made her come back, only to be arrested over and over?

"What are we looking for?" Shiloh asked.

I shrugged. "Your grandfather says she used to talk about 'washing the past with fresh air,' and I remember her saying

31

something similar to me. Otherwise, I have no idea."

This was the room where John Lennon stayed with his first wife, Cynthia. It would have been luxurious then, with a gorgeous view of Miami Beach. I glanced out the rattling windows. In the hurricane, the black ocean looked angry.

The room had been stripped of its bed and other furniture long ago. Squatters had graffitied the walls in blue and black, and the carpet was torn in patches, revealing concrete. Yellowed wallpaper fell in strips from where its glue had given way in the humidity since the air-conditioning had been shut off.

I pictured Oma cleaning up after the Beatles, perhaps even talking to them in the hallway.

Nonsense. She was just a maid. Why would they—or any other guests—take time to befriend her? The only time anyone ever addressed her was probably just to ask for new towels.

"Next room," I said.

Shiloh followed me to 1215 ("Ringo Starr and Paul McCartney roomed together here," she said) and then 1218 ("George Harrison slept here").

We checked the bathroom, where the wallpaper had been stripped bare. When I trained my light on it, I saw a graffitied yellow flower on the gray wallboard.

Outside, a door opened and closed, and an accented male voice—deep and menacing—shouted, "Stop what you are doing!"

I gripped Shiloh's arm, pulled her to the floor.

Rain pelted the windows, heavy footsteps moved away from us down the hall, and the voice shouted, "Drop whatever it is you're looting and get out of here!"

"Come on," I whispered. "Quick." Desperate to escape, I pulled open Room 1218's door—to find a flashlight beam drilling into my eyes. Those footsteps had been a trick, and I'd fallen for it.

There was an ominous click, and I made out the shape of a pistol held by a blond man in an overcoat. His forefinger tightened on the trigger, and I swung a fist wildly.

The man grabbed me and threw me against a wall. I fell, my head smashing against a metal grate that covered an air-conditioning vent near the floor.

Shiloh shrieked as the guy gripped my throat. He bashed my face against the grate, which buckled, one edge gashing my forehead. He pressed the barrel of his gun into my nose, his knee heavy on my chest. I gasped—and then he collapsed to the floor beside me, his flashlight twisted to illuminate a pair of yellow eyes that fell slowly closed.

Shiloh pulled at me. "Dad! Get up!"

I struggled to my feet, ears ringing. My daughter was holding the monkey wrench I'd given her earlier.

The man on the floor lay motionless, the back of his head bleeding.

"We have to go, Dad, before he comes to."

Something glinted in the light of Shiloh's flash. She knelt and retrieved a tarnished metal key that had been taped to the inside of the metal grate I'd fallen against.

Back at our trailer, Shiloh pulled open the freezer, wrapped a bag of frozen peas in a dish towel, and handed it to me.

"That guy was not Security," I muttered, touching the cold pack gingerly to my forehead.

"Look at this," she said.

Stamped into the key she'd found hidden behind Room 1218's busted A/C register—from which "fresh air" had once flowed—were the words "5TH ST. GYM."

The next morning, right around the time the Deauville finally imploded, Shiloh and I stepped into the 5th Street Gym, a haven for prizefighters.

An old man limped toward us, looked me up and down, and said, "Looks like you lost."

I nodded, "Maybe. Does this key mean anything to you?"

He squinted at it, and then his rheumy eyes went wide.

"How that come to you?"

"We found it."

"Where?"

"The Deauville Hotel," Shiloh said.

The man sniffed. "What's your name, son?"

"Craig Van der Veen."

The corners of his lips twitched, and he blinked rapidly. "I can't believe it." Turning away, he called over his shoulder, "Come with me."

In his office, four metal lockers were bolted to the wall. He pointed at the one on the far right. "Some little old lady rented that one, long ago. The owner told me the story when he retired and I took this place over, said a man named Craig had the key and would show up someday. I moved these lockers here when the old place across the street was leveled."

I slid the key into the lock and twisted, and the door swung open.

There were three packages inside the locker, and on top of them a white envelope with the words READ ME FIRST on the outside.

I tore open the flap and slid out a sheet of paper. In faded ink, in a handwriting I recognized, I read:

My dearest Craig,

I trust that you have learned to love yourself, and to love and care for your children. (Oh, I pray that you have been blessed with children!)

One of these things was a gift, but the others I brought with me when I left Germany. Perhaps their loss caused my captor some pain. I hope so. Please sell them or destroy them, which-ever you please—but do not return them to that monster.

I am pleased that you found my treasure. You were always a bright boy, much smarter than your father. Please forgive him. I know that, in his own way, he loved us both.

Oma

Shiloh removed the three packages and set them on the old man's desktop.

The first was swaddled in black cloth and clinked in my palm as I unwrapped it to reveal two gold wedding rings and a necklace with an embossed swastika.

The second package contained a small painting of a boy and a girl standing beside a seated couple who were obviously their parents. Their father wore a Nazi uniform. I stared at their faces, a lump rising in my throat. This must be the commandant and his wife and children, the family who lived in the big house, up the twelve steps.

The final package was wrapped in a *Stamp Out the Beatles* sweatshirt and held a boxing glove that bore the signatures of John Lennon, Paul McCartney, George Harrison, Ringo Starr, and Cassius Clay in blue marker on the red leather.

Had she stolen the glove from the Deauville, as she had stolen the other items from the commandant's home? Was it this that had gotten her fired? And had she returned to the hotel so many times after her dismissal to retrieve the key she had hidden?

"There's something inside the glove," Shiloh said.

I eased out a sheet of hotel stationery, yellowed with age.

Patricia,
It was a pleasure chatting with you. Here is a gift from the five of us. Hang onto it—it might be worth money one day. (Hopefully it won't be long!) I'll never be the same after hearing your story.
Best wishes,
George

Oma Patricia had seen people living high in the world. She'd taken her Nazi captor's wedding ring, his wife's ring and necklace, and their family portrait to avenge her captivity. She'd stashed these items at the gym—along with the signed glove

George Harrison had given her—and hidden the key to the locker in what had been George's room at the Deauville. But she'd also stolen—or was believed to have stolen—from the hotel's guests, which led to her being fired before she could retrieve the key…which led in turn to her trespassing and multiple arrests.

Somehow, someone—the commandant's son? his grandson?—had learned of the existence of the locker and key, and it was our bad luck that he'd gone after it on the last night of the Deauville's existence.

The old man whistled at the items laid out on his desk. "What you gone do with all these things?" he asked. "Sell 'em, like she say?"

"Not a chance," Shiloh announced.

And I realized in that moment that Oma had been right: sometimes it's okay to be a bad boy.

I pulled my daughter to me, holding her tight, happy to have her by my side—and happy to have a part of my grandmother back in my life again, too.

The Beatles' Second Album
Released April 1964

"Roll Over Beethoven"
"Thank You Girl"
"You Really Got a Hold on Me"
"Devil in Her Heart"
"Money (That's What I Want)"
"You Can't Do That"
"Long Tall Sally"
"I Call Your Name"
"Please Mr. Postman"
"I'll Get You"
"She Loves You"

"Roll Over Beethoven" is by Chuck Berry.
"You Really Got a Hold on Me" is by Smokey Robinson.
"Devil in Her Heart" is by Richard Drapkin.
"Money (That's What I Want)" is by Janie Bradford
and Berry Gordy, Jr.
"Long Tall Sally" is by Enotris Johnson, Richard Penniman,
and Robert Blackwell.
"Please Mr. Postman" is by Brian Holland, Robert Bateman,
William Garrett, Georgia Dobbins, and Fred Gorman.
All other songs are by John Lennon and Paul McCartney.

I Call Your Name
Josh Pachter

You have to keep in mind that I'm a cop—and as corny as it may seem, a *good* cop. It's easy to put us in a bad light these days, what with Rodney King and Eric Garner and Tamir Rice and Breonna Taylor and Tyre Nichols and all the rest of them, but most of us are horrified by the atrocities committed by a comparatively small number of bad apples in blue, and we truly *believe* that our job is to protect and serve.

I grew up in WaKeeny, Kansas, where my father was a Trego County sheriff's deputy. For my sixth birthday, mama and papa gave me one of those twelve-piece Fisher-Price uniform sets, complete with hat, badge, and plastic sidearm, holster, nightstick, cuffs, and walkie-talkie, and from that moment on I knew that I wanted to be a peace officer like my dad when I grew up. I think the proudest moment of my life was when I graduated from the academy. Papa was county sheriff by then, and he gave me my first job. I'll never forget the pride in his eyes when he pinned that star above the left pocket of my uniform shirt.

Someone was shaking my shoulder, and I rolled over, groaning.

"Denny, wake up!" It was my wife Michelle. "You're doing it again, babe."

"Wha—?" I said blearily.

"You're having that nightmare."

Ever since we moved into the house we bought when we got married, I can't sleep at night, and when I *do* manage to drop off, bad dreams keep me tossing and turning.

"Sorry," I mumbled. "I don't know why—"

She stroked my cheek, soothing me. "It was different this time, though, honey."

I came fully awake and sat up in bed, my mouth dry, my tongue furry. "Different how?"

"You were talking. You kept saying something about *cats*."

"Cats?"

"Cats. Were you dreaming about cats?"

"I don't know. Maybe. I guess."

"You seemed so sad."

"Really? Was I crying?"

"No, you never weep at night."

"Cats," I said, shaking my head. "That's weird."

But it *wasn't* weird, not really. Because I wasn't muttering "cats" in my sleep. I was calling your name, Cass.

I find myself thinking about you more and more lately, Cassie, about *us*, about our history. You know the story as well as I do: we grew up across the street from each other in WaKeeny, went through grade school and junior high together, were teenage sweethearts and tied the knot less than a year after graduation.

In retrospect, we should have waited. We were *kids*, practically children, certainly too young to get married.

We each knew what we wanted individually. You'd played the female leads in our high-school productions of *Bye Bye Birdie* and *The King and I* and had the standard small-town dreams of going to Hollywood and making it in the movies. And of course I knew what I wanted: a *real* uniform and badge.

You were there at the Trego County Courthouse the day I got them, and I think you were every bit as proud of me as my father.

But we didn't know what *we* wanted, for us together as a couple, and I suppose it was inevitable that our marriage would fall apart.

After it did, WaKeeny just held too many memories for me. So I kissed my mama's cheek and shook my papa's hand and came up here to the Dakotas—South Dakota, to be exact— where I'd applied for and gotten an offer to sign on with the Minnehaha County Sheriff's Office in Sioux Falls.

It was a chance to start over, and I didn't think the fact that I'd spent two and a half years married down in Kansas was anybody's business, so I never told anyone about you, about us.

But I thank you, girl, for a lot of wonderful memories. I miss you, Cass, and though I love Michelle, I'm sorry things didn't work out for us. I guess that's why I've been calling your name in my dreams. Even when I'm asleep, you've still got a hold on me.

When I parked the cruiser in the driveway the next night and popped my Billy Joel CD from the player and went into the house, all the lights were out and Michelle was planted in front of the television, a bowl of popcorn beside her on the sofa. On the screen, three guys were sitting at the bar in a bowling alley, heads-on to the camera, and the heavyset goateed one on the right was gesturing with a cigarette and telling the other two something that sounded like, "Say what you want about the tenants of National Socialism, dudes, at least it's an ethos."

"Whatcha watchin'?" I asked.

"I don't know," she said. "Some movie. You want pop-corn?"

"Nah," I said. "I'm pretty whipped, Mish. I'm gonna go to bed."

"Don't dream about cats, you hear?"

"I'll do my best." I leaned over the back of the sofa and

41

kissed the top of her head, and she made a smooching noise with her lips without taking her eyes off the TV.

The thing is, see, when my partner Elliot Doherty and I worked the night shift back in WaKeeny, we got in the habit of hitting the bar after we clocked out. We'd have a couple of beers, maybe a shot or two, kill an hour before he took off for his doublewide and I headed home to the upstairs half of the century house you and I rented on Junction Avenue, Cass.

And that meant you wound up spending a lot of evenings alone. I guess I was being unfair, selfish—fine, let's just stipulate I was an asshole—and I suppose that means I was to blame for your getting involved with Phil Johns. Thinking back, I imagine you reached a point where you just couldn't take the loneliness anymore. And to be honest, I don't know who *could* have, under those circumstances.

Michelle and I met a few weeks after I started my job in Sioux Falls. She was waiting tables at the Bread & Circus Sandwich Kitchen, right across the parking lot that serves the Sheriff's Office, the SFPD, Animal Control, and the South Dakota Association of School Resource Officers. I used to go in there for lunch when I was working days, and after a while she and I got to talking, the way you do. There was no ring on her wedding finger, and I finally got up the nerve to ask her out.

We dated for a while, the way you do. She was two years younger than me, a pretty little thing, I don't know *why* she wasn't already married.

Neither one of us was religious, so we didn't want a fancy ceremony. We got hitched late one Friday morning, outdoors, in the Japanese Gardens next to Covell Lake, us and her parents—she was an only child—and a preacher we found online. We invited Rev Deb to join us for lunch at Parker's Bistro after, but she had another commitment, so it was just the four of us. Then Mishie and I got in her car and drove the two hundred and forty miles northeast for a long weekend at a nice bed and breakfast in Minneapolis.

Like I said, we weren't religious, but Michelle was old-fashioned enough that we didn't move into the house we'd bought until we returned from our honeymoon.

Everything was fine for a while. We worked our jobs, took turns cooking supper and cleaning up the kitchen after, ate popcorn in front of the TV, laughing at syndicated reruns of Jerry, George, Elaine, and Kramer. We went to bed together, like you do, and that was soft and warm and good.

But then the nightmares started. I would toss and turn and moan and groan, and of course Mishie couldn't sleep through all that commotion, so she'd get up and go back out to the living room and stare at the tube until I settled down.

The nightmares got worse, though, started earlier and lasted longer, and we got in the habit of me going to bed first and her waiting until I'd finished wrestling my pillow before she slipped in beside me.

And now things had taken a new turn, and I was talking about "cats" in my sleep.

When I found out about you and Phil Johns, well, that tore it for me. We were supposed to be faithful to each other till the end of time. Once I knew you were cheating on me, Cass—well, I couldn't stay married to you. That was flat-out not an option.

And then, before I had time to divorce you, you turned up dead. You and Phil thought you were keeping your affair on the down-low, but at least half a dozen people had spotted you together in dim-lit bars, all lovey-dovey, and practically everyone in town knew Phil had a terrible temper. Thank God the jury didn't buy his melodramatic protestations of innocence and sent him away for twenty-five to life.

After the verdict came in, I couldn't stick around WaKeeny any longer. The pity I saw on people's faces just—man, I knew I wasn't going to make it if I stayed there. So that's when I started applying for other jobs in other places, and when the offer from Minnehaha County came in I grabbed it, packed my bags, and left.

"What *is* it with you and cats, Denny?" Michelle asked, the fourth night in a row that my nocturnal struggles had roused her from her slumber. "You're not allergic, are you?"

I fisted my eyes and shook off the cobwebs. "I never used to be," I said. "We *had* a cat, when I was a kid. Louie, we called him, I don't remember why. I wasn't allergic then, and I don't think I am now."

"Why *cats*, then? What's giving you these awful nightmares?"

"I don't know, Mish. I have no idea."

She wrapped her arms around me and drew my head to her shoulder. "You think maybe you ought to see somebody? See if you can get this figured out? It'd be nice if we could actually *sleep* together."

I took a deep breath and sighed it out through my nostrils. "Maybe so," I said. "We can't go on like this much longer."

I know what you're thinking, Cass. You think you've figured out what happened next, and I'm about to tell you I killed Mishie, too.

Well, no, I haven't—and I won't. First of all, my cop skills made it easy to frame poor Phil Johns for *your* murder, but who've I got to pin Michelle's on? Nobody, that's who. She loves me for who I am, and I know she would never cheat on me, no matter what.

But there's more to it than that. I don't give a damn about

44

Phil, but what I did to you, Cassandra, that was terrible, and I regret every day of my life that you're not there anymore.

But if you can believe your eyes and ears or not, I swear to you that what I did back in WaKeeny was an aberration. Honest, Cassie, I'm not that kind of man. I'm a cop, remember? One of the *good* ones.

And Michelle's a good woman, a fine woman, and it is my job to protect her and serve her.

I just hope she doesn't figure out it's not "cats" I call in my sleep, after all, and start digging into my past. I don't think I could take it if she made me do to her what you made me do to you.

A Hard Day's Night
Released July 1964

"A Hard Day's Night"
"I Should Have Known Better"
"If I Fell"
"I'm Happy Just to Dance With You"
"And I Love Her"
"Tell Me Why"
"Can't Buy Me Love"
"Any Time at All"
"I'll Cry Instead"
"Things We Said Today"
"When I Get Home"
"You Can't Do That"
"I'll Be Back"

All songs are by John Lennon and Paul McCartney.

Can't Buy Me Love
Vaseem Khan

1

It's amazing how stupid people can be. You'd think that with the endless warnings, the conveyor belt of online dupes you hear about on the news, they'd be aware—or at least attuned to the *possibility* that they're being scammed.

But that's human nature for you. We're a trusting species. We live in hope—and hope, they say, makes fools of us all.

I'm a professional conman. There are, of course, those in my line of work who take things too far, get greedy, make silly mistakes. But there are rarely second chances in this business. When you fall, you fall hard. Some never get up again.

That's why I've always been careful. Every mark well vetted, every step measured. I have a tried and trusted formula, and I don't deviate from it.

The most important lesson I've learned?

Always be ready to walk away.

It's the elderly, the lonely, the destitute who tend to fall into my net. Those for whom the Internet is still an enticing world of stimulation and opportunity.

Men are far more common than women. Widowers, and those whose wives have walked out on them, slamming the door, screeching off in the family sedan, one final kick in the nuts. Once they pick themselves up off the floor, they get a second wind.

This time, they promise themselves, *I won't make the same mistakes. This time I'll be in charge. I'll control the script.*

They're old enough to have built up a little nest egg, even after the ex has taken her slice of the pie—that's the first thing I check—and they're going to use that pot of gold to buy the life they *should* have had, a life that invariably involves a much younger woman with an accommodating attitude toward sex.

A geisha. That's what they want, and that's exactly what I offer them.

I can pretend to be anyone. If there's one skill I have, it's the ability to inhabit the skin of my avatars. Tall, short, black, white, long hair, short hair, dressed like a nun... I can be anything they want me to be. Their darkest desires, their hidden fantasies made flesh.

Ah, the wonders of modern technology.

The technical term is "deep fakes." But to those of us who wield the wand—the wizards behind the curtain—it's all just code. Lines and lines of code.

There's a lot more to it than that, of course, but that's what differentiates me from some dilettante sitting in a Third World Internet café and preying on pensioners.

I'm what you might call a *connoisseur.*

Besides, half the work is done by the mark. They *want* me to be real. They need me to be real. I am the answer to their prayers. I am exactly what the doctor ordered, the balm for their broken hearts.

Why do I do it? It's not as simple as you might think.

Like the Beatles sang, I don't care too much for money. In my case, it's the thrill of the chase that gets me off.

And it's only when I finally lower the boom that the little voice that's been trying to warn them off suddenly becomes audible. That-
    -moment-
        -when-
           -it-
              -finally-
                  -hits-
                     -home.
That's the moment I live for.

Call me perverse, call me cruel, but the fact is I take pride in my work.

After all, am I not entitled to a *frisson* of pleasure as I watch their faces when I deliver the *coup de grace*? Bloated faces, shimmering on my screen, the uncontrollable blinking, the red flush spreading across trembling cheeks, the hands grasping futilely at emptiness?

The tears, when they come, are pitiable, the rage understandable.

And then there are those who simply collapse onto their keyboards or slip from their chairs in a daze. Sometimes, I can hear the thud as their bodies hit the floor. I don't laugh. But I'd be lying if I said I don't feel a wicked amusement bubble up inside me.

I can't help but sign off with a final flourish. You might call it unnecessary, but I think of it as my little warning not to get caught out again. I'm practically doing them a service by leaving these words flashing on their screens:

Didn't anyone ever tell you, angel?...You can't buy love.

2

I don't see many *female* suckers in my line of work, certainly not attractive ones. They don't need *me*. They can stroll into a bar and walk out again two hours later with the answer to their problems, or download an online dating app designed to provide tailor-made service. You want a forty-something six-one guy with black hair, a Christopher Reeve chin, impeccable table manners, a six-figure salary, and no ex-wives in the rear-view mirror? Coming right up!

But sometimes....

This one's name was Olivia.

I came across her on Facebook. That's my happy hunting ground. The dating apps have been infiltrated by organized gangs, buffoons blundering around like bulls in a china shop. I stay well clear of them.

But Facebook, for all the negative press it gets, is the preserve of those who joined it back when it was shiny and new. This is where they play out their games of suburban one-upmanship. This is where they share their highs and wallow in their lows— the lower the better. Trauma porn, anyone?

This is also where they're at their most unguarded.

Hundreds—sometimes thousands—of posts, an endless reel of photographs and videos and links to everything that matters to them. I don't even have to pore through the litany of soul-numbing dullness myself. A few lines of code, and my AI assistant can do the job in a fraction of the time.

Of course, if it were *that* easy, any half-decent coder could do it.

No. The real skill comes in what happens next. Sucking up all your tell-tale data, letting it whisper your darkest secrets into my ear, and then using it to create a tailored plan of action, fine-tuned precisely for *you*.

In typically Neanderthal fashion, the authorities have given my approach a vulgar name: "fattening the pig." What they mean is that a professional like me takes his time with the mark, raising the "pig" before ultimately slaughtering it. It takes skill, patience, and nerve to do what I do. Convincing a sophisticated mark that you're not after their money but seeking a soulmate is no mean feat.

So: Olivia Callaghan.

Forty-four years old. Blond, beautiful, with a dead husband who'd left her a good-sized townhouse in a nice London suburb, a lovely diamond ring, a decent stock portfolio, and no children.

Perfect.

And who was *she* looking for, I wondered?

According to her profile, she wasn't looking for anyone. She was on no dating apps and, judging from her social media, made a point of resisting her friends' attempts to set her up with other friends.

She liked:

- books (Elizabeth Strout, Rachel Joyce, stories about strong women with turbulent emotional lives, cookbooks by Stanley Tucci),
- indie cinema (though without Dead Husband, that was now a source of pain, not pleasure),
- long walks in the woods (when he wasn't playing Big Cheese in the City, Dead Husband had been a nature lover, a patron of various conscience-salving eco-charities; pillage the earth by day, build wells in Africa by night, a Gordon Gecko for the new millennium), and
- her job (lecturer at a university, teaching ancient Mesopotamian history, a subject as dead as her husband).

A woman like this would require a very particular type of bait. No ordinary man would do.

Hmm...how about *this* guy?

Meet Robert Irving, forty-seven, a widower with one daughter (who emigrated to Australia a decade ago). Darkly handsome, but rakishly unaware of his charm. Impeccably dressed, with a certain tweediness to his outfits. Bespectacled? Sure, why not?

A man of intellect. An art historian—though not employed by any institution where his credentials might easily be verified. No, our Mr. Irving works for himself. He is a consultant, a man whose services are quietly hired by museums and galleries around the world, a man who makes a great deal of money but is prudent in the way he spends it.

A man of taste and refinement, of learning and culture.

A Renaissance man.

3

Olivia only appeared on Facebook a year ago, two years after her husband died.

Prior to that, she'd never even dipped a toe into the murky world of social media. Never needed to. Her social life was rich and full. Blessed.

But post-Dead Husband, she became something of a recluse. Stopped going out. Stopped answering the phone. Her friends began to worry.

And then someone suggested the Book of Faces. Hail, hail, the gang's all here—along with a limitless supply of *new* friends. All the social interaction you could ever need at the click of a mouse.

She took the plunge.

Her early posts made me smile. Shy, tentative, self-conscious. And then, as the power of the *like* took hold—as others appreciated her posts, her pictures, and by extension *her*—her sense of self-worth grew. She began to *participate*, to reveal more of herself, until finally her life was an open book.

It takes a special kind of person to read that book.

There are companies hiding in the darkest corners of Silicon Valley that specialize in it. Organizations that make a fortune from analyzing your every post, every like, every click. And they are frighteningly good at it.

I should know—I used to work for one of them. Until—well, we don't need to go into *that*.

They can strip you down to your essence, those organizations, with the help of a few algorithms.

And that's what I did with Olivia.

I first became aware of her when she reacted to a post I'd shared.

It was bait, of course. Chum in the water. An opinion I—or rather Robert Irving—expressed about the lack of governmental will to properly fund the arts. He was hot under the collar about a certain small-town museum facing closure, the loss of local culture, local access to art. Robbing the young of their right to sup at the cultural table.

Cry me a river.

But a certain type of woman finds a man with such opinions irresistible. Especially when he comes in such attractive packaging.

I didn't agree with her response to my post. Not entirely. I didn't want to seem too keen. I've found that a little resistance to begin with works wonders. A gentle rebuff, like smacking a dog on the nose with a rolled-up newspaper. They always come back for more.

In this case, she stayed away for several weeks. I didn't rush her. "Robert" kept putting up posts, until at last he hit another nerve.

This time, my response to *her* response was magnanimous.

Conciliatory.

And that's where it began. The start of the yellow brick road. Pretty soon, we were texting. It was *You've Got Mail* on steroids—except there's never a happily-ever-after in my version of the script.

Inevitably, there came a moment when we crossed the line between professional and personal. I've been there many times before, but still, every time it happens, every time I breach the walls, I have to stop myself from leaping up and giving a fist pump.

I made the first move, told her about my darling dead wife. Dead of cancer that ate her away to the bone.

Watching her go was the hardest thing I've ever endured. It almost broke me.

Sure enough, that's when Olivia began to reveal her sad story. Quid pro quo. This is the part I always find most fascinating. It never gets old, peeling back the emotional skin of a mark, one layer at a time, learning exactly how much of what I've predicted accords with their behavior, their beliefs, their actions.

She told me about her late husband, also dead of cancer. (What a coincidence!)

I deserve an Oscar.

4

There was a sadness in Olivia that I had rarely encountered. Dead Husband had truly meant something to her. She'd loved him in a way it was difficult for me to fathom. I'd never experienced love of that kind, never knew it existed outside of Hollywood. This forced me to display a similar passion for my dead wife.

It's called "mirroring," a standard technique in my business.

We began talking on the phone, recommending books to each other, followed by intense literary discussions. And then she introduced movie night. We'd watch the same film, at the same time, on our laptops. We'd buy upmarket popcorn and crunch away, dissecting the film afterward, frame-by-frame, with a glass of wine in hand.

Months passed.

I never mentioned money, not once. That took restraint, more of it than was usual for me.

The truth was that I was enjoying myself.

Olivia was an attractive, genuinely interesting woman. Watching her bloom, regain some of the life she'd lost when Dead Husband had gone the way of the dodo, was something to behold.

Don't get me wrong. I wasn't going soft. I hadn't forgotten my ultimate goal. It just so happened that this journey was pleasanter than most.

And then *it* happened. A moment when everything changed.

We were chatting on the phone, as had become our nightly ritual. I could tell that she was drinking. It was Dead Husband's death anniversary, and she was emotional.

I listened, then tried to divert her thoughts—her hanging onto Dead Husband was no good for my mission, for obvious reasons—by reading out wacky news stories from around the country. This was now a regular feature of our conversations, a way to lighten the mood.

She laughed at my tale of the woman caught pleasuring herself outside a supermarket with adult toys she'd bought from the store.

"Let me read *you* one," she said, her voice slurred. "Listen to this headline: *Church collapses on congregation of elderly women in Cornwall.*"

And she burst out laughing.

"I'm sorry," she spluttered. "But the *thought* of those old dears lined up in prayer, beseeching God to make their dreams come true...and He replies by dropping a roof on their heads."

There are two sides to all of us. And not even the most effective algorithm, the most perceptive intellect, can always plumb the depths to reach the far shore. We all keep some part of ourselves hidden.

I suppose that was the moment I fell in love with her.

For me, it was a new feeling. It burst over me in an agony of white heat, an insane cocktail of exhilaration and terror.

Did she feel the same way?

That question kept me awake through most of the night.

I needn't have worried. I am good at what I do. And besides, what woman could possibly resist Robert Irving?

And therein lies the rub.

Because once Olivia acknowledged that she had begun to fall in love with me, too, it became obvious that a face-to-face meeting could no longer be avoided. That would be the next logical step in our relationship.

When she first suggested it, I ignored her calls and messages for an entire week. I was in a panic, a poker player whose bluff had been called.

I had two choices. The obvious one was to walk away. Never contact her again. Remove all evidence of Robert Irving's existence from the Web. Erase every trace of our digital interaction.

And then what?

Go back to being *me*. The puppet master. In control. Untouchable.

And alone. Utterly, indescribably alone.

This life I lead, it confines me to a fortress of solitude.

And I realized I couldn't do it anymore.

5

On the day we agreed to meet, I paced my living room in nervous anticipation.

I'd suggested meeting in a public place; I thought she'd expect that. Instead, she'd said, "We're past that stage by now, aren't we, Robert? I'd like our first real encounter to be more...intimate."

How could I say no to *that*?

I marveled at myself. Had I really taken this irrevocable step? Was I about to meet a woman I could truly care for? A woman I had spent *months* lying to?

Truth. It's an over-rated concept.

Yes, I had lied to her, but *every* couple lies, don't they?

In my defense, I'd come clean about certain things, the things that simply couldn't be hidden.

I need to tell you the truth, I'd said. *I don't look like my pictures. I used a special software that alters my appearance. My real name isn't even Robert Irving.*

I could *hear* her eyes widen.

Don't misunderstand me, I said. *I wasn't trying to—*

I lied to you, Olivia. I'm sorry. After my wife died, I tried online dating, but I was badly hurt. And then a friend showed me how to use this software, as a way of protecting myself.

I never expected to fall in love with you.

Everything else I've told you about myself, though— everything that matters—*is true.*

And now, here we were.

I felt like a schoolboy. Giddy. Terrified.

How would she react, when she finally came face-to-face with me?

I had refused to share an authentic image of myself, claiming I was too afraid of rejection. Perhaps that was simply a residual cautiousness, a product of my years of flying below the radar.

She'd argued, and then reluctantly accepted. She claimed she didn't care what I looked like. She hadn't fallen in love with me because I *looked* like "Robert Irving."

She was late.

Finally, just when I thought she wasn't coming, I heard a car pull into the driveway.

My house—a good-sized detached property—is the last on the street, a quiet, leafy road in Westminster, a stone's throw from the famous Abbey Road.

The bell rang; my heart lurched.

I steeled myself, then swung the door open, smiling.

She was every inch the vision I had imagined her to be.

And then her hand swung up, faster than I could track.

Whatever she was holding touched my neck. A lightning bolt of pain shrieked through me; my body convulsed, my legs buckled, and I fell backward, my head striking the hardwood floor.

Drool escaped my lips.

My last thought as I saw her approach was that I had been very, very stupid.

6

Her name was Francine.

Not Olivia's name, but the name of her friend, one of the women I had duped. The friend who had killed herself, having fallen in love with a man who turned out to be a figment of my imagination, who had robbed her of her life savings—and, more importantly, of her belief in humanity.

Olivia had known Francine since high school. They had been through thick and thin, had planned to grow old together, from bridesmaids to grandmothers.

And I'd taken that away from her.

Francine had left her a letter. A detailed, blow-by-blow account of how an online conman had groomed her, then cheated her.

Olivia had vowed to come after me. She'd planned it for a year, and then she began to search Facebook, waiting, watching, crafting a profile to lure me in, knowing the type of prey a predator like me was on the hunt for.

I had to hand it to her. She had been masterful.

And so here we were: me trussed to a chair in my own living room and this woman—this brilliant, beautiful, *dangerous* woman—with a knife in her hand and a wild look in her eye.

"You don't have to do this," I pleaded. "I have money. More than you can imagine. Everything I took from Francine and more. Much, much more. We can share it. Together. What I feel for you is real. I love you, Olivia."

"But I don't love *you*," she said. "I loved my friend, you see—and that's something your money just can't buy."

Something New
Released July 1964

"I'll Cry Instead"
"Things We Said Today"
"Any Time at All"
"When I Get Home"
"Slow Down"
"Matchbox"
"Tell Me Why"
"And I Love Her"
"I'm Happy Just to Dance With You"
"If I Fell"
"Komm, Gib Mir Deine Hand"

"Slow Down" is by Larry Williams.
"Matchbox" is by Carl Perkins.
All other songs are by John Lennon and Paul McCartney.

I'm Happy Just to Dance With You
Tom Mead

London, 1964

Years later, all it took was a couple of bars of that silly old tune and Nell was back on the dance floor at the Seven Stars. Smoke in her nostrils, arms about her waist, as though she and her partner were the only two people on the face of the planet. Funny how music does that to you.

But really the dance was just the beginning. A prelude to the rest of it.

The night it started was Nell's night off, but she popped into the Seven Stars anyway, just to see what was what. George and Albie were drinking in a booth. Fred was behind the bar, looking busy. Old Harry Whispers was on a barstool, staring down into his whisky. The whisky was staring back.

Nell had a knack for latching on to interesting people, and she got a good feeling about the fellow nursing a pint of something at the other end of the bar. She immediately christened him "the professor," on account of his thick-rimmed National Health specs. He looked like one of those eccentric genius types: tufty fair hair and keen dark eyes.

"Buy you a drink?" he said, being polite, when she took the stool beside him.

"I'll have a Newcastle Brown."

The professor ordered two. Fred the barman pulled the pints, and Nell toasted them both with a wink. She even toasted Harry Whispers, but he didn't look her way. It was hard to get much sense out of the old man these days. Since the stroke, his voice—which had been left hoarse by a gas attack in the trenches during the war—was almost non-existent. It scratched like claws on concrete.

"What's your name?" she asked the professor.

"Jack Clayton."

"Pleased to meet you, Jack. I'm Nell."

Fred, polishing glasses behind the bar, didn't take much interest. Soon enough, he drifted over to Harry Whispers and started on about the cricket.

"Don't think I've seen you 'round here before," said Nell.

"No. I'm a friend of Pam's."

"Ah." Nell's smile turned solemn. "Sorry."

"You knew her, did you? You know what happened to her?"

They'd found Pam in a storage shed on an Acton trading estate about eight months prior, her clothes littering the floor, a scarf knotted round her neck—same as the others. It was getting heavy, girls dropping like flies. How many was it now?

Nell decided to change the subject. "Care for a dance, Jack?"

He grinned. That was a nice sight—it took some of the shadow out of his thin face, made him look like a happy kid.

She slipped a coin in the jukebox, a disc rolled into place, there was a warm crackle, and the music began.

"I'm bad at this," Jack said, nearly stepping on her toe.

"You are, aren't you? That's all right, I'll teach you." She pulled him close and breathed his boozy scent.

There was something about a dance like that. Maybe it was the smoke, the heave of the bodies, the heat, the chilly trickle of sweat. And Nell was a good dancer. All it took was one spin, one twirl, and she could make you feel like she'd known you all your life.

She knew the song well. It was a sweet number they played on the radio sometimes. By the time it ended and they were back at the bar, she could tell that Jack had fallen in love with her.

He lit a cigarette for her and asked, "How well did you know Pam?"

She cocked her head, puffing smoke up at him. "What's it to you?"

"She came here, didn't she?"

Nell shrugged. "Sometimes."

"She came here the night she died," he said. "Didn't she?"

Nell tried to pull away, but he leaned closer.

"Come on, Nell," he said, "don't play dumb. You know she was here. You saw her, didn't you?"

"Who are you, anyway? A copper, or what?"

"You saw who she was with," he went on.

Nell frowned. "You're a funny sort, aren't you? Anybody'd think it was *you*."

He finished his pint. "I'd like to find *out* who it was."

"That's why you've come here, is it? Looking for a murderer?"

"Sort of."

"Well, we've no shortage." Nell was in a playful mood. She downed half her pint in one go. "Maybe George can help you."

"George Cornell?"

"That's the chap."

George was a bad lad. He'd done his share of time, including a recent stint for slashing a girl's face with a razor blade. But he was all right, really. And he had connections. Everyone in this part of London knew about the Richardsons and their infamous kangaroo courts in the abandoned warehouses of the dock-lands, where transgressors were tortured into submission with pliers, electricity and other tools of their illicit trade. These streets belonged to them, and George Cornell was their golden boy.

Jack shook his head. "It's not him."

"How do you know?"

"Well"—Jack signaled to Fred for another drink—"let's just say the killer's M-O doesn't match the stories I've heard about Cornell."

"Yeah?" said a voice. Jack and Nell turned, and there he was. "What stories would those be?"

George Cornell was an intimidating, square-shouldered physical presence, but Jack was unfazed. "Nothing, Mister Cornell," he answered calmly.

"I could have sworn my ears were burning."

Albie Woods, George's crony, sidled over. "Everything all right, George?"

"Hunky-dory," answered the gangster.

A long, ugly silence hung between them. Even the music seemed to fade away. Nell's heart thundered.

Finally, Jack spoke. "Whoever's killing these young women," he said, "has no motive."

"What are you on about?" scoffed George. "Of course he does. There's only one reason a bastard would do a thing like that, and then keep *on* doing it. Some sad sacks, it's the only chance they're going to get to have a woman."

"Maybe whoever it is can't get it up any other way," Albie added. "Some old geezer like Harry Whispers. Eh, what about that, Harry? You been throttling these girls, have you?"

Harry grumbled, flapping his good right arm. The left hung limply at his side, wrist slightly crooked, as it had been since his stroke a few months earlier. The stroke had left him vague, scarcely able to conjure complete sentences, partially immobile. But he was thirstier than ever and got through half a bottle of whisky each evening. He came in the club because there wasn't anywhere else for him to go.

"No," said Jack, "you're wrong. These aren't sex crimes." He spoke slowly, eyes fixed on his beer.

"Know a lot about it, don't ya?"

"I'm interested, is all." He took a sip, still not looking at George.

George was studying Jack. He cocked his head to one side, as though trying to puzzle out some bewildering piece of modern art. "You're Old Bill, aren't you?"

"No."

"You sure? You act like a copper."

"Leave him alone, George," said Nell.

"You shut your mouth."

The air crackled with ice. George looked Jack up and down, not taking his eyes off the younger man. "Why don't you piss off, jamrag? This ain't your sort of place."

"Gents," said Fred, "no trouble, please."

"Leave it, George," said Albie.

And all at once, George snapped his gaze away from Jack. "Ah, we're just having a little chinwag, aren't we, mate? Nothing major. No need to get your knickers in a knot. Come on, Albie."

He stalked back to his booth and, before following his master, Albie leaned in and said confidentially, "You want to watch yourself with George. He's not himself at the moment."

Fred the barman explained. "One of the victims—not Pam, but one of the other ones—George had a bit of a thing for her."

"Lucy," said Nell. "Poor Lucy."

They'd found Lucy in a car park in Kensington about a year ago. That was the thing about this fellow, whoever he was—he liked to space out his murders out. He'd commit one of his atrocities, then disappear for months at a time. It had been going on since 1958. He'd leave it long enough for people to start wondering if he was done for good, and then he'd strike again.

Everyone knew about the traces of industrial paint found on two of the bodies. They knew that one of the victims had been seen climbing into a Ford Zephyr just before she disappeared. They knew all the victims had been found nude but unmolested. The only thing they didn't know, it seemed, was whodunit.

Nell and Jack parted ways soon after that. But she thought about him long into the night. She wished she had asked him more questions—and listened closely to his answers.

＊

The following night was a work night, but the Seven Stars was half empty, so Fred let Nell off early. He could tell she was distracted.

When she emerged from behind the bar, there was Jack. "Got time for another dance?" he asked her.

She made the time. Truth was, she found him interesting. Not at all her usual type.

He came into the Seven Stars every night that week. Every night, they danced to the same songs. Fred indulged her but kept a close eye, made sure this Jack fellow didn't try anything untoward.

When they weren't dancing, they drank, smoked, and talked. Nell told him what it had been like growing up in Brighton, told him about her brothers and sisters, told him how she had ended up here. But getting Jack to talk about himself wasn't so easy.

"Tell me about you and Pam," Nell prompted. "I know she had boyfriends. Were you one of them?"

Jack gave an unpleasant laugh. "No," he said, "you've got that wrong."

"Then you'd better tell me the truth, hadn't you?"

He sighed. "The truth is, I'm her brother."

Nell looked him up and down. "She never said she had a brother."

"I get the feeling there's a lot she didn't say."

"So you want to find out who killed her?"

"Too right I do. And LaGrange has gotten nowhere." Inspector LaGrange had been in charge of the case from the beginning. "He's out there now, scouring bedsits and bordellos. But I'll bet they *all* came in the Seven Stars, didn't they? All the victims, every last one."

"You think you're the first to suss that out? Use your noodle, Jack. LaGrange and his boys have been in and out of here for months. Undercover men. Digging. Asking questions."

"They came on too strong," said Jack. "Scared him off. He waited for things to cool down, then he came back for Pam. You know what they say: softly, softly, catchee monkey. And that's where *you* come in."

"Where exactly?"

"You know the regulars well enough, don't you." It was an observation, not a question.

"What if I do?"

"What if I told you that one of your regulars has been killing these girls? Think about it, Nell. Stands to reason, doesn't it?"

"What if it does?"

"Look at yourself, Nell. You're his type, aren't you? You're young, you're pretty. Just the sort he goes for. Like my sister."

"Much obliged, I'm sure."

"Think about it. You and me, we could nail him. We could put a stop to all this."

"How?"

"You chat up the blokes who come in here. You dance with them. But all the time, I'll be watching, see? I'll keep an eye on you, make sure nobody takes any liberties."

She scowled. "How are you going to do that, Jack?"

"Trust me."

And, in spite of herself, she did. They shook on it, his warm hand clasping hers as he studied her through his bottle-glass lenses.

That was how it began. Night after night, man after man, Nell chatted with the customers, learned about their lives, danced with them—and listened.

The Seven Stars was one of those not-quite-fashionable London establishments, full of people who were on their way either up or down. Nell didn't discriminate; she danced with both kinds. And all the time she was conscious of Jack's eyes on her. He was never obtrusive, but he was always there, usually sitting in one of the booths along the far wall.

Sometimes she made eye contact with him. His expression never changed. He watched, he smoked, and he drank. He did not seem to blink.

One night, George Cornell pulled her aside. "I know what you're doing," he said, "and I think you're a bloody dope."

"Charming."

"Let me finish, will you? I think you're a bloody dope, but I don't want what happened to Lucy and them others happening to you, right? So as soon as you spot anything a bit iffy, you give me a shout. Yeah?"

Nell cocked her head; she had not anticipated this. She cast an involuntary sideways glance in Jack's direction. Then she nodded.

"All right," she told him. "You can count on me, George."

It was about a fortnight later that the man in the gray suit came into the Seven Stars. A few people recognized him and gave him a wide berth. He made for the bar and ordered a scotch. Nell served him.

"Haven't seen you for a while," she commented.

"Been busy."

"I thought you'd forgotten about us."

"Oh, I couldn't forget you, sweetheart," he said, as she handed him a glass. "What time do you get off?"

"About ten minutes."

"Good. Come and find me."

She found him in a booth. He lit a cigarette for her and said, "Well?"

"Well, what?"

"Nell, don't piss me about. I want to know about George Cornell."

"It's not George."

"Why, because he's a happily married man? Trust me,

sweetheart, that counts for nothing."

"Whoever it is, he's brighter than George. George is just a bruiser."

The man tapped the side of his nose with a stubby, tobacco-stained forefinger. "Maybe that's what he wants you to think. You watch yourself, Nell. Don't believe everything people tell you. I'd hate to see you get hurt."

"Don't worry about *me*," she protested. "I can look after myself."

But he just sighed. "Listen, that bloke you've been hanging around with. How well do you know him?"

She shrugged and glanced involuntarily across the room at Jack. "Not that well. He's Pam's brother."

The man in gray smiled. "That's what he told you, is it? Well, maybe he is and maybe he isn't. It doesn't matter. The point is, he's *here*, and he's sniffing around places he shouldn't be. Don't you get mixed up in anything you can't get out of."

When the man in gray was gone, she drifted back to Jack. "That was Benny LaGrange," he told him. "*Inspector* La-Grange."

Jack responded very seriously. "That counts for nothing. Think about it: LaGrange is a regular at the Seven Stars, too."

But Nell was unconvinced. "You really think it could be a Met officer?"

"It could be *anyone*."

"True enough. It could be *you*, couldn't it?"

"Don't be daft."

"You said it could be anyone. Well, it could. Maybe you had a reason for killing your sister. Maybe you set it up to look like the other killings, what they call a copycat, and now you're looking for a scapegoat."

"No," he barked. Then, sensing eyes on him, he moderated his tone. "I would never have hurt Pam."

"Maybe you did all of them," said Nell. "Maybe *that's* why you've been sniffing around."

"You've got it all wrong, Nell. Listen, I'm getting close. I mean it. I've been doing some digging. Going through archives, newspaper reports. I'm closing in on him. I am."

"You're full of shit, Jack. And I don't want you to come in here anymore. Understand?"

He jumped to his feet and reached across the table to grip her by the wrist. "Nell—"

"There a problem?" said George Cornell, stepping from the throng of nearby drinkers.

"I think there is," said Nell. She stood and watched as George and Albie hauled Jack away.

Fred had called time, and Nell was helping him mop up the tables as the boozers filed out into the night. George and Albie were long gone, and she hadn't seen Jack since they'd escorted him from the premises. She did not doubt that they'd given him a good kicking, but he had been asking for it.

Harry Whispers—who had been propping up the bar all night, gazing vaguely into smoky space and downing whisky after whisky—was by now noticeably the worse for wear. The last straggler at the bar, he mumbled, "Got to see a man about a dog."

"What's that, Harry?" Fred called out. "You off home?"

The old man was clambering cautiously from his bar stool. The whiskies had taken care of his shakes, but he was still slow and unsteady.

He almost made it to the door before careering into a booth. There was a thump, a crash of shattering glass, a pool of spilled beer.

"God Almighty," Fred said. "Nell, would you see to him?"

She nodded, slipped an arm under Harry's, and heaved him to his feet. "You're all right now, aren't you? Look at all this glass. Have you hurt yourself? Just wounded pride, is it?"

Harry murmured an unintelligible response and slumped into

the booth.

"You want me to call you a cab, Harry? Get you home safe?"

She heard the creak of the door, soft footsteps on the beer-stained carpet, and whirled around. "What the hell are you doing here?"

Jack had indeed taken quite a beating. He had a black eye and blood crusted around both nostrils. But he was alive and upright. "Nell," he said. "You need to listen to me."

"I don't," she answered, before bellowing: "Fred!"

The barman emerged from behind the bar. "I thought I'd seen the bloody last of you."

Jack raised his hands defensively. "Wait!" he said. "Please. You have to listen to me. Both of you."

"Take Harry home," Fred growled at Nell. "He lives 'round the corner. Bryson Mews. I'll sort *this* out."

Not waiting to be told twice, Nell wrapped an arm around Harry's waist and got him to his feet.

Bryson Mews. All the years Harry had been coming into the Seven Stars, and Nell had only now learned how close the old drunk's house was. The mouth of the mews yawned darkly at the other end of the road.

She didn't want to think about the fate that awaited Jack. Fred was in pretty tight with George Cornell, Frankie Fraser and the rest. In many ways, the Seven Stars was "their" place.

As they headed along the mews, Nell studied the housefronts and tried to imagine which of the terraced properties might be Harry's. "What number is it?" she asked him.

"Nine," he told her.

They reached the house and, after a moment's hesitation, Nell helped him up the stone steps, one at a time. Then she fished in his pocket and emerged with a key.

Depositing him in a ratty armchair beside a two-bar electric fire, she said, "There. You can look after yourself now, can't you?"

She didn't wait for an answer and headed back out into the brisk night air. She shuddered a little as she walked, the metronomic tick of her heels on the cobblestones echoing about the mews.

She could not have said precisely when she first suspected that she was being followed. But when she rounded the corner into Cherry Blossom Lane and heard the alien footstep, she knew for certain.

She paused. Whoever it was had been making an effort to keep his steps in time with hers, but he'd slipped out of rhythm. She carried on walking, careful not to alter her pace. Her flat was a quarter of a mile along the road. She dug in her handbag for the key.

Stupid, she thought, *bloody stupid*.

"You asked me if I know who it is," said Jack hoarsely. He was clutching his ribs, and his nose was bleeding again.

She turned to get a proper look at him. "Looks like Fred made a mess of you. You want to be careful. Normally they don't give blokes like you a second warning."

Jack gave a rattling exhalation. "I know who's been strangling these girls," he wheezed.

She gritted her teeth and, with her right hand behind her back, wrapped her fingers around her flat key so it protruded between her knuckles. It was sharp enough to do some damage.

"It's Harry," Jack said.

"You *what*?"

"That's why I came back, why I followed you. I wanted to make sure he didn't try anything."

"Have you *seen* Harry Whispers? He's just a poor old man!"

"He is—now. But he wasn't when he killed Pam. He had the stroke a few weeks after. You know what his real name is?"

"Harry Simmons, I think."

"That's what he calls himself. His *real* name is Arthur Driscoll. He was born in Antrim. I've got all the records back at my flat. In the summer of 1911, he killed two women. Didn't know *that*, did you?"

"I don't believe it."

"The whole thing is public record, if anyone could be bothered to look. Well, *I* bothered, and today I found out all about it. He was too young for the death penalty, so they gave him life. He got out after sixteen years, supposedly reformed. Changed his name, came to London, and disappeared."

"You're daft. He's just a sweet old man."

"He's anything but," Jack said with a hollow laugh.

That was when the car coasted up behind him, a pea-green Jaguar. As it rolled to a halt, two men climbed out.

"Wait," said Nell. "Wait!"

But they didn't wait. In an instant, George and Albie were out and on him. Five seconds later, Jack was in the back of the car and they were roaring away. Nell could do nothing but stand there and watch them go.

Word would get out. People would see his photograph in the newspapers, would remember seeing him around, asking questions about the murders. They would put two and two together. *Jack Clayton*, they would say. *I never thought it was* him.

By the end of the 'Sixties, London was a different place. Eventually Nell returned to Brighton, moved back in with her parents for a while, got a job in another, quieter bar. Eventually, she got married.

But her London days came back to her in waves, quick stabs of memory, like a song on the radio. All it took was a few bars, and she was there again. Back in the Seven Stars, in her best frock, eyeing the man in glasses at the other end of the bar. Once again, she danced with him. Once again, she watched from the curb, too startled even to scream, as Jack was hauled into the waiting car.

He didn't seem to realize what was happening until he was already in the back of the Jag. George slammed the door as Jack was starting to protest. Nell couldn't hear what he was saying, but she could tell from the grotesque pantomime of his flapping arms. He looked frantically from side to side, then his gaze latched back onto her as the car pulled away. He craned his neck to stare at her. His eyes were a pair of dark, damp globes, and his mouth was a sad O as the Jag rounded the corner and disappeared from view.

George Cornell might have satisfied her morbid curiosity about what happened to Jack. But before she got around to asking him, he was shot dead in a bar. Not the Seven Stars but the Blind Beggar.

Harry Whispers died around the same time. Nothing dramatic, just another stroke. They found him when his neighbors complained about the smell. Nell never did learn whether Jack had been right, whether Harry really had been Arthur Driscoll, the murderer, or if the murderer had been Jack himself, after all.

But once Harry and Jack were gone, no more girls were strangled.

Beatles '65
Released December 1964

"No Reply"
"I'm a Loser"
"Baby's in Black"
"Rock and Roll Music"
"I'll Follow the Sun"
"Mr. Moonlight"
"Honey Don't"
"I'll Be Back"
"She's a Woman"
"I Feel Fine"
"Everybody's Trying to Be My Baby"

"Rock and Roll Music" is by Chuck Berry.
"Mr. Moonlight" is by Roy Lee Johnson.
"Honey Don't" and "Everybody's Trying to Be My Baby"
are by Carl Perkins.
All other songs are by John Lennon and Paul McCartney.

I'll Be Back
Christine Poulson

"Do you want the good news or the bad news first?" Julian asked, when I got home from work.

I guessed that both good and bad news would be about our holiday. We were due to leave the following morning.

"Worst first," I said.

"The agency rang. We can't have the cottage in the Lake District. They've had a flood."

"Oh, no!" I dropped my briefcase with a thud. "But there's good news?"

"They've offered us another place, Lindsay. It's bigger and more expensive, but they'll cover the difference."

"That sounds great."

"Yes, but—"

"What's the problem?"

He screwed up his face to indicate that I wouldn't like what he was about to say. "It's not in the Lake District. They're holding it for us, but we can have a refund instead."

"Well, where *is* it?"

He angled his laptop toward me. "It's an early Nineteenth Century manor house in a little village in Lincolnshire. It's not far from Lincoln, and you can get to the coast quite easily."

I looked over his shoulder at the photograph on his screen. The house looked fine, and Lincoln *is* a nice old cathedral city.

The name of the village seemed somehow familiar, but I couldn't put my finger on just when and where I'd heard it before.

Lincolnshire is not a picturesque county, not a patch on the Lake District, but it didn't seem reasonable to object. We'd booked the time off work, and we needed the break. We run a small printing business, and it's not easy for us to get away.

It didn't occur to us to wonder why such a desirable holiday rental would be available on such short notice.

It was late in September and unseasonably warm when we arrived in the village. At first, we couldn't find the place, not even with our GPS. So we stopped at a little general store, and I went in to ask.

"North Lees Hall?" the woman said doubtfully.

"We're renting it for a week."

"I don't think," she began, but then something occurred to her. "Unless you mean the Manor House? I did hear they changed the name. And you're staying there, are you? Well, if it's the place I'm thinking of—"

And she gave me directions. Turned out it was up a drive between two houses, which was why we'd missed it.

I was laughing when I got back in the car and told Julian what she'd said. "It was her tone of voice," I explained, "like in one of those corny old horror movies where the locals know more than the newcomers."

When we arrived at last, my first impression of the house was of red brick and white paintwork and a white-pillared portico framing the front door. There was a date of 1836 on the wall above the entrance. My spirits rose.

We had a code for the key box and retrieved the key. Julian opened the door and gallantly gestured for me to go in first. I had my foot on the threshold when—for just a moment—I felt as if someone had placed the palm of their hand on my chest to hold me back. But the sensation passed, and I stepped inside.

Opposite the entrance was a lovely curving staircase, but that turned out to be the house's only original feature. Otherwise, the interior had been completely redone, luxuriously, in the style of a boutique hotel. King-sized beds. Three bathrooms, one with a free-standing bath. Fluffy towels. A vast kitchen. Three TVs, one with a huge screen in a separate room like a small cinema. The place had been renovated by someone with a lot of money, and in the process the *character* of the house had been lost.

There was too much space, somehow. A house like that should be cluttered with books and nice old furniture, but everything was too new, as if no one had ever lived there.

After we brought in our luggage, I went into the kitchen to make a cup of tea and found half a dozen flies buzzing around. The blue light of a fly killer glowed in the corner, its bars studded with little black corpses.

Julian armed himself with a folded newspaper and set about swatting.

"Must be a pig farm nearby," he commented, as I looked for the kettle.

A *zap*, and another fly was incinerated.

"How can there not be a kettle?" I said, after I had opened every cupboard and drawer, revealing a vast array of pans and enough cutlery for a small army.

"I wonder," Julian said, going to the sink. "Yeah, thought so. It's got one of those fancy taps that dispenses boiling water."

"Oh, Lord, this is all wrong," I said, waving a hand. "Not just the tap. I mean all of it. I expect it was once a real family home—"

"I know what you mean: a bit shabby, freezing bathrooms, drafts everywhere—"

"—overstuffed sagging sofas, an Aga with a whistling kettle—"

"—a cat or two, and a dog."

"Definitely a dog," I said. "In fact, more than one. A couple of golden Labs."

And a picture came into my mind, so vivid that I could actually *see*, just for a moment, two dogs flopped down in front of the Aga, tongues lolling, tails thumping the floor.

Later, we explored the grounds. They were a disappointment, too. They'd been designed for low maintenance: no flower beds or shrubs, just lawn and the odd tree.

There was only one place where I got any sense of the people who'd once lived there, and that was in what was once the stable block. It ran alongside the drive, a long red brick building covered in ivy, with a dustbin store at one end. About halfway down, French windows had been let into the wall. We found ourselves looking past a notice taped to the glass—POOL CLOSED DANGEROUS DO NOT ENTER—into a room with more French windows on the other side and beyond them an empty swimming pool in a courtyard.

What interested me most were the framed photos of weddings and other family events that crowded the walls of the room. I cupped my eyes to see past my own reflection in the window. It wasn't easy to make out the details, but I could see enough of the clothes people were wearing and the way the colors had faded to guess that the pictures weren't recent.

There is something melancholy about old photographs, isn't there? A wave of sadness swept over me—no, more than sadness, a sense of desolation. The hairs on my arms stood up, and I shivered.

"What's up, love?" Julian asked.

"Someone walking over my grave," I said, shaking it off. "Let's go in and get supper started."

* * *

Later that evening, I was brushing my hair in the bathroom mirror when Julian came over and put his hands on my shoulders. He leaned in and planted a kiss on my neck.

"Looking good," he said.

I smiled up at him. We were on our best behavior, each of us making an effort. This trip was meant to be a chance for a new start. A second honeymoon, if you like.

It was the usual story. Working hard to establish our business, we'd neglected our relationship and drifted apart. Finally, though, we'd decided that our marriage was worth saving, and we were working hard to get things back on track.

Was he right? *Was* I looking good?

I examined myself in the mirror. Not bad for nearly forty. I hadn't started to go gray. The one white lock in my dark hair wasn't due to age, but to an accident that had happened years ago, a decade before Julian and I first met. I didn't think much about it anymore, but tonight I found myself remembering.

They'd had to shave my head, and my hair had grown back white where the stitches had been, a memento of the crash—as were the headaches that still afflicted me from time to time. Everyone said I wasn't the same person afterward. I'm told a head injury can do that.

I wasn't sure that I would have *liked* the old me very much.

Apparently I'd been drinking that night, but I don't remember anything leading up to the accident. I'd been alone in the car, thank God, and I hadn't hit another vehicle or pedestrian.

I don't drive now, and I don't drink much, either.

"Are you coming, love?" Julian called from the bedroom, and I went to join him in the gigantic bed.

I was making breakfast the next morning when he came rushing into the kitchen with his laptop.

"Lindsay, look at this. You'll never guess." He sat down at the kitchen table. "I was curious, so I typed 'the Manor House' and the name of the village into Google, and look what came up."

I peered over his shoulder and read "The Manor House Murders."

"No wonder they changed the name," he said. "Just imagine—"

"You mean there were murders *here?*"

"Surely you remember. It's one of *the* famous unsolved crimes. No one was ever even arrested."

And now it did ring a bell, though my memory was hazy. It must have happened around the same time as my accident.

"Twenty years ago, almost to the day," Julian said. "The police received a 999 call in the early hours and got here to find a bloodbath. Three people dead and one survivor—he was the one who phoned it in."

His face was alive with interest, and my heart sank. In my view, Julian's interest in true crime verges on the morbid. Oh, I don't mind watching the occasional episode of *Poirot* or *Vera*, but nothing too graphic—and certainly nothing about things that have happened to real people. Julian is fascinated, though. He even belongs to an online group that discusses unsolved crimes and offers solutions.

He settled back in his seat, and I groaned inwardly as I realized I was going to hear all about the Manor House murders, whether I wanted to or not.

"They were a farming family, the parents and their two sons, both of whom lived and worked on the farm. On this particular weekend, the parents had gone away. The two brothers didn't get on—that's important. The older one, Damien, was in line to inherit the farm, and the younger one, Michael, resented it. That's why he avoided the poolside party Damien threw in their parents' absence. Also, he knew there'd be hard drinking and drugs, and he wanted to be well clear of it. At least that's what he claimed, afterward. We're not talking teenagers here, by the way. Damien was in his mid-twenties, and Michael was a couple of years younger.

"Michael's story was that he spent the evening in his room, watching TV, then went to bed. You mentioned Labradors when we arrived—well, they *did* have a couple of dogs that were shut in the kitchen at night. Michael was awakened by their howling and thought there might be an intruder. He looked out the landing window and saw that the floodlights were still on by the pool. He couldn't see very much over the roof of the stable block, but what he *did* see was a foot—someone lying on the far side of the pool. He rushed over there and found the bodies of his brother and two of his friends. They'd all been stabbed."

I was drawn into the story despite myself. "The police never found out who did it?"

"Right. Never found the murder weapon, either. Probably that was part of why they couldn't make a murder charge stick. Michael was the prime suspect, of course, but he claimed that someone else—apart from the three victims—had been there that night. He'd heard a car drive up, had briefly glimpsed someone and heard a woman's voice. Or so he said, though there was no evidence to support his story. Michael had motive and opportunity—and plenty of time to get rid of the murder weapon before he called the police. But there wasn't enough evidence to charge him. Wait till I tell the guys in the group we're actually *staying* here!"

No wonder the name of the house had been changed. This also explained the reason the place had been done up—to obliterate all traces of its past—and the reason that the family, or what was left of it, didn't live here anymore.

Did it *also* explain the sense of desolation I'd felt by the swimming pool and the unease I'd felt even before learning of the murders?

Perhaps I was psychic.

"Come on," Julian said. "Let's have a look."

"At what?"

"The pool, of course. The scene of the crime!"

Without giving me time to object, he was out the door.

I followed reluctantly, and by the time I reached the stable block he'd disappeared. I called him, and he poked his head around the door to the bin store.

"There's a door in here, and it's not locked. You can get through to the swimming pool."

He disappeared again, and I went after him into what had originally been the stable yard. It was surrounded by red brick buildings with white trim. The pool was in the center, and one line of stables had been converted to changing rooms. Sheltered from the fierce east-coast winds, this must once have been a delightful spot. But now the deep end of the pool was half full of rainwater, dank and opaque. Weeds were growing through the paving stones. Dead plants trailed from cracked stone urns.

Julian was looking into the building we'd seen from the other side, and I joined him. One end had been fitted with a kitchen and bar, and it was still much as it must have been in the days when the happy shrieks of splashing children filled the air and gin and tonics were drunk around the pool—except that dust had settled everywhere, and wicker chairs with floral cushions that matched the curtains were stacked up inside. Thinking about what had happened here, the hair went up on the back of my neck.

I turned to Julian. He was looking around, scrutinizing the paving stones as if there might still be blood stains. And maybe there were. If so, I didn't want to see them.

"We can't stay here," I said. "Not now, now that we know what happened."

Julian was silent, and I guessed that he was pondering the best line to take.

"Please," I said. "Let's just pack up and go."

"Look, Lindsay, we don't believe in ghosts, do we? And even

if we did, we're staying in the *house*, and that's not where the—"

"Oh, God, you *want* to stay?"

"It just seems a pity to give up our holiday—and you must admit, it's interesting."

In the end, we compromised. I agreed to stay on for a bit longer and see how I felt. And Julian agreed that, if I felt the same after a couple of days, we'd go home. Perhaps we'd even be able to get some money back from the holiday company.

That evening, we ate a long boozy dinner and ended up in bed. We made love, and I fell asleep.

I was awakened by Julian shaking my shoulder. He was standing by the bed.

"Are you all right?" he asked. "You were groaning."

I squinted at him in the dim moonlight that filtered in through the curtains. "I'm fine. Must have been a bad dream."

"I've made you some tea," he said, putting a mug on my bedside table. He got back into bed and began tapping on his laptop.

"What are you looking at?" I asked. He didn't reply. "Not another article about the murders?"

"Actually, I think you might be interested in this one. There are photos of the inside of the house as it was before it was renovated. They *did* have an Aga. But listen, sweetie"—he cleared his throat—"now that I've had some time to think about it...if you're not happy here and you still want to go home—"

"Really?"

"I suppose it *isn't* the best place for a holiday. So why don't we do what you said, pack up and go?"

"When were you thinking?"

"Tomorrow morning?"

I was surprised by this sudden capitulation, but I was hardly going to object to getting my own way.

"That's settled, then." Julian sat up and swung his legs over the edge of the bed. "You stay here and relax. I'm going to straighten up downstairs, and then I'll be back."

He left the laptop. I propped myself up on the pillows and sipped my tea. For a while, I resisted temptation, but in the end I couldn't help but be curious. As I scrolled through the photos, I saw that the house *had* been pretty much as I'd imagined it. *Just* as I'd imagined it, really. The kitchen range was an Aga, but that was standard issue for a farmhouse. And there were dogs, and—

My temples were throbbing. I had one of my headaches coming on.

I searched in my bag for painkillers and found that the packet was empty. I'd used the last ones without realizing.

Julian kept some in his washbag, I knew, so I padded into the bathroom and rummaged around in it. I did find the aspirins, but I also found something else: a basic pay-as-you-go phone. Why did he have a hidden second phone, when he owned an iPhone?

I had no trouble unlocking it. What a careless fellow my husband was: the password was the same as on his office computer. And the text messages I discovered were positively pornographic. It was like a punch in the gut.

As I scrolled through them, a new one pinged in: "See you tomorrow. Can't wait."

And now I understood why my husband was suddenly so keen to go home. Our reconciliation, our fresh start: it was all a sham.

He was having an affair.

"You can't do this to me," I heard myself say out loud, still staring at the phone.

When Julian called up to me, I slowly descended the stairs, as if in a dream.

It was hot down there, because we'd closed the windows

against the flies. Still, there were several of them buzzing about. Everything might have been different if it hadn't been for the heat, and if Julian hadn't been slicing a lemon for a gin and tonic.

Because it was the sharp citrus scent rising from the chopping board that broke the log jam in my mind and took me back to that sultry evening twenty years ago.

I knew at last what had happened in those missing hours before my accident. I still couldn't quite remember how I had ended up at the Manor House or where I had met Damien. In some bar, no doubt. No matter. The unidentified woman who was there that night? That was me.

So I hadn't been imagining what our holiday home used to look like. I already *knew*. I'd been here before.

As for the killings, may I say in mitigation that they began as self-defense?

Damien wouldn't take no for an answer. He grabbed me and forced me back against a table—the others were laughing, egging him on—I was terrified—and I grabbed the knife—the one he'd used to cut up lemons for the gin we'd drunk earlier. I was only trying to stop him, but it all happened so fast. When I realized what I'd done and saw the look of horror on the faces of the other two, I panicked.

They were too far off their heads on drink and drugs to put up much resistance.

No wonder I had been driving erratically. I drove as fast as I dared, desperate to get as far as possible from the scene of the crime. At some point, I stopped to throw the knife into a ditch.

And then, not long after that, the accident that wiped out all memory of what had gone before—though perhaps some vestiges of it explained my headaches and bad dreams?

As the memories returned, so did my old self, the person I had been before the accident, the wild child who lived dangerously, the risk-taker who had been hungry for experience. Had she ever really gone away? Hadn't she always been there, waiting in the shadows for this moment?

She was back now, back with a vengeance. And she wasn't going to take any shit from anyone. If Julian thought he could cheat on me and get away with it, he was making a very big mistake.

"Are you okay?" He had put down the knife and was staring at me. He looked puzzled. "You seem...I don't know... *different.*"

"I'm fine," I said. And I was. I reached for the knife. "You'll be interested to know that I've solved the mystery of the Manor House murders."

He didn't know how to take that. "Really?"

"Really. *I* was the woman who was here that night. I killed the bastard who tried to rape me and the friends who were going to let him. Rotten to the core, the lot of them. I killed them all. And I'm not sorry."

He gazed at me, his mouth open, incredulous. I suppose he thought I was making some tasteless joke. Because as I moved toward him, he began to laugh.

Well, he's not laughing now.

Beatles VI
Released June 1965

"Kansas City/Hey-Hey-Hey-Hey"
"Eight Days a Week"
"You Like Me Too Much"
"Bad Boy"
"I Don't Want to Spoil the Party"
"Words of Love"
"What You're Doing"
"Yes It Is"
"Dizzy Miss Lizzy"
"Tell Me What You See"
"Every Little Thing"

"Kansas City" is by Jerry Leiber and Mike Stoller,
and "Hey-Hey-Hey-Hey" is by Richard Penniman.
"You Like Me Too Much" is by George Harrison.
"Bad Boy" and "Dizzy Miss Lizzy" are by Larry Williams.
"Words of Love" is by Buddy Holly.
All other songs are by John Lennon and Paul McCartney.

You Like Me Too Much
Michael Bracken

"Sheriff, we got a domestic at the Roadrunner Mobile Home Court," said Martha Radisch, dispatcher.

"Send Clayton."

"Can't. He's on the other side of the county at the Dahl Ranch."

"Well, damn." Sheriff Victoria "Vic" Benson snatched her Stetson from the coatrack in her office and headed out the door. Twenty minutes later, she stood on the rickety wooden porch of a fourteen-by-seventy-foot mobile home that tilted slightly toward the northwest and was rented to Joseph Carter. She rapped on the door with her nightstick.

The ruckus inside stopped, the door jerked open, and a greasy-haired man shouted in her face, "What the fuck do you want?"

As she pressed the flat of her hand against his chest and pushed, she said, "Manners, Joe. I want to see some manners."

He staggered backward.

"Ma'am," she called through the open door. "One of your neighbors phoned, said she was worried about you. Can you come out here on the porch and talk to me?"

A moment later, a slender blonde ten years Vic's junior stepped into the doorway.

"All the way," the sheriff said. "Don't you worry none about him."

The woman followed the sheriff down to the hard-packed caliche that served as a driveway, and they stood next to an eighteen-year-old Chevrolet Silverado.

"That's quite a shiner you got there. He do that to you?"

The blonde glanced back at the mobile home. "No, I—"

"—ran into a door," the sheriff said, completing her sentence. "Appaloosa Spring seems to have an epidemic of accidents involving women and doors."

"Yeah, well, Joe can get himself another girl, but *we* don't have too many choices around here, do we?"

"More choices than you realize, Miss—?"

"Amy," said the blonde. "Amy Wyatt."

The sheriff motioned toward the man standing in the mobile home's doorway. "You want to press charges?"

"I can't," the blonde said as she shook her head. "He's my ticket to ride."

The sheriff eyed her and asked, "You work over at the Bluebonnet Grill, don't you? I've seen you on Tater Tot Tuesday."

"I'm there breakfast and lunch."

"I'll stop by tomorrow morning, have a cup of coffee, see how you're doing."

Amy swallowed hard. "That's okay. I don't need your help. I'll be fine."

The sheriff left her standing next to the truck and climbed onto the porch again. She cupped a beefy hand around the back of Joe's neck and pulled his face close enough that she could smell the alcohol oozing from his pores. She whispered into his ear, "If I get called out here again, Joe, it'll be the *last* time I get called out here."

Then she returned to her cruiser and left the two of them to work out their differences.

Appaloosa Spring, county seat and largest city in Mescalero County, Texas, had once been a brief stop for Pony Express riders, and a town had grown up around the swing station where riders exchanged mounts. Things changed over the years, and the change was never more evident than when Victoria Benson was elected sheriff. She was a bulldog of a woman who had served twenty years as an M.P., then been encouraged to retire rather than face punishment for extramarital sexual conduct that had adverse effects on her military unit. After discharge, she had moved to Appaloosa Spring to live and act naturally in ways she could not during her military career.

Monday morning, she straddled a counter stool at the Blue-bonnet Grill and watched as Amy Wyatt moved easily from customer to customer, a smile on her face that didn't reach her eyes. She appreciated the way the blonde filled out her pink-and-white uniform but didn't let her thoughts stray too far in that direction.

"I didn't expect to see you this morning, Sheriff," Amy said, filling Vic's coffee cup.

"I always keep my promises." Vic stared at the other woman and noted the thick layers of foundation and concealer around her left eye. "Once you get to know me, you'll realize that."

Amy laughed uneasily. "Unless you're coming back for Tater Tot Tuesday, I hope I don't need to get to know you."

The sheriff left it at that, finished her coffee, and slipped a generous tip under the saucer. On the trip through town to her office next to the Dairy Queen, she drove the length of Main Street, past the food co-op, a Mexican restaurant, five art galleries, two antique shops, and the renovated Bijou.

Martha greeted her with a wry smile when she walked through the door.

"What're you looking at?"

"I've just seen a face on you I ain't never seen before."

"And?"

Martha shrugged. "Sunshine's running late," she said. "The baby has colic, and she's over to Doc Pritchard's."

"Can't her wife take care of the kid?"

"Carol went up to Dallas yesterday to meet with a new artist she wants for the Lonestar Gallery and won't be home until tomorrow."

The sheriff swore under her breath. Her six officers were the only law enforcement for the entire county. When one of them called out, the others had to pick up the slack.

"It's okay," Martha said, "Clayton's covering."

All the deputies on staff when Vic took office had either retired, changed careers, or moved on, and Clayton was fresh out of the academy. Martha, one of the department's two civilian dispatchers, was the only remaining staffer who had worked for the previous sheriff.

Broad-shouldered, small-breasted, and shaped more like a barrel than an hourglass, the sheriff wore her black hair cut high and tight. The tops of her ears and the back of her neck were perpetually sunburned, and she rarely wore makeup. Tuesday morning, she applied a hint of eye shadow and mascara, and she touched it up in the ladies' room before heading to lunch.

Chicken-fried steak and all-you-can-eat tater tots kept the Bluebonnet employees busy on Tuesdays, and the sheriff had to wait for a booth to free up before being seated.

As Amy offered Vic a lunch menu, she asked, "You here for the special?"

The sheriff smiled. "Bring on the tots."

She took her time eating, and most of the lunch crowd had dissipated by the time she worked through two helpings of tots.

When Amy came to drop the check and clear the table, she asked, "Why are you here, Sheriff?"

Vic liked looking at the younger woman but couldn't admit it. She said, "I was hungry."

"That isn't why."

"I'm concerned about you. Everything okay at home?"

"Tell me what you see."

"You're healing," the sheriff said. "Joe treating you right?"
Amy shrugged. "Wouldn't do me any good to complain."
"But you'll call if things change?"
"It's only love, Sheriff. Some things *never* change."

The sheriff lunched at the Bluebonnet Grill every day for the
next few weeks, monitoring the healing progress of Amy's eye
and watching for other signs of abuse. She also pulled the file
on Joseph Carter, a lowlife with a string of petty crimes to his
name. Appaloosa Spring wouldn't miss him if he were gone, but
until he did something stupid or Amy was willing to press
charges, the sheriff had to keep her distance.

Six weeks after the first call, Martha stepped into her office.
"It's a domestic, and you'll want to handle it yourself. It's at the
Roadrunner Mobile Home Court."

"The Carter trailer?"

"Yes, ma'am," Martha said. "And don't be so obvious about
it. You got to do a better job of hiding what you're thinking."

Vic grabbed her Stetson and twenty minutes later stood on
the rickety porch outside Joseph Carter's mobile home, pound-
ing on the door with her nightstick.

"Go away," Joe shouted from the other side of the closed
door. "You got no call to be here, Sheriff."

"Open up, Joe, or I'll bust in."

She waited a moment, then backed up until she stood a leg's
length away from the flimsy door. She turned slightly and
kicked the heel of her cowboy boot just below the knob. The
door cracked, the frame cracked, and the door swung open.
Someone scrambled inside the mobile home, and a door at the
opposite end slammed. Vic stepped into the living room.

"Amy," she called. "Get on out here."

Amy stepped into the living room wearing a faded blue robe,
holding it closed with one hand.

"Show me," the sheriff said.

Amy let the robe fall open. Bruises covered her torso.

"Get dressed and come with me."

The sheriff drove two hours to the community hospital in Chicken Junction, checked Amy in through the emergency room, and asked the doctor to examine her for internal damage. Before returning to Appaloosa Spring, she left Amy with enough cash to purchase a bus ticket home.

Amy was back at the Bluebonnet Grill two days later, but she avoided Vic until the end of the lunch rush.

"Something's happened to Joe," she said, slipping into the seat opposite the sheriff. "He's disappeared."

"When's the last time you saw him?"

"The night you took me to the hospital. When I returned home, Joe was gone, and so was his truck. I haven't heard from him since."

"Isn't that a good thing?"

Amy shook her head. "When he shows up, he's going to be drunk and pissed. That won't be good."

"Have you filed a missing-person report?" the sheriff asked, knowing she hadn't.

"You think I should?"

"I'd be remiss in my duties if I didn't," Vic said. "Swing by the office after your shift and talk to Martha. She'll take down your information, and we'll get on it."

Amy reached across the table and touched the back of Vic's hand. "Thank you," she said. "I should have said this sooner but thank you for caring."

Eight weeks later, Deputy Clayton responded to a call about a pickup truck at the bottom of a ravine at the western edge of Mescalero County, not far from the Dahl Ranch. The license plate identified the truck as belonging to the missing Joseph

Carter, and the body inside was later identified as his. The Justice of the Peace conducted an inquest and attributed Carter's death to blunt force trauma to the forehead, likely the result of striking his head against the steering wheel when his Silverado hit the bottom of the ravine. A surfeit of empty beer cans and a broken Jack Daniel's bottle led Clayton to suggest in his final report that Carter had been drunk when he drove off the road and into the ravine.

The only people to attend the funeral were Amy Wyatt, the sheriff, and the pastor of the non-denominational church. After the brief graveside service ended and the pastor expressed his condolences to Amy, only the two women remained.

"I'm sorry for your loss," Vic said.

"I'm not." Amy's answer didn't surprise the sheriff. "I should be, but I'm not."

"What are you going to do now?"

Amy shrugged. "I'll swear off men. They've brought me nothing but pain and heartache."

"Mind if I check on you now and again?"

"You see me every day at the Bluebonnet, Sheriff. Ain't that enough?"

It wasn't. A month later, Vic invited Amy to dinner at Jose's Cantina, followed by a movie at the Bijou. The theater was offering a summer series of pre-code films hosted by a local movie buff who introduced them by discussing their subtle and not-so-subtle sexual subtexts.

Amy had never heard of any of the movies but told the sheriff she was happy to do something other than sit around Joe's trailer, where she still lived. The lease had nine months on it, she earned enough to pay the rent, and she had nowhere else to go.

Friday evening, the sheriff, dressed in low-heeled ropers, Wrangler jeans, and a black T-shirt, parked her black F-150 on the caliche drive and made her way onto the porch. The door she had kicked open had been repaired, and for the first time she knocked politely. A moment later, Amy answered. She wore a sleeveless light-yellow knee-length sundress that accented her figure, and she had her hair in a ponytail. Her bruises had faded. She said, "You clean up pretty good, Sheriff."

"So do you," Vic responded, gazing appreciatively at the younger woman. "And tonight I'm not the sheriff. I'm just Vic."

Amy tilted her head to the side. "That'll take some getting used to."

By the time they finished dinner, Amy had used the sheriff's name half a dozen times and it had begun to sound natural. They walked a block to the Bijou and sat in the back row, where the theater was darkest. That evening's movie was *The Sign of the Cross*, and the host encouraged the audience to watch for Claudette Colbert's first scene, in which she swims naked in a milk bath.

As the movie began, the sheriff took Amy's hand, engulfing it in hers. Amy stiffened but didn't pull away, nor did she resist when the sheriff entwined their fingers.

After the closing credits, Vic drove Amy back to Joe's mobile home, walked her to the front door, and waited while she unlocked it.

Amy turned. "Thank you for dinner and the movie and—"

Vic cupped her hand around the back of Amy's neck and held her as she leaned in for a kiss. Amy resisted at first, then relaxed and pressed herself against the sheriff. When the kiss ended, she said, "I—I have to go in now."

"We'll do this again soon," Vic said.

Amy stopped, took a deep breath, and said, "When I told you I planned to swear off men, this isn't what I had in mind. I'm not—I've never—I don't—"

"That's okay," Vic said. "I am, I have, and I do."

* * *

Little changed in Appaloosa Spring during the seven years following Joseph Carter's death. Two boarded-up buildings on Main Street were renovated and occupied by a faux antiques store and yet another art gallery, the old motor court hugging the highway north of town was turned into an artists' retreat, and new owners of the Roadrunner Mobile Home Court evicted the remaining tenants and turned the site into an RV park. The revolving door in the Mescalero County Sheriff's Office continued until Clayton and Martha were the only employees other than Vic Benson who had not moved on—Clayton because no other department would have him and Martha because she knew everything about everybody.

When Amy was evicted from her dead boyfriend's mobile home, she moved into the sheriff's three-bedroom brick ranch, and their relationship began the roller-coaster ride that often defines relationships born from the disconnect between the needs of the rescued and the desires of the rescuer. Amy still waited tables at the Bluebonnet Grill, and the sheriff still lunched there each day.

One Tater Tot Tuesday, Vic stood at the register and looked around the diner. The night before, she'd argued with Amy about the attention she'd been paying to other women.

"She didn't come in this morning," said the Bluebonnet's octogenarian owner. "Didn't call, either. I swear, Sheriff, you're going to lose that girl one of these days."

Amy had tried to leave several times, but each time Vic had tracked her down and brought her home. She returned to her cruiser and radioed dispatch. "I need eyes out for a white Equinox, license number—"

Martha interrupted her. "Again, Sheriff?"

"This time it's different. She didn't go to work, and she didn't call in sick."

"Her car's parked in the alley behind the Lonestar Gallery."

"She's with Carol?"

"Don't know," Martha said. "I just know I saw her car there earlier."

Sunshine and Carol had separated four years earlier, when Sunshine had taken a position with the Houston Police Department and left with their daughter. Vic drove down Main Street and parked at the curb in front of the gallery. She stepped from her cruiser, hitched up her gun belt, and settled her Stetson atop her head.

When she entered the gallery, Carol stepped from the back room. "May I—?"

"I know she's here," Vic said. "I want to see her."

"She doesn't want to see you."

Vic pushed past Carol into the back room, where a counter separated her from Amy. She leaned over the counter. "I was worried about you. You weren't at the diner."

"I wasn't," Amy said. She had a smear of lipstick on her cheek, and it didn't match the color on her lips. "I'm leaving."

"You'll be back tonight. I know you will."

"Not this time," Amy said.

"You've tried before. Where will you go? Who will have you? Everybody knows you're mine."

"Sheriff?" The gallery owner put her hand on Vic's arm.

Vic spun around. "Back off, Carol. This is none of your concern."

"Maybe it is. I've told Amy she can stay with me until she figures things out."

Vic turned back to Amy. "You going to leave me alone? Just walk out and leave me? I know you won't do that. You like me too much. And I like you, Amy, I really do."

"Maybe that blinds you to how you treat me."

"Wherever you go, I will find you, and I will bring you home. That's a promise, and you know I always keep my promises."

"You're just like Joe was," Amy said.

"I've never hit you."

"You don't have to hit me to hurt me, Vic. I want more than this."

"More? I give you everything you want!"

"Everything but love. You don't love me. You love *possessing* me."

Vic had no response.

"Sheriff, perhaps—"

Vic spun around. "You stick your nose in one more time, Carol, and I swear to God it'll be the last time."

Carol held up both hands, palms forward, in placation.

"Just think about it, Amy," Vic said. "I'm the best thing that's ever happened to you, and you know it." She straightened her Stetson and adjusted her gun belt. "I'll see you tonight."

She spun on her heel and strode out of the gallery.

That evening, Vic was sitting at the kitchen table nursing a bottle of Shiner Bock, reviewing a stack of applications for the perpetual openings in her department, when Amy's Equinox pulled into the driveway. She put down her beer and was standing at the door when Amy pushed it open. "I knew you didn't have the nerve to leave."

"Carol said I should come back. She says I'm not ready, but I'll always be welcome when I am."

"No matter where you go, Amy, I will follow you and bring you home."

"You think I belong to you, like I belonged to Joe?"

"No, I—"

"This is the last time," Amy said. "If you don't treat me right, Vic, the next time I really will leave. I swear."

Vic's cell phone rang. She glanced at the table, saw that the incoming call was from the station, and reached for it.

"Clayton's stuck in Chicken Junction," Martha Radisch said, "won't be back for a couple of hours, and his shift's about to start. I wouldn't have called you on makeup night if I could have found someone to cover for him."

The sheriff considered her response. The intensity of intimacy with Amy following an argument or on a day when the younger woman had run off and been brought home couldn't be denied. But something was different this time. Amy believed she had options, and if she had options, the sheriff could never fully have her. That had to change. Into the phone, she said, "I'll cover until Clayton returns."

She disconnected the call and told Amy, "I have to go. You be here when I get back."

She cupped her hand around the back of Amy's neck and kissed her. The kiss was not returned with the same level of enthusiasm.

By the time Vic returned, several hours later, Amy was curled up in bed. Vic put her uniform in the washing machine and showered. When she climbed into bed and tried to spoon the smaller woman, Amy stiffened.

"I won't ever let you leave me," Vic whispered.

The next morning, Martha Radisch stuck her head into the sheriff's office. "Carol Stemmons didn't open her gallery this morning. The insurance agent next door is concerned. Think we should send a welfare check, see if she's okay?"

Vic knew Carol wouldn't be home, and she knew it might be weeks before anyone found her in the ravine at the western edge of Mescalero County, but she said, "Send Clayton."

Help!
Released August 1965

"Help!"
"The Night Before"
"You've Got to Hide Your Love Away"
"I Need You"
"Another Girl"
"You're Going to Lose That Girl"
"Ticket to Ride"
"Act Naturally"
"It's Only Love"
"You Like Me Too Much"
"Tell Me What You See"
"I've Just Seen a Face"
"Yesterday"
"Dizzy Miss Lizzy"

"I Need You" and "You Like Me Too Much"
are by George Harrison.
"Act Naturally" is by Johnny Russell and Voni Morrison.
"Dizzy Miss Lizzy" is by Larry Williams.
All other songs are by John Lennon and Paul McCartney.

Ticket to Ride
Dru Ann Love and Kristopher Zgorski

NOW

Perhaps Lizzy's recent doctor's appointments are weighing on us. Whatever the reason, this morning I feel an overwhelming sense that I am losing her, that she is drifting away, and my usual melancholy descends deeper into sadness.

The ancient television on our chipped Formica kitchen countertop flickers into life. Its black-and-white picture rolls, then comes to rest.

"...a memorial will soon be erected to honor the thirteen individuals who lost their lives on that tragic day in 1993. Later in this special edition, we'll talk with several experts who will explain how a senseless act of violence changed the city of New York...."

I snap off the set in disgust and shake my head, the only sane response to the naiveté of these clueless newscasters.

I mustn't let today's anniversary get to me. Lizzy will know something is wrong, and that's the last thing she needs in her condition.

Though I know I shouldn't, I let my mind drift back thirty years....

THEN

The Monday afternoon humidity followed me like a shadow, coating my dark brown skin with a sheen of moisture, like dew on morning leaves. I was on my way to a job interview, and it was hard to tell if the sweat was from nerves or the weather. A teaching job at one of Manhattan's prestigious high schools would be great—I'd always wanted to make a difference in the lives of young people. At my current school, I was little more than a glorified babysitter.

I darted down the subway stairs, found a token in my pocket, and passed through the turnstile. I felt the breeze of the approaching train and smiled as its sliding doors stopped right in front of me.

A crowd streamed from the train, and I pushed against the flow like a salmon swimming upstream and made it aboard before the doors closed. I found a seat next to a young woman about my age. Her alabaster skin glistened in the dim lighting.

"Do you happen to have the time?" I asked. I almost shook my head at the triteness of the line.

"It's one twenty-five."

"Thank you," I said.

At the next stop, several people got off, leaving the half-full car with some breathing room. A young man stood by the door as if guarding it. I had a weird feeling that something wasn't right. There were empty seats, so why wasn't he sitting down?

"A warm day, isn't it?" I asked, attempting to prolong the conversation with the beautiful woman seated next to me.

Before she could respond, the young man began pacing up and down the aisle, mumbling angrily. I locked eyes with him, and his stare was intense and erratic. The woman beside me wrapped her arms protectively around her black purse. Was it possible that her white skin had become even paler?

I was leaning over to assure her that things would be okay

when I heard a *pop-pop-pop.*

The kid was waving a gun with a randomness that bordered on chaos, and the train exploded with the sounds of more bullets being fired.

"Get down," I screamed, diving for the floor.

The shooting continued, and the passengers scrambled for cover, screaming for help. Blood splattered on the car's windows, poles, and floor, and the screams faded into moans, like the drone of a wasp's nest before a swarm.

When the train finally stopped again, the young man dropped his gun and raced out the automatic doors, running toward the stairs.

There were screams and tears all around me. All I wanted was to escape being trapped for even a moment longer, but I remembered the woman who had told me the time just before the carnage began. Seeing her huddled on the floor, I reached for her hand—and that's when I noticed the blood darkening her blouse.

NOW

The sizzle of bacon beckons Lizzy to the kitchen. I pour cocoa for both of us and set a plate before her.

She smiles. "Lester, it smells so good! How do you make the bacon this crisp?"

"Years of practice, my dear, years of practice."

She laughs and eats her breakfast, staring off into space, enjoying the new day.

When we finish, I clear the table. While Lizzy gets dressed, I wash the dishes. She considers the simple chores I do to make her life easier the acts of a knight in shining armor, but they're really just my way of showing her my love. What would she think if she knew how far I've taken my devotion?

Once I complete my kitchen tasks, I find Lizzy sitting on the

111

edge of the bed in a blue sweater and a pair of black slacks, looking just as beautiful as the day I married her.

"Are we going to have fun today?" she asks.

I chuckle. "Yes, my love, I thought maybe we'd head to Coney Island and recapture our youth."

I can see her delighted reaction to the idea of fun and frolic, but I worry that, somewhere deep in her mind, she is remembering the neurologist's most recent report.

Her repetitive questions, increasing confusion, and general anxiety are warnings that her condition is worsening, but most concerning of late have been the memory lapses.

Sure enough, she almost instantly forgets my suggestion of an excursion to Coney Island and drifts off to that magical place where she has no concerns. I hate to disturb her, but the doctor has told us that mental stimulation and exercise will be good for her—and the process of getting out the door takes time.

"Honey, let's go," I say, and immediately see the tics that begin when she realizes we'll be leaving our building. "It's safe out there, remember? I'll never let anyone hurt you again."

I felt the same way thirty years ago, when I first walked into her hospital room....

THEN

I held the woman's damaged body until the paramedics arrived. I could feel her energy level dropping. Her face was swollen where she'd slammed against the metal seat on her way down, and the bullet wound wouldn't stop bleeding. Thankfully, I heard her whisper her name to the EMTs as they wheeled the gurney away. They wouldn't let me ride with them, of course, but at least they told me where they were taking her.

The chairs in the hospital's waiting room were calming shades of blue and green, but I was unable to control my nerves enough to sit. Instead, I paced the floor like an expectant father. I knew there was no way the ER staff would give me any information, much less allow me to visit a woman I'd met only a few hours earlier. Yet something compelled me to stay as close to her side as I could.

Sometime in the middle of the night, a nurse tapped my shoulder, waking me from a fitful nap. "Miss Lizzy is asking for you," she said.

I followed her down antiseptic halls, past beeping machines and their whispering operators. Behind an ugly green curtain, I found Lizzy in bed, bandaged and bruised. Despite the ordeal she had undergone, she was still beautiful.

When the nurse left us alone, Lizzy gave her best effort at a smile. "The nurse told me someone was in the waiting room. I knew it had to be you."

I approached her bedside. "How did you convince them to let me see you?"

Her cheeks flushed. "I might have told them you were my fiancé," she said, unable to disguise the giggle behind the words.

"You did not! Well, in that case, I'd better introduce myself. I'm Lester Evans."

"I'm glad you're here, Lester Evans," she said. "I don't have anyone else."

"You have me," I said, taking her hand. "You'll always have me."

I didn't know at the time how prophetic those words would become.

NOW

A taxi blares its horn to alert some slowpoke to its presence, and Lizzy hunches over and covers her ears at the sound. I stroke her hand reassuringly.

These moments of comfort are what have sustained us for

three decades. Our life today bears little resemblance to what we had envisioned. After we got married, Lizzy decided she couldn't bear to bring a child into a world so dominated by gun violence. There were periods when she felt that living with me was bringing her down—seeing me was a constant reminder of that tragic morning on the subway. But we endured, and now, at last, we are happy.

From the vestibule of our building, flashing headlights alert us to the arrival of our Uber. I carefully navigate Lizzy outside, open the door for her, and make sure she is settled before circling the car to get in on the other side.

I put on my seat belt before turning to help Lizzy with hers. To my surprise, I see her mimic my movements, proudly buckling herself in without assistance.

It may seem silly to consider such a simple act as an accomplishment, but survivors of traumatic events are much more likely to develop early-onset dementia. Now that my wife is headed in that direction, I relish those moments when the old Lizzy, the independent Lizzy, re-emerges from the gathering fog.

I will go to my grave blaming that subway gunman for what he did to her, what he *took* from her, from us.

Just thinking about it makes what I did all the more understandable....

THEN

It was happenstance, the day I saw him again, twenty-five years after his rampage. I had walked to our neighborhood convenience store to pick up a few items, and there in line before me was that face, a face I could never forget. Like me, he had aged—but his cold eyes had not changed.

My first instinct was to call the cops, but something stopped me. Justice is served less and less often these days—some legal loophole or lawyerly b.s. gets in the way. So I followed him instead, as if I were Easy Rawlins deep into an investigation.

To my dismay, I learned that, after the psychiatrists had judged him rehabilitated and released him from his long confinement to a mental institution, he had rented a place just two blocks from our apartment. That was almost certainly a coincidence, but its nature didn't alter its impact.

The subway gunman hadn't a care in the world, while just a few corners away Lizzy's deteriorating cognitive health was a constant challenge. Unsure what to do, I returned home, but soon found myself lingering outside his building night after night.

I had become a stalker, and at last I decided to approach him directly, to tell him I was there that day he destroyed so many lives, including my wife's.

When I did, he threw back his head and laughed.

My blood boiled, the anger that lurked behind the veil of our life together burst loose, and before I knew what I was doing, my hands were around his neck. I strangled him without a second thought, and when I was sure he was dead, a sense of calm settled over me.

We were only a few steps from the Gowanus Canal, and I felt confident it would be virtually impossible to discover a body there.

NOW

"I love this stretch of road," I say as we turn onto Ocean Parkway, using landmarks as a distraction from the doctor's diagnosis. *Deterioration is progressing faster than we would like.* We knew for some time that this was inevitable, but hearing it said so matter-of-factly still came as a shock.

I lean closer to Lizzy. "We're approaching the curve that gives you a view of the Aquarium, sweetie." I watch her face light up at the sight of the building.

"And there she is," I say, a moment later, "the Cyclone,

standing tall for ninety-five years. Isn't she majestic?"

"I'm going to ride her today, Lester," Lizzy says.

"I'm not sure that's such a great idea, darling. You've always been afraid of heights."

The car pulls up to the Luna Park entrance, and Lizzy's grin tells me I made the right choice for our day out.

She barely waits for the car to come to a full stop before unbuckling her seatbelt and throwing open the door with youthful abandon.

I take her arm, and we head for the stairs that will lead us to the boardwalk. The sounds of happiness float on the air as people whoop and holler on the rides while others play carnival games along the midway.

As we climb the steps, I reflect on the strange trajectory of our lives. That one act of violence, all those years ago, still echoes.

When we reach the top, the sight of the Atlantic Ocean stops us in our tracks. It is moments like this that make our journey worthwhile, our lives worth living.

We walk hand in hand along the boardwalk, past Deno's Wonder Wheel and Nathan's Famous. Just seven miles to the north lies the Gowanus Canal, where I pushed the shooter's body into the water five years ago. In many ways, that night feels like ancient history, an eon away from where we are today.

We begin to retrace our steps, and suddenly I feel compelled to confess my crime. "You know how I'm always telling you the shooter can never hurt you again?" I take a deep breath. "Well, Lizzy, I did something...."

She shrieks, but not from shock. We have reached the legendary B&B Carousell, and Lizzy's excitement tells me this will be the perfect ride for her. I let my confession fade with the wind and say, "Look, dear. You can pretend you're riding high, soaring through the air on the back of a stallion!"

I encourage her to approach the booth alone and hear her ask the attendant, "Can I get a ticket, please? A ticket to ride your horses?"

He hands her the ticket, and I take care of the payment.

With fifty hand-carved wooden horses and two majestic chariots to choose from, I am not surprised by Lizzy's choice of the most brightly painted steed. I worry that she will struggle to hoist herself into the saddle, but she makes it look easy, like someone half her age.

As the music begins, the carousel starts to turn. I lose sight of Lizzy for a few moments as her painted horse reaches the back of the ride, but then she appears again, a brilliant smile on her face, galloping around to the front of the circle, the horses rising and falling in time to the music.

Eventually, the carousel slows to a stop, and Lizzy dismounts, noticeably wobbly. As she comes through the exit gate, I take her arm.

She looks up at me, confusion and fear on her face.

"Do I know you?" she says, and my heart breaks into a million pieces.

I know the spell will pass in a matter of moments, but one of these days Lizzy will permanently forget who I am, who *she* is. Her mind will fly off to some faraway place where I won't be able to reach her.

She will forget the life we have built together. But she will also forget at last that horrible day on the subway, the day we met.

I take a deep breath and guide Lizzy to a nearby bench, where we sit and watch the birds glide on the wind and the sun begin its slow descent.

Rubber Soul
Released December 1965

"Drive My Car"
"Norwegian Wood (This Bird Has Flown)"
"You Won't See Me"
"Nowhere Man"
"Think For Yourself"
"The Word"
"Michelle"
"What Goes On"
"Girl"
"I'm Looking Through You"
"In My Life"
"Wait"
"If I Needed Someone"
"Run For Your Life"

"Think For Yourself" and "If I Needed Someone"
are by George Harrison.
"What Goes On" is by John Lennon, Paul McCartney,
and Richard Starkey.
All other songs are by John Lennon and Paul McCartney.

Run For Your Life
Paul Charles

1

"Early this morning, I woke up with a fright," the woman standing on the general public's side of the polished dark wood counter in North Bridge House, the home of Camden Town's Criminal Investigation Department, began calmly. "I checked my phone—it was two eighteen—and I experienced an overwhelming anxiety about my sister Barbara, more like a premonition. When we were teenagers, I *always* knew when something was wrong with her. We're twins, you see."

Desk Sergeant Timothy Flynn offered tea and sympathy to the stunning bottle blonde. She was nearing the end of her twenties, about five-five, slim but not thin, perfectly made up, dressed in skin-tight black jeans, a white T-shirt under a red military-style jacket, red Converse sneakers, a black leather rucksack slung over her shoulder.

DS Flynn wrote her name—Brigitte Baker—at the top of a report sheet. The other particulars he included were age (twenty-eight), occupation (travel agent), address (100 Regents Park Road, Primrose Hill, NW1), and marital status (single). He added Barbara Stanley's details: age (twenty-eight), occupation (dental hygienist), address (16 Chamberlain Street, Primrose Hill, NW1), and status (married to Sean Stanley).

121

"I wonder," Flynn said. "In the past, when you experienced those episodes, how would they—?"

"On one occasion," Brigitte interrupted, "we went for an early morning dip in the Ladies Pond on Hampstead Heath. Barbara had her suit on underneath her clothes, and she immediately peeled off and jumped in, while I found a sheltered spot to change. As I was unpacking my swimwear, I had an episode. The works: cold sweat, acute shivers, difficulty breathing. Fully clothed, I raced to the side of the pond.

"Barbara was waving her arms frantically and splashing. I swam out to her, remembering our mum's advice: in life, as in the swimming pool, the more you splash and make waves, the slower you'll go. Barbara was pointing under the water. I went down and discovered her difficulty. Her left foot had become lodged in a bicycle frame some idiot had dumped in the pond, and the frame was caught in some tree roots. I freed her foot and dragged her to the bank, and we collapsed in each other's arms sobbing."

Telling the story had forced Brigitte Baker to relive the episode, and Flynn now found himself fearing for Barbara Stanley's wellbeing.

2

A missing person is not officially a "Misper" until they've been missing for at least twenty-four hours. Flynn fast-tracked this one by visiting the office of his boss, Detective Inspector Christy Kennedy. He relayed his concern, and they both returned to the interview room.

"When did you last see Barbara?" Kennedy asked, in his gentle Ulster brogue.

"We see or at least phone each other every day."

"And you last *saw* her when?" Kennedy continued, as DS King entered the room.

"We had a quick coffee in the Coffee Jar on Parkway after lunch yesterday."

"Were you due to see her today?" King asked.

"Well," Brigitte replied, "I was actually at her house at six this morning."

"Was that prearranged?" Kennedy asked.

"No, it was because of the premonition I had."

"Was she at home?"

"No." Brigitte paused. "At first, her husband Sean—he's a surgeon—refused to answer the doorbell. He eventually stuck his head out their bedroom window and hissed, 'Babs is not home. She didn't come home last night. And, no, I don't know where she is, and, no, I don't know when she'll be back. Now eff off, I'm going back to sleep.' He closed the window. I put my finger on the doorbell and left it there. He finally came down, and I ran past him into the house and searched every room, even his sacred basement, but Barbara wasn't there."

"Did Sean threaten you?" Kennedy asked, looking for an excuse to visit the house without a warrant.

"No, he didn't."

"Did he look concerned that his wife had stayed out all night?" King asked.

"Not in the slightest."

"Did he suggest where he thought she might be?" Kennedy continued.

"He said he hadn't a clue, though he admitted they'd had an argument yesterday evening and she'd run off."

"Had she run off before?" King asked.

"When she did, it was always just around the corner to me. I found these on her bedside table," Brigitte said, rummaging through her rucksack and producing a blue spectacles case, which she opened to reveal a pair of glasses with thick lenses.

"Barbara's?" King guessed.

Brigitte nodded.

The three of them eyed the spectacles.

"It wasn't just that she *wouldn't* go anywhere without her glasses," Brigitte said. "She *couldn't*. She even had to have prescription lenses in her swimming goggles."

"Did she not have a spare pair?" Kennedy asked.

"She did,' Brigitte acknowledged, and produced a red case from her rucksack. "Blue is her normal pair, and red is the backup. Without either pair, she couldn't see a thing."

3

"So you're convinced Barbara must still be somewhere in the house?" Kennedy asked.

"She's never far from her glasses," Brigitte Baker said.

"Okay." Kennedy stood. "Let's go to Chamberlain Street."

"Will we need a search warrant?" King asked.

"We will, but we don't have time to wait for one. We'll see how Mister Stanley reacts to our visit. If he refuses admission, we'll leave a couple of constables on guard—one front and one rear—until Sergeant Flynn can find someone to sign a warrant."

4

The first three things Kennedy noticed about Sean Stanley were his earnest brown eyebrows, his pointed chin, and his "please believe me, I always speak the truth" eyes, which were magnified by his National Health wire-frame specs. He wore a black polo-neck sweater under a blue denim jacket, with a matching pair of jeans and black canvas slip-ons that minimized his five-nine frame. His head and face were clean-shaven. A shadow betrayed the extent of his rapidly receding hairline.

"A bit early for bobbies on the beat?" he said in a singsong, clocking the two constables behind King and Kennedy.

"Good morning, sir," Kennedy began, producing his warrant

card. "This is"—he paused to allow his colleague to present her
I.D. for inspection—"Detective Sergeant Dot King, and these
are Constables Ian Ward and Thomas McDonald."

"I'll bet my batty sister-in-law is behind this."

"Actually, it's your wife we're concerned about," King offered, opening her pink notebook.

"That makes three of us," Stanley said. "Five if we include
your two bobbies, six if we include Miss Concerned of Camden
Town." He strained on his tiptoes to see if he could spot Brigitte Baker, but Kennedy had insisted she remain at home.

"Have you any idea of her whereabouts?" Kennedy asked.

"Na, na, na," Stanley grunted.

"You don't seem concerned, sir, if I may say," King continued.

"Indeed you may, Dorothy. Indeed you may." Stanley
grinned. "But I'd like to add for the record that we all show
concern in diverse ways."

"Can we come in, sir?" Kennedy asked politely.

"They say a man's home is his castle, and I officially declare
this castle open to the bobbies," Stanley said, bending forward
and swinging his right arm in an exaggerated arc.

Sean Stanley's "castle" was a deceptive building. From the
outside, it looked like any other house on the small cul-de-sac in
the heart of Primrose Hill. On the inside, however, it was furnished tastefully and sparingly with expensive modern furniture.

"Have a look 'round, officers. I'll see if I can rustle up some
tea and meet you in the study. I'd usually have Babs fetch it, but
sadly she's disappeared."

The house had three bedrooms—two with en suite bathrooms—a family bathroom on the top landing, a small home
office, a spacious kitchen and dining area, a large sitting room,
and the aforementioned study.

By the door to the home office was a spiral staircase leading
to an open-plan basement. The basement was covered in white
tiles—floor, ceiling, and walls. It was extravagantly decked out
with gym apparatus, with a power shower in one corner.

What struck Kennedy about the gym was the smell of disinfectant and the sound of what appeared to be an air-conditioning unit. The longer he remained in the basement, the less he noticed the sound of the A/C—but the more he noticed the smell.

"Is that the mark of a leather shoe sole?" King asked Kennedy, noting a blemish on the tiled floor. "Or a rubber one?"

Finding no sign of Barbara Stanley, Kennedy and King made their way to the study.

Atop an antiquated record player, Kennedy noticed an Elvis Presley seven-inch single ("Baby, Let's Play House") and three LPs (Nancy Sinatra's *Boots*, Johnny Rivers' *And I Know You Wanna Dance*, and Gary Lewis and the Playboys' *She's Just My Style*). All were vinyl, in their original sleeves, and appeared to be in mint condition. Kennedy noted numerous medical volumes on the shelves of the book-lined wall behind Stanley's desk. He was still examining the books when Stanley came in with a tray laden with tea, milk, sugar and Penguin biscuits.

"Has your wife ever disappeared before?" Kennedy asked.

"Na, na, na," Stanley replied. "I mean, you'd hardly call doing a runner for an evening as missing, would you?"

"Well, Brigitte is very worried about her," Kennedy said.

"Ah, sisters," Sean sighed. "Girls who don't like each other very much but have to pretend they do."

"Absolute crap," King whispered, but Stanley heard her and glared.

"What was the argument about?" Kennedy inquired.

"Sorry? What argument is it you speak of?"

"You told Brigitte this morning that you and Barbara had a fight yesterday evening, and that was why she ran off."

"Ah, that one. Why are men and women both put on this earth if not to be in constant conflict with one another?"

"I'm not sure I agree with that, sir," Kennedy said.

"I think John Wesley said we'll agree to disagree," Stanley smirked. "What I say is, I'll let you be in my dreams if I can be in yours."

"I believe that was Bob Dylan," Kennedy offered, remembering his girlfriend's favorite artist.

"So what was the fight about?" King asked.

"Hardly a fight," Stanley said. "Merely words spoken in anger between a man and his wife."

"Yet when Brigitte Baker visited your house this morning," King said, checking her notebook, "you told her your wife had run away because you had a fight."

"It was nothing," Stanley said.

"It was hardly nothing, sir, if your wife ran off late last night and hasn't yet returned."

"What's the best way to put this?" Stanley mused. "Oh, I'll just say it. I believe my wife was cheating on me." When neither King nor Kennedy reacted to this, he continued. "I happened to see her getting very friendly with a malevolent character in a dark corner of the York & Albany two nights ago."

"Did you know the gentleman?" Kennedy asked.

"One should never address a scoundrel as a gentleman," Stanley lectured. "It only affords them the cloak of decency they crave."

"Nonetheless," Kennedy prompted.

"As it happens, I do know him," Stanley admitted. "He's a former friend of mine, William Turner, sometimes known as Bill or Billy or even, when he's on the ale, Willie."

"Would you know where we could find him?" King asked.

"I believe he is currently sofa-surfing in an apartment on the top floor of the tower block overlooking the Hill. It's on Primrose Hill Road, on the right as you go up."

"You mean Hill View?" King guessed.

"Indeed I do, Dorothy. Indeed I do."

"What time did your wife leave yesterday evening?" Kennedy asked, no longer amused by Brigitte Baker's brother-in-law.

"I would say seven of the clock."

"And did you hear from her later?"

"No, I did not."

"Did you go looking for her?"

"No. To be found, a person must needs *want* to be found."

"Not if she's dead, sir," Kennedy suggested.

"Touché, officer."

"What did you do for the rest of the evening?"

"I never have difficulty entertaining myself."

"What did you *do*, sir?"

"I watched TV, I read, I listened to music."

"What did you watch on TV?" Kennedy asked.

"The only watchable program *on* TV, *Mortimer and Whitehouse—Gone Fishing*."

"What did you read?"

"The newspaper."

"Which one?"

"*The Times*."

"What was on the front page?"

"Putin, if memory serves."

"What music did you listen to?" Kennedy pushed, hoping for a radio station.

"The Beatles."

"Which album?"

"My favorite, *Rubber Soul*."

"Good choice, sir. The last track, 'Tomorrow Never Knows,' is a favorite of mine."

"Yes, a very impressive song, Inspector," Stanley replied, clearly enjoying the conversational tone of the questioning.

"Did you ring anyone?" Kennedy asked, moving back into gear.

"No."

"Did anyone ring you?"

"No!" Stanley snapped.

"Okay," Kennedy said. "We're going to leave Constables Ward and McDonald to protect the house until we return, sir. We're waiting for a search warrant. In the meantime, we'll pay a visit to Mister William Turner."

5

As luck would have it, William ("Call me Willie") Turner was on the premises—not sofa-surfing but in fact the owner of a top-floor flat with spectacular views.

"Was Missus Barbara Stanley here yesterday evening?" Kennedy asked, post introductions.

"She's *never* been here," Turner said. He was not quite six feet tall, a wiry, effervescent man in his fifties with curly brown hair and a permanent smile.

"Were you at home last night?" King asked.

"Yes, I had a few friends 'round for dinner. They arrived at eight and left well after midnight, probably closer to one."

"Could you give us the names and contact details of those in attendance, please?" King asked.

"Francie Schwartz and Walter Rhone," Turner replied immediately, adding their phone numbers.

"And would you mind telling us what you did on *Wednesday* night?" Kennedy asked.

Turner looked a bit awkward.

"We have a witness claiming he saw you in the York & Albany with Barbara Stanley," Kennedy offered.

Turner grinned. "Actually, I *was* in the York & Albany on Wednesday, but I wasn't dining with Barbara Stanley."

"Oh?"

"I was with her sister, Brigitte Baker."

6

Five minutes later, King and Kennedy were knocking on the door of 100 Regent's Park Road.

Brigitte Baker showed them into her busily furnished living room, its floor-to-ceiling windows looking out on the foot of Primrose Hill. As King took a leather stool by a white marble mantlepiece supporting a giant mirror, Kennedy was distracted by the reflection of a large council waste-truck making its rounds, emptying the man-high wheelie waste bins that were strategically placed around the Hill.

"Any news?" Brigitte asked.

"Nothing so far," Kennedy apologized. "Sean Stanley told us that he and Barbara argued yesterday evening over her affair with William Turner. He spotted Mister Turner and his wife together in the York & Albany, he said, two nights ago."

"What?"

"We've just been to visit Mister Turner, and he told us—"

"Sean told you that Willie Turner was out with *Barbara* on Wednesday?"

Kennedy nodded.

"The daft ape. Sean, like my sister, is blind as a bat, but *un*-like my sister he refuses to wear his glasses in public. If he'd had his glasses on, he'd have seen that I was the twin who was out with Willie on Wednesday evening."

"Are *you* having an affair with Mister Turner?" King asked.

"I believe the phrase 'having an affair' implies deceit," Brigitte smiled. "Neither Willie nor I have any other romantic commitments, so 'affair' is not the correct term. Perhaps 'relationship' would be a better word. Mister Turner and I are in a relationship."

"Was Sean Stanley aware of this relationship?"

"We keep it low-key. Sean and Willie are old friends. Willie dated my sister before Sean did. In fact, it was Willie who introduced Sean to Barbara."

"But you and Turner dating—what's that got to do with Sean Stanley?" King asked.

"Barbara didn't want Sean to know about Willie and me."

King shook her head, not understanding.

"Early in their relationship, Sean admitted to Barbara that he was a wicked man, born into this life with a jealous mind. He warned Barbara that, if he ever caught her cheating, it would be all over for her—and she worried that someone might see me with Willie and mistake me for her."

King frowned, putting the pieces together. "And now you think Mister Stanley thought he saw his wife cheating on him with Mister Turner and—and has done her some harm?"

"Has he ever hit your sister?" Kennedy asked.

"I believe so, but she never admitted it. She occasionally had visible bruises, but she always had the clichéd excuses—she'd walked into a door or slipped on the floor."

7

When Kennedy and King reached 16 Chamberlain Street, they found DS Flynn ready with a signed search warrant.

They returned to Stanley's white-tiled basement gym, and Kennedy was again distracted by the sound of the air conditioning and a strong smell of disinfectant. Oddly, there was no A/C unit—but he discovered a MeacoDry ABC portable dehumidifier unit amongst the fitness apparatus. Using its single finger-hole, he slid out the collection tank—which holds the excess moisture drawn from the air in damp buildings—from under the grill and shivered at its contents.

He slid the tank slowly back into the unit, then sent DS King on a chore and found Sean Stanley in his study.

"Beautiful house you have here, sir," he started.

"Thanks. I like it."

"Have you been here long?"

"A good few years."

"It's in wonderful condition," Kennedy said. "Maybe a wee bit of damp in the basement?"

"Damp?"

"It's just that I noticed a dehumidifier unit down there."

"Oh, that. Surgery can be quite strenuous, you know, so I work out to keep in shape. I find the dehumidifier keeps the air fresh for me, if you see what I mean."

8

A few minutes later, Kennedy said, "You know, sir, I'm a bit surprised."

"Oh?"

"Yes, well, we've been chatting for some time, and you haven't asked me about your wife."

Just then, DS King entered the study and nodded.

"You told us you were in the York & Albany on Wednesday evening and thought you saw your wife with William Turner."

"I did see Babs with Turner," Stanley snapped.

"Actually, sir, that was her sister Brigitte."

"Impossible!" Stanley barked.

"Both Mister Turner and Brigitte acknowledged to DS King and myself that they've been dating for quite a while."

"But then—"

"Mister Sean Stanley, we're arresting you for the murder of your wife," Kennedy said, standing. "DS King will read you your rights."

"Na, na, na!" Stanley shouted, shaking his head furiously. "There's no body!"

"Dehumidifiers collect the moisture out of the air, sir," Kennedy offered.

"And?"

"Well, the moisture collected in your dehumidifier is pink, sir. Despite your efforts to clean up the mess you made, I bet we'll find traces of your wife's DNA in that pink liquid."

"But you won't be able to compare the DNA with a body."

"Well, two things about that. One, your wife has a twin sister, and twins' DNA is close enough for confirmation."

"But still no body," Stanley crowed. "No body, no crime, Inspector."

"Yes, and that's my second point. As you well know, there are large waste bins by all the gates into Primrose Hill. Those bins were just now emptied into a refuse truck for the first time since yesterday. DS King here intercepted the truck and diverted it to North Bridge House for closer inspection of its contents. We expect to find the remains of your wife in several bin bags amongst that rubbish."

9

"You were prepared to arrest a man because he didn't know the name of a Beatles song?" Dot King said, as Sean Stanley was taken into custody.

"No, Detective, he was caught out because he lied. He claimed that *Rubber Soul* was his favorite Beatles album, yet when I mentioned 'Tomorrow Never Knows' as being the final track on that album, he agreed that it was. If *Rubber Soul* was indeed his favorite album, he would have known that 'Tomorrow Never Knows' isn't even *on* that record. It's on *Revolver*. So he lied about the fact that he was listening to music. I just needed to work out *why* he was lying."

"Just out of curiosity, sir, what *is* the final track on *Rubber Soul*?"

"'Run For Your Life,'" Kennedy replied.

"If only she had," King whispered. "If only she had."

Yesterday and Today
Released June 1966

"Drive My Car"
"I'm Only Sleeping"
"Nowhere Man"
"Doctor Robert"
"Yesterday"
"Act Naturally"
"And Your Bird Can Sing"
"If I Needed Someone"
"We Can Work It Out"
"What Goes On"
"Day Tripper"

"Act Naturally" is by Johnny Russell and Voni Morrison.
"If I Needed Someone" is by George Harrison.
"What Goes On" is by John Lennon, Paul McCartney,
and Richard Starkey.
All other songs are by John Lennon and Paul McCartney.

We Can Work It Out
John M. Floyd

"There they are," I said. "Right on time."

Cecil interrupted his study of his iPhone screen to look up at me. We were sitting in the moonlight on the open tailgate of my truck, which I'd parked on a hill overlooking the local high school's football field. I handed him the binoculars and pointed.

In the parking lot below, three people—an older man in a fringe coat, a tall guy built like a weightlifter, and a young woman with curly blond hair—had climbed out of a Mercedes SUV and were headed for the field. They disappeared from view behind the end-zone bleachers, then emerged and settled in near the fifty-yard-line on the far side. The Friday-night lights were blazing, the crowd was sparse, and the game was already underway. I watched Cecil as he watched the three new arrivals.

"They brought the bodyguard," he said, as if I hadn't noticed.

"As usual." I took the glasses back and focused again on the seated trio—Lawson, his hired help, and his daughter. "You ready?"

"Dern right," he said.

I hoped so. The truth was that Cecil Prescott—my second cousin on my mother's side—was seldom ready to do *anything* that required physical or mental exertion. Since leaving the Army, both of us seemed to have grown heavier in the gut department and lighter in the brains department, and we were barely twenty-five.

But tonight we had to depend on each other, the way we did in Afghanistan, and we both knew it. Cecil and I were roommates at a trailer park just down the road, both of us single and out of work and out of options and with only one vehicle between us.

If tonight panned out, our financial problems would be solved, and there was no reason it shouldn't go well. I might be a failure at gainful employment, but I'm a good planner. Anytime a problem pops up, my go-to thought is, *We can work it out.*

So far, we always had.

"Go on down," I said. "I'll call you when she heads your way."

Cecil pocketed his phone and trudged into the trees. I didn't bother trying to track him with the binoculars—he'd be in thick woods down the hill and around the back of the cinderblock building that housed the restrooms and concession stand. I checked the time and went back to watching the three spectators.

I felt certain that at some point, the blond girl—Everett Lawson's twenty-two-year-old daughter Hartley, known far and wide as "Honey"—would get up and walk down to the long, low building at the east end zone. There she would visit the ladies' restroom and then the snack bar, where she would buy a Coke and return to her seat. She'd done exactly that on each of the three Fridays Cecil and I had cased the situation, and she'd been accompanied every time by her father's oversized bodyguard, who lumbered along behind her the whole way and waited in the hall outside the restroom during her pit stop and by her side at the snack counter.

I wasn't worried about the guard. The ladies' room, which he wouldn't be entering, was where everything would happen.

The key to our plan—pun intended—was something I'd

found on the floor outside a broom closet at the concession stand one night two months ago during a game: an unmarked metal key. Sneaky guy that I am, I pocketed it, returned after the building was closed, and tried it in all the outside doors. It wound up fitting a back door to the ladies' restroom, which rendered it useless to me, because (1) there was nothing I wanted in the ladies' room and (2) the restrooms and the hallway outside them were unconnected to the rest of the building, which contained things that I *might* have wanted. Disappointed, I saved the key anyway, just in case.

And, lo and behold, it had become useful. With that key, Cecil would be able to enter the women's restroom through the back door, hide in one of the rear stalls, wait for our target to enter the room, clap a hand over her mouth, and whisk her back out to me and my truck on the far side of the woods. And that little package, one Honey Lawson, would be our ticket out of Dry Springs, Texas. Her widowed father owned almost everything in the county, and paying us for her safe return would be as easy and painless for him as paying one of his flunkies to polish his Benz.

A word of explanation: if it seems that Cecil would be doing most of the evening's work...well, he would be. But that was necessary, because (1) there was the chance somebody might spot him in the ladies' room, and with his long feminine eyelashes, a clean-shaven baby face, a ball cap pulled low on his forehead, a baggy coat, and his ponytail sticking out the back of his cap, he might pass for a jeans-and-cowboy-boots farm girl, which I couldn't, and (2) he was bigger than me, so if our target put up a fight he'd be more able to get her through the hundred yards of pine forest between the building and my truck. He understood all that and didn't mind. After all, he'd be getting half the ransom.

I was so caught up in thinking all this as I sat there with my binoculars and watched Lawson and his daughter and his bodyguard that I almost missed our cue. Halfway through the first quarter, much earlier than expected, Honey Lawson stood and climbed down from the stands and walked alone down the sideline. The hulking bodyguard stayed in his seat for a change, but Dry Springs had the ball, first and goal on the visitors' five, and I guess he didn't want to miss a home-team score. I snatched my phone from my pocket and texted one word: "Go!"

It took me two minutes to drive down off the hill and along the winding dirt road to the remote spot we'd picked. When I got there, I stopped and sat with the motor running and watched the woods in the direction of the ball field. I could hear the half-hearted cheers in the distance. As long as nothing catastrophic disrupted the mission—like a witness strolling into the ladies' room at exactly the wrong moment—it wouldn't be long now.

I was right. Five minutes later, Cecil emerged from the trees, hurrying a young woman in a black fleece coat beside him, her curly hair gleaming gold in the moonlight. I leaned over to open his door, and he boosted the girl onto the seat between us. I had a bandana ready, which I tied securely over her eyes. Once she was blindfolded, Cecil and I whipped off the ski masks we'd put on at Zero Hour and exchanged a quick triumphant look, and then he buckled her in and I took off.

It had worked. And since the bodyguard for once hadn't been waiting for her outside the restroom, her absence might not even be noticed for a while. As I drove, I let out a sigh of relief. The hard part, I thought, was over.

I couldn't have been more wrong.

At a quarter to eight, we escorted Honey Lawson into the back bedroom of our trailer and removed her coat and blindfold. Cecil tossed the coat into the closet as I carefully patted her jeans pockets. Nothing. Not even a phone.

"You relocked the back door," I asked my cousin. "Right?"

"Right."

Good. The cops—and Lawson and his guard—would wonder how someone had gotten her out without being seen, and any confusion on their part would be to our advantage.

I was trying hard not to smile. Like the bear raiding the beehive, we'd stolen the honey and gotten away clean.

"Sit down, Miss Lawson," I said. She did, on the side of the bed. Cecil took the room's only chair, and I remained standing. For some reason, she didn't seem all that upset.

After a hesitation, she asked, "Who are you? What's going on?"

"You've been kidnapped," I said.

She looked around. "Where am I?"

"In a safe place, about half an hour from your house."

"I asked you who you are."

"We're your abductors. You can call me Woody." I nodded toward Cecil. "He's Buzz."

She gave each of us a hard look. Her eyes were as cool and blue as a November sky.

"We're not gonna hurt you," I said. "I promise."

"What is it you want?"

"Money. From your daddy, in exchange for you."

"From my daddy?"

"That's right. Everett Lawson." This time I smiled. "I have a feeling he can afford it."

At that, she lowered her head and chuckled, as if I'd told an especially good joke.

"What's funny?"

"You are. Everett Lawson can afford it, all right. He can afford just about anything."

"I'm glad you agree."

"Problem is," she said, "he ain't my daddy."

The room went dead silent.

"Excuse me?" I said.

141

She shook her head. "You screwed up, boys. I ain't Honey Lawson. I'm a stand-in."

I just stared at her. "A what?"

"A lookalike. A double. My name's Brittany. Believe me, Honey and me's from different sides of the tracks. Didn't you idiots think it was strange he didn't send Carl to the john with me?"

"Carl?"

"The bodyguard. Big guy. You musta noticed him."

I gulped.

"So you mean—you and Honey are twins?"

"No, we ain't twins, Einstein. We ain't even kin."

"She's lying," Cecil said. "She's Honey. Nobody could look that much like somebody else. The eyes, the walk, the hair—"

He stopped. She had gripped the hairline above her forehead and pulled backward. The blond wig came off easily, exposing short jet-black hair. She was still a beauty—she'd be a beauty if she were bald and cross-eyed—but she no longer looked like Honey Lawson.

My head was spinning, my heart sinking. Cecil sat frozen in his chair.

Our captive stared calmly back at us, wig in hand. "I earned my pay tonight, you dipweeds. You scared me, I admit that, but what you pulled is exactly why he hired me."

"But, if that's true—"

"It's true." She tossed the wig aside. "Honey was tired of going to all them ballgames, and she finally told her daddy she wouldn't. He worries all the time about him or Honey getting kidnapped, and since two of his security guys quit last week and Lawson didn't want nobody knowing she was home alone tonight, what does he do?" She pointed to herself. "He takes good old Britt with him to the game in Honey's place. Sorta like a decoy. Not the first time I filled in when little Honey got a bug up her butt and wanted to skip some event Everett thought she oughta be seen at. And wouldn't you know it, he was right to be worried. Guess I oughta be glad I got snatched instead of shot." She frowned at that thought. "You don't plan to shoot me, right?"

This was too much to process. "Buzz and I need to talk," I said.

"Yeah, well, while you do, I gotta whiz. If you recall, my potty break got delayed."

"In there," I said. Cecil and I were already headed down the narrow hallway. "Then back in the bedroom, okay?"

She snorted. "Whatever you say, *Woody*."

When she was locked away in the can, Cecil and I put our heads together. "What have we done?" he said.

I drew a shaky breath and let it out.

"You believe her?" Cecil asked.

"Yeah. What she said makes sense. She's a looker, but she's not Honey."

"So what do we do now?"

That was the big question. As the self-appointed leader of our crack criminal team, I voted to admit defeat and let her go. After all, (1) she'd been blindfolded for the drive to our trailer and could be blindfolded again, and (2) I'd had the rare foresight to mislead her about our location. Our place was actually only about ten minutes from the Lawson ranch.

Cecil disagreed. He thought we should go ahead and call Lawson and ask for the ransom and see if he'd pay us *something* to get his employee back. Anything would be better than nothing.

As expected, our abductee had her own views on the issue. When we reconvened, she sat on the bed and said, as if reading our minds, "He won't pay you a penny. He barely pays *me*, and I work for him."

"You're just trying to persuade us to let you go," Cecil said.

"No, I'm telling you like it is. Everett Lawson and me ain't overly fond of each other. He'll probably be glad I'm gone." She seemed to consider that. "In fact, *I* oughta be glad I'm gone."

"What?" I asked.

She focused those blue eyes on me. "I been looking for a way to get out of Dry Springs, but I ain't got enough saved to do it. And working for Lawson, I'll never have enough."

She paused again and then continued, dead serious: "You guys messed up, for sure. You got it wrong, but no harm's done. You could just turn me loose—we'll say good night, I'll keep quiet and go my own way, and you two go back to being losers. No offense. That's one solution."

Cecil and I exchanged a puzzled look. I said, "There's another one?"

She hesitated, studying my face. "Life is very short, Woody. You ever heard that? And there's no time."

I broke out a tiny smile. We had ourselves a fellow Beatles fan here. "For fussing and fighting, you mean?"

"For a lot of things," she said.

I just watched her, waiting.

She raised her chin and said, "I know where the impersonatee is."

"The what-now?" Cecil said.

"The real Honey Lawson. I know where she is at this moment."

We gaped at her. "You said she stayed home at the ranch," Cecil said.

"Yeah, but I know exactly *where* at the ranch."

I was beginning to understand.

"Think of what I'm saying," she said. "You can still 'nap her." Brittany leaned forward, pinning us with her eyes. "Snatch her quick, right now while Lawson and the cops and everybody are still at the ballfield, runnin' around looking for the daughter's stunt double—if they even realize yet that I'm gone—and then demand whatever ransom you want. Lawson don't care about me, but he sure cares about his little blond darlin'. He'll pay anything to get her back."

"And—let me guess—we cut you in on the payoff?"

"Yep. Three-way split. Then you give her back and the three of us really do go our separate ways, fat and dumb and happy." She looked us over and added, "Well, in my case just happy."

Again the little room went quiet. Brittany was watching us, and we were watching her. I liked her idea. Maybe we *could* work this out.

Cecil abruptly said, "'Scuse me, I don't feel so great," and stepped into the hallway. I heard the toilet door open and close.

"Delayed reaction," I said.

Brittany and I sat there thinking. The only sounds were the eerie hoot of an owl somewhere in the woods behind the trailer and the sickening noise of Cecil throwing up everything but his shoelaces behind the bathroom door.

Finally, I took a long breath. "Look, I'm—well, I'm sorry about what happened."

She shrugged. "You guys are actually okay, criminal-wise. That was a pretty neat getaway. Sorry about the 'idiot' comment."

"We deserve it," I said.

Her eyes twinkled. "And you're extremely polite to your hostages."

"Except that you look cold. My apologies—our thermostat's broken."

"That's okay. My coat's over there, I can bundle up." She tilted her head and studied me a moment. "You don't even have guns, do you?"

"We didn't want anybody getting hurt."

She nodded. "I believe you."

After a pause, Brittany asked me what we did when we weren't kidnapping people, and I told her about our military stints and our odd jobs around town. "We're good with weapons and such—but that's about all we're good at, and it doesn't translate too well into civilian life."

She nodded as if she understood and told me she'd been a

waitress at one of the greasy spoons nearby until Lawson spotted her last year and saw she was the spittin' image of Honey—who, according to Brittany, is a nice-enough girl—and hired her as a part-time impersonator. "Looks like all three of us are square pegs in round holes," she said.

Cecil had returned by then and was standing there looking pale and embarrassed. Brittany and I looked up at him.

"My name's on my shaving kit," he said.

She nodded. "Cecil Prescott. I saw it."

"So much for secrets," I said. "I'm Andy Williams."

"Like the singer? 'Moon River'?"

"No relation."

"Well, I'm Brittany Ainsworth." She looked at the two of us. "You know, you guys don't really seem like crooks."

"We're just doin' what we got to," Cecil said. "To get by."

"What if you had a chance to go straight? Would you take it?"

"Any openings at the greasy spoon?" I asked.

We all chuckled at that. But she appeared to be waiting for an answer, so I said, "There just aren't many jobs around here for folks like me and Cecil."

Nobody replied, and after a while she said, "So what about my proposal? For the real and sweeter Honey." She looked from me to Cecil and back again. "What do you think?"

"In other words, try to see it your way?"

She shrugged. "Only time'll tell if I'm right or wrong. Are you up for it?"

Another long silence.

"Yes," we said.

She nodded and held out her hands. We each clasped one of them. "Partners in crime," she said.

"So what's next?" Cecil asked, as we released hands. I held onto Brittany's a little longer than necessary.

She thought a moment. "You got a pencil and paper?"

"In the other room," Cecil said.

We said nothing while he was gone. She had the most beautiful eyes I had ever seen—and they stayed on me, unwavering.

At last I leaned forward and said, "When this is over—"

"Yeah?"

I didn't finish. But she was smiling.

Cecil returned with a tablet and pen, and when the three of us were gathered around the kitchen table she drew a map of the ranch.

The Lawson place was no longer a working ranch, but it had a sprawling house and barn and a dozen outbuildings. One of those was a cottage that Brittany told us contained offices and a media room. That was where she said Honey would be, either reading or watching DVDs. It was almost nine and, according to Brittany, nobody else would be there.

Cecil and I went alone. I parked nearby, and we stepped onto the porch and rang the doorbell. We were as nervous as a politician in a confessional.

"Grab her soon as she answers the door," I whispered.

But she didn't answer the door. The man who did was tall and broad-shouldered, with a Sam Elliott mustache and a square chin and a two-toned forehead from wearing a hat all day in the sun. He looked us up and down, then turned and growled "Come on in" over his shoulder.

I think Cecil and I were beyond surprise by now. I followed the Marlboro Man on trembling legs, and Cecil followed me. Our host settled into a chair behind a huge walnut desk.

"My name's Dave Brigman. I got a call awhile ago that you'd be here soon. I assume you're Williams and Prescott."

A call? I felt my shoulders sag. *The coat,* I thought. *Her phone was in her coat. Which we forgot to search.*

"Have a seat, boys. Don't stand there gawkin'. She asked me to pass along a message." He scooted a notepad across the desk toward us. The message read: SURPRISE, SURPRISE. "I didn't

147

ask her what that meant."

I knew what it meant.

"Anyhow," Brigman said, "I believe you know her. She's a friend a mine named Hartley Lawson. Everybody calls her Honey."

I cleared my throat. "We do know the caller, Sir, and I don't doubt she probably sounded like your friend. She also looks like her, except I know Honey Lawson's a blonde. This lady's got short black hair."

"So does Honey," he said.

I blinked. "What?"

"Honey's hair is black as night. Always has been. She just wears a blond wig."

I thought I heard Cecil fart. His eyes were bulging. Mine probably were, too.

"Excuse me," I said. "Who'd you say you are?"

"I work for Honey's father. I'm the head of security for Lawson Enterprises."

I slumped a little farther into my chair.

Even in the face of this new disaster, I couldn't help admiring good old Brittany—or, more accurately, Honey. I could see it all now: first she'd tricked us into believing we had nothing worth ransoming, and then she cooked up a plan to reel us in. Good Lord. *She* ought to be head of her daddy's security.

Think of what I'm saying, she'd told us. I knew now that we should've thought about it a lot longer. Cecil and I hadn't worked *anything* out. *She* had.

And I could sense that more was coming. I took a couple of deep breaths and waited.

"I need to explain something to you boys," he said. "Honey Lawson's a sweetheart and smart as a fox, but she's also a wild child. You see, I got word from Everett Lawson earlier tonight that he and one of my men—Carl Morgan—were at the high-school ballgame pullin' their hair out, lookin' for her. Said they let her outa their sight for a while—we had the ball on the five, and Carl didn't want to miss the home team's score."

Bingo, I thought. *At least I got that right.*

"Anyway, she up and disappeared. Well, just as I was about to head over there, I got a call from Honey herself, telling me she's safe and sound. Said she'd met a guy at the concession stand and left with him, but then the guy abandoned her and two strangers saw her and rescued her and took her to their place to let her rest up." He paused, watching us. "Mister Lawson was plenty surprised when I passed that information along to him a few minutes ago."

Not any more surprised than I was. My mouth had gone dry as the Sahara. *Rescued her?*

"She told me she's still there, at their place—your place. And said you two were coming here and I should give you her message."

I swallowed and tried to figure this out, but I couldn't.

"So what now?" I asked. "Are we being arrested for something?"

"No." His craggy face changed, and I realized the new look was amusement. "You're being recruited for something."

I felt my brain go blank. Beside me, Cecil spoke for the first time. "Recruited?"

Brigman did a palms-up. "I told you, Honey said you helped her out. She said you boys were good to her—thoughtful, resourceful. She also said you've had military training." He paused. "The thing is, I had two employees quit this past week. I could use a couple of guys like you two, and I'd pay you well. How about it?"

I took another long breath. Things were happening too fast.

Brigman was waiting for an answer. I looked at Cecil and he looked at me, and I realized this was a no-brainer. I turned back to Brigman and said, "We accept."

Five minutes later, I decided to take a chance. I stopped and looked Brigman in the eye and said, "How did all this really happen?"

He smiled. "To be honest, Honey asked me to trust her and

not pose too many questions. But I got the feeling she might be a little sweet on one of you boys."

"Must be me," each of us said.

On the way home, my cell phone buzzed. I glanced at Cecil, who looked as surprised as I was. Nobody ever called us. Keeping my eyes on the road, I held the phone to my ear.

"You forgive me?" she said.

I felt a warm glow that had nothing to do with my truck's heater. "For what? Causing two heart attacks?" I pressed the speakerphone button so Cecil could hear.

"You don't sound dead to me. How about Buzz? Did he get sick again?"

"I think he's just hungry. How'd you know my number?"

"I found your phone bill." She paused, and I thought I could hear our TV in the background. *Shark Tank.* "I understand you two just made a career change."

I couldn't help chuckling. "We have friends in high places."

"Apparently."

I swallowed, took a breath, and said, "Why the change of heart?"

"Like I said before: life is short." After a pause, she said, "Why don't you stop by Pizza Hut. I just called 'em and ordered two larges, and a salad for me."

"Supremes?"

"I spared no expense."

When I'd disconnected, Cecil said, his eyes fixed on the windshield, "Know anybody who needs a spare key to a ladies' restroom?"

"Not offhand. But I think I got an idea for our new boss."

"What's that?"

"Find somebody who looks like Everett Lawson and use him as a stand-in when the big fella don't feel up to being seen out in public. What do you think?"

"Stupidest idea I ever heard."

We were still grinning when we got back to the trailer with our supper.

And so was Honey.

Revolver
Released August 1966

"Taxman"
"Eleanor Rigby"
("I'm Only Sleeping")
"Love You To"
"Here, There and Everywhere"
"Yellow Submarine"
"She Said She Said"
"Good Day Sunshine"
("And Your Bird Can Sing")
"For No One"
("Doctor Robert")
"I Want to Tell You"
"Got to Get You Into My Life"
"Tomorrow Never Knows"

"Taxman," "Love You To," and "I Want to Tell You"
are by George Harrison.
All other songs are by John Lennon and Paul McCartney.

(NOTE: The three songs in parentheses did not appear
on the original North American release of *Revolver*,
but were included for all other markets
and ultimately added to the 1987 CD release.)

Eleanor Rigby
John Copenhaver

Christmas 2001

Holding his Cape Cod up, he wound his way through the crowd. TLC's "Sleigh Ride" was bouncing in JR's speakers, and the bar's patrons—mostly men older than him—smiled in his direction and scanned his body. He liked their greedy eyes. He was the type they wanted, with his twinkish good looks and prep-school boyishness. They saw him as a young buck, a cherry to pop, which gave him the upper hand.

"Use what God gave you," his mama always told him. And after she called him a fuckin' faggot and kicked him out of the house during his senior year of high school, he did just that. He took the first bus from Wythe County to D.C. and hustled for a while, turning tricks for cash and saving up until he landed a legit job. He'd often stand in front of his mirror and thank God he was beautiful—not because he was vain, but because otherwise he'd probably be dead by now.

After sliding through two handsy guys, he pushed open the door to the cramped, musty bathroom. The stall was occupied, and an older dude was at the urinal. He waited, setting his drink on the edge of the sink next to another half-consumed Cape Cod and glanced in the mirror. He was still wearing his Dupont Video "uniform" of khakis and a navy-blue Izod, and he'd forgotten to remove his name tag.

The pissing guy finished and turned. He was handsome, classic-movie-star handsome. Put together, well groomed, great hair.

"Sorry to make you wait," Movie Star said.

On reflex, he covered his name tag with his hand. His name embarrassed him, the name of the boy his mama shunned. "It's cool," he said, and switched places with the dude.

"I haven't seen you at JR's before," Movie Star said.

"Not my usual scene."

"Which of these drinks is yours?"

He wasn't sure. "The closer one, I think."

"You with someone?"

He often fantasized about landing a wealthy older dude, someone who would take care of him. So, sure, he'd link up with the Cary Grant lookalike and bat his eyelashes. Who knows what would happen? Maybe tonight's the night he'd find love—or at least a Sugar Daddy. So he said, "No, I'm on my own. Name's Jason." When he turned tricks, he used Jason, like Jason Priestley. It suited him.

"Join my friend Bax and me," Movie Star said. "We won't bite...too hard."

Christmas 2022

As I climbed out of my Uber, I saw him: his forehead like an Easter Island monolith and the distinctive bump on the bridge of his nose. In the glow from the entryway, he appeared ghostly, a memory in flesh. His thinning gray hair was tangled, his eyes blurry, restless.

Over the rush of traffic on 14th Street, I called out, "Baxter? It's me, Jimmy!"

But he didn't hear me—or chose not to. Was he coming from our building? Was he visiting Clark? I fumbled my Christmas purchases, the rope handles biting into my palms. I closed the car door with my hip. When I looked again, he was gone. I hadn't seen him in nearly twenty years.

He and Clark ended their friendship in the early 2000s—a falling out over money or something. I didn't know. At the time, I was falling in love with Clark—Clark Rhys the writer, not yet the man—and I didn't want to fuck it up by asking too many questions. I was twenty-two, pretentious, and, worse, a huge fan. *The Dry Sea* had been nominated for a Pulitzer, and I was obsessed with Clark's lyrical prose and subject matter: the glamour and darkness of gayness!

God, I was so serious.

Before the split, I'd met Baxter several times. He was flamboyant, foul-mouthed, fond of recreational drugs, and witty. He'd spill into a room, gather an audience of plastered and pliable gay men, and read us. Although wary initially, I liked him; he understood that my interest in Clark ran deeper than a boyish infatuation.

After hauling my bags to the fifth floor and dropping them at our wrapping station, I found Clark staring out of his office window with his hands in his lap. He was a young sixty-two, the result of a good diet, daily exercise, a skillful hair colorist, and an expert tailor, all of which I orchestrated for him. Great minds need time to think, to dream, and shouldn't be fretting over the best protein blends or designer sportswear. As our lives had merged, our ten-year age gap seemed to dissolve. For good or ill, marriage has that effect. We were no longer "slender, bespectacled grad student" and "handsome, disheveled-yet-masterful man-of-letters."

Today, though, he looked every bit of sixty-two. As I approached him from behind, his reflection in the window was shielded, withdrawn. I said his name twice before his eyes lifted to meet mine.

"The shopping is done," I said with a huff. "I had to torture the clerk at Bloomy's until she gave me a discount on your gift. Hope you like camo Crocs!"

Levity flickered in his expression, but he didn't banter back.

"What's wrong?" I said. "Don't you like camo?"

He looked away. "I've had a morning."

"Want to talk about it?" *Was his funk about Baxter?*

He shrugged. "Not really."

I placed my hand on his shoulder and kissed his head. The spicy, leathery scent of the cologne I'd bought him for his birthday wafted up. "You'll never guess who I saw on the sidewalk outside our building."

He twisted his chair around and said, forcing a chatty tone, "Tom Cruise? He's shooting an action film in town. Say what you will about him, that man is beautiful when he runs."

"No, a blast from the past."

He shuddered.

"Baxter Davies."

"Jesus," he said, shaking his head. "What rock did *he* crawl out from under?"

Unease crept into my gut. Call it instinct, but now I was sure Baxter had visited him. "He seemed...old."

"He was never kind to his body."

By our early thirties, most of us had stopped partying hard, but from what I'd heard, Baxter had kept on. Clark reached for his computer—a signal for me to scram—but I continued to pry: "Are you *sure* you're okay?"

"I'm fine," he said firmly. "I read my Goodreads reviews of *Token Heart.* A stupid thing to do."

I walked away, rumbling with anger. Clark never read Goodreads reviews. Even if he did, he wouldn't care what they said. His contempt for the use of crowdsourcing to judge the value of literature—or anything, for that matter—was unambiguous. He was a snoot—which I'll admit I usually admire. "You can't be a trendsetter if you're a trend follower," he always said.

I'll be the first to tell you: my relationship with my husband is a lonely place. I've wrestled with this truth over the years. After many therapy sessions, many therapists, and even a few flings, I'm at peace with it.

Pros: a beautiful apartment in downtown D.C., travel to exotic locales, delicious food, interesting friends, good sex—sometimes *great* sex—and above all else, security. I grew up poor. Not dirt poor, but close. So spare me your bourgeois notions about romance. Security can't be cast down and trampled on. Clark knows about my flings (we're open with each other), but he doesn't know I've weighed our relationship on occasion. I've loved him since I first pored over *The Dry Sea*, and, sure, loving the man versus his art is a separate (although not easily differentiated) matter. But love is there.

The chief con—the only real con—is that he's remained hard to know. It's like staring at a bright-flecked pet goldfish. You admire it, feed it, clean its bowl, but you can't quite reach it. After all, you breathe air, while it breathes water. That's what you sign up for when you marry a writer.

The day after Baxter's visit, I overheard Clark on his phone: "What more do you want?" When I asked if everything was okay, he said, "Just a telemarketer."

That was a weak lie and he knew it, so he switched on a seductive smile. He had a bit of the George Clooney about him, a sweep of salt-and-pepper hair, a close-cropped beard, dark eyes. He can be irresistible. He drew me close, kissed me, and ran his hands down my back. I pulled away. What was he thinking: if he fucked me, I'd get amnesia?

I told him I had chores to do.

"Are you seeing that guy again?" he said, despondent. "What's his name?" He was trying to make me feel guilty.

"I would've told you," I said.

When he left to do errands, I began snooping. I wanted to talk to Baxter and arm myself with evidence before confronting my husband—who was, as you may have gathered, a master of deflection. I searched his address book, day planner, and desk but found no contact information for Baxter. Clark had erased him from his life. I couldn't search his phone, which was always with him. In the top drawer of his desk, however, I discovered a photo I'd never seen before and recognized a crowded JR's, circa 2000. In the foreground, happy, handsome, and drunk, Clark had his head on Baxter's shoulder. Baxter's face was beet-red, his lips pursed on the verge of an outburst of laughter. A pretty blond boy in his early twenties leaned into Clark, his eyes glazed with alcohol. Next to them, a drag queen in a floral-print A-line and a massive bouffant smirked through a Holly Golightly cigarette holder. The drag queen, Dinah something, was on rotation at JR's, and her real name was Case. Someone, perhaps Baxter, had scrawled on the back of the photo: "How did he know his name?" Was this a message to Clark? If so, what did it mean? A chill ran through me. I flipped through Clark's address book and found Case's number.

Case seemed unsurprised to hear from me and agreed to meet at Cafe Saint-Ex. I found him outside, wrapped in a bulky tweed overcoat, green scarf, and fingerless gloves, warming himself with a latte and a cigarette. Seeing his long body folded over the cafe table, I recalled how tall he was, particularly in drag. With heels on, his armpits met most of our heads, and his bouffant had its own micro-climate. "Hello, Dinah," I said with a bit of a swish. "I see you're still smoking those death sticks."

He swung his arm out, cocked his wrist, and in a husky Jewish accent, said, "Name's Dinah Cansah, not Dead of Cansah, sweetie. I am and always will be Dinah Cansah!" He offered me a package of Marlboro Reds. "Want one?" His fingernails were lime-green, the polish chipped.

I eyed the graceful stream of smoke from his cigarette. "No, I shouldn't."

"You look good," he said. "Have a seat."

Case was a recovering addict. After several trips to rehab, he had stabilized, thrived, and began managing the front office of Arena Stage. He and Clark never fell out, but Clark distanced himself from that friend group as they plunged from recreational to habitual drug use, about the same time I entered his life.

"So," he said, leaning back, a slender hand dangling his cigarette below the table's edge. "Let me guess. This has to do with Baxter Davies."

I was taken aback. "How do you know that?"

"Baxter showed up on my doorstep the other day."

"That's unusual?"

He nodded, blowing out a cone of smoke. "I haven't seen him in ages. Five years? Six?" He frowned. "He's still using. Looks terrible."

"What did he want?"

He raised his sculpted eyebrows. "Why, to find your hubby, the great Clark Rhys!"

"You gave him our address."

"I was shocked I still had it."

I sat with that information. "Do you know why he wanted it?"

Case's lean face drooped, but his crystalline blue eyes didn't waver. "Look," he said, "he was in a state, so he wasn't making much sense, but he kept saying, 'I don't know why that motherfucker did it.' That sort of thing."

"Jesus." My heart lurched, and I thought of Clark's troubled expression and the writing on the back of the photo: *How did he know his name?* "Did what?"

"He didn't say, but he was shaking Clark's latest book like he was pissed off at it."

"He's out of his mind," I said, relieved.

"I gave him your address, and he went away."

"Can you think of anything else?"

He ashed his cigarette and sipped his latte. "Why don't you talk to Clark?"

I pictured a goldfish slipping away through dark water.

"He doesn't know you're here, does he?"

I explained that I'd seen Baxter and that Clark had pretended he hadn't met with him.

He smirked and said, "Your hubby's hiding something."

"No shit."

Then, with an eye roll: "Such the happy couple."

I didn't appreciate his sarcasm and stood up.

"It's just that you two, well...everything's gone your way. I'm surprised you never had a kid. That would've been the icing on top."

I adjusted my coat. "How do I get in touch with Baxter?"

"He manages a secondhand store on Rhode Island Avenue. Sylvia's." Case tossed his butt into the dregs of his latte. "What's *Token Heart* about?"

"A murder of sorts. Two men fight over a woman and kill her in the process."

"A murder mystery?"

"No," I said, pushing in my chair. "A tragedy."

On the check-out table just inside Sylvia's, someone had encased a 1950s mannequin head in an upside-down glass jar, the kind that once held pickled eggs. It wore a fluffy pink tam, and a scarf had been wrapped around its neck to suggest shoulders. Then—with great care, I imagined—the jar had been lowered over the assemblage. It drew your eye, like something from a Victorian cabinet of curiosities. So much so that I didn't notice Baxter emerge from the back of the store.

"She's our mascot," he said. "Sylvia—"

I glanced up, and I could see the look of surprise on his face as he recognized me.

"—P-Plath," he stammered, unnerved to see me.

"A bell jar," I said, and thought about it and added, "That's not funny."

Although he looked drained, Baxter was still striking. Hard living had carved away the extra flesh from his face, and now the twitchy energy of the muscles and tendons underneath was visible, like vines creeping up an abandoned building. He pursed his lips. "Why are *you* here?"

"When I called to you the other day, you heard me, didn't you?"

He studied me. "I don't know what you're talking about."

"You were visiting my husband."

He turned away. "Talk to him about it."

I stepped toward him and touched his arm. "Clark told me he hadn't seen you."

He put space between us. "Good for you, Nancy Drew."

"I've talked to Case. That's how I found you."

"Well," he said, "I'll have to tell him to fuck himself the next time I see him." He waved me off. "I've got work to do."

"Did you call Clark this morning?"

He glared. "I'm not having this conversation, Jimmy. Go home to your husband and keep living in a dream." He shook his head, pantomiming pity.

"What do you mean, 'living in a dream?'"

His eyes sharpened, and his forehead crinkled. "One day, you'll realize who you married."

Was he fucking with me, or did Clark have a secret? Case's words echoed: "*Such the happy couple.*" Was this just petty jealousy, or something worse? The dread was too much, and I snapped and grabbed his wrist. "Explain yourself," I growled, digging my fingers into his arm's sinewy ridges. "What did you and Clark talk about?"

He stared at me defiantly.

"Tell me," I spat. "Did it have something to do with *Token Heart?*"

He shrank under my grip. He was trembling, frightened. His watery, bloodshot eyes glared up at me. I imagined how he spent his days sorting used Old Navy T-shirts, chipped Fiestaware, and wobbly IKEA lamps. He was a discarded man among discarded things. But he was the key to this mess, whatever it was, and I wasn't going to let him go. I applied pressure to his spindly arm and said, "What is it about the book?"

He jerked away, crashing into the table behind him. His arm flew out and knocked Sylvia and her bell jar to the floor. The thick glass didn't break but rolled away, the mannequin caught like a severed head in a basket.

"Goddamnit," he said. "Look at what you did."

I wasn't going to beat the truth out of him, so I changed my tactic. In a voice more pleading than enraged, I said, "Was it something he wrote in *Token Heart*?"

He went to Sylvia and hoisted her jar back onto the table. The upside-down mannequin's eyes stared out, profoundly empty. "Ask your hubby about Avery."

"The woman in the book?"

"The victim." He reached into the jar, wrapping his hand around Sylvia's face.

"What are you saying?"

"Get the fuck out of here." He squinted at me. "That's what I'm saying."

Avery Rogers is the twenty-something ingénue about whom the plot of *Token Heart* pivots. The novel's dueling protagonists, Jordy and Jack, use beautiful, idealistic, outspoken Avery as the rope in their tug-o-war. Each man wants her, gets her for a time, and loses her. When one of them has her, his life soars—Jordy becomes a successful artist, Jack a rich entrepreneur—and when he loses her, he schemes to weaponize her against his rival. Eventually, Avery wrenches this way and that, unravels, and kills herself. Sensitive Jordy realizes the horror of what he's done, but brutal Jack stages her death as a murder and frames Jordy. As the book ends, Jordy has lost his freedom, Jack his soul.

When he finished edits, Clark told me that the novel was really about an unrequited love affair between the two men, and that Avery was a symbol of the swagger of straight male culture, the false stamp of male virility, the blonde on the arm of an "impressive" man. Her presence anoints him as desirable, successful. "She's token and therefore tragic," he added, and I wondered about her being purely symbolic. Was that fair to her? Or maybe that's how I feel now, knowing what I know.

It was evening when I returned. Clark was sitting in a pool of light at our kitchen island. His head was bowed, and he held a tumbler in his hands. His mind was elsewhere. I didn't know what to say to him. I had googled "Avery Rogers" in the Uber on the way home and what I discovered had left me speechless. I took off my coat, grabbed a glass of wine, and positioned myself across from him. With as much composure as I could muster, I sipped my wine and said, "I know who Avery is. The *real* Avery Rogers, not the one in your book."

He lifted his head but didn't seem surprised. Had he planned to tell me? He must've known I'd sensed his lies.

"The other day," he said, "I read a New Yorker article about Paul McCartney writing 'Eleanor Rigby,' that great meditation on loneliness." He swirled his drink—unable, it seemed, to look directly at me. "He named Eleanor after Eleanor Bron, who the Beatles had worked with on the film Help!, and Rigby was the name of a local shop. Paul felt the name fit the tone of the song. Years later, a fan discovered that 'Eleanor Rigby' was the name on a gravestone in a churchyard in Woolton, which Paul and John had wandered through as young men, talking about their future." He sipped his bourbon. "That couldn't have been a coincidence. Paul must've absorbed the name subliminally, and it eventually worked its way to the surface. There's even a church in the song."

"Why are you telling me this?" I said, my frustration showing.

His face grew dark. "If you know who the real Avery is," he said, "you know he went missing in 2002."

"So says Google."

"But you don't know what happened, do you?" He paused, pained by a memory.

I glared at him. "Do you? Does Baxter?"

He moved his lips, trying to form the right words. "Yes," he muttered, "but I didn't know who the real Avery Rogers was until yesterday." A cloud shaded his expression, as it had Baxter's earlier. His muted shame was infuriating—no, it was his evasiveness that was too much. Out with it, all of it! He owed me the truth; he owed Avery Rogers the truth.

"What do you mean?" I fumed. "And what the hell does this have to do with a Beatles song?"

Clark crossed to the sink and leaned against the counter. He wanted distance between us, as if the truth would land more gently if it had further to travel. The shadows obscured him, making him oddly alluring. But I wanted to see him warts and all—a husband's privilege—so I crept nearer.

"He told me his name was Jason," he said. "I spotted him in the bathroom at JR's at their Christmas bash. Thick blond hair, startling blue eyes, very preppy. He had that innocence and youthfulness that drove me crazy back then." He took another swig of bourbon. "The same quality that drew me to you."

I shivered. I'd met Clark just weeks after this. I was Avery's age at the time. Had I been Version 2.0? I was blond then, and young and silly and adoring.

"Do you *really* want to hear this?" he asked, sensing my apprehension.

"I do."

"I was celebrating. *The Dry Sea* was a huge success, and I'd just sold the second novel. Baxter had GHB; we'd doctored our drinks and were flying high. My libido was surging. When we came out of the bathroom, Bax swooped in, and after some inane chitchat, we decided to go to the Deluxe, where Bax was renting a suite while he was having his apartment remodeled." He cleared his throat. "I dumped some of Baxter's GHB in the kid's gin and tonic. I don't remember doing it—I was pretty drunk—but Bax saw me."

"Jesus, Clark."

His eyes flickered. "He swilled his drink like a sailor, turned up the music, and pulled off his shirt. We joined him. It was lovely. Not ugly." He met my gaze. "None of this was *supposed* to be ugly, Jimmy." He sighed, his irritation dissolving. "Within minutes, Jason was slurring his words and tottering. He began to shake, then suddenly he collapsed and vomited. We panicked. I tried"—pain rippled across his face—"I tried to clear his mouth and throat, but he choked to death. I was too drunk and out of it to do CPR." He dropped his chin. His thick gray hair swirled out from the center of his scalp. He seemed at once impossibly foolish and impossibly vulnerable. "It was awful. This beautiful boy ruined on a hotel floor."

I wasn't going to let him deflect: "Why didn't you call for help?"

He shook his head and looked up. "The GHB made us bold, arrogant. We undressed him, wrapped him in sheets, wheeled him to the end of the hall in a laundry cart, and sent him down a trash chute."

"Now, *that's* ugly," I said. I couldn't imagine Clark doing those things.

He stepped forward, the light from the overhanging fixture revealing the ridges and hollows of his face, still striking, still handsome. "When Bax picked up his clothes to take them to be destroyed, the kid's wallet fell out. He opened it and told me Jason wasn't his real name, but I stopped him before he could tell me what it was. Knowing his name would have made it too real, too horrible."

My stomach churned. "Wasn't it reported in the news?"

"The police never made the connection. The body they discovered must still officially be listed as a John Doe."

"You weren't curious? At all?"

"I avoided the news for months—and of course I was distracted. You'd come into my life. The crew at JR's thought they saw *you* with us that night. You looked like Avery back then, and the partying clouded everything."

"That photo," I said, trembling. "The blond boy is Avery."

"Yes."

"You're a coward," I whispered.

He frowned. "I was," he said. "I was so ashamed."

"You didn't want to fuck up your career. Your precious career."

He covered his mouth. Was it to muffle a scream or to stop himself from contradicting me? I couldn't tell. Jesus. I should hate him. I should walk out and never look back. Instead, a twinge of lust vibrated through me. After years of being an outsider, I was now inside.

"If you didn't know his name," I asked, "how did it end up in *Token Heart*?"

His eyes were glossy. "Bax read the book, and of course *he* knew the kid's real name. He showed up yesterday in a state, shoved the photo in my face, and told me I'd destroyed both him and myself. But I had no idea what I'd done. My use of 'Jason's' real name was a crazy coincidence, like Eleanor Rigby—or maybe I heard it that night. Maybe he mentioned it, and the booze and drugs erased it...or seemed to." He gripped the counter edge to stave off a sob. "Fuck, Jimmy, it was an accident."

"You drugged him without his consent." I kept my voice low. Despite my desire to reassure him, I refused to offer him sympathy or forgiveness. "You dumped his body in the trash."

"I was high as hell." He wiped his cheeks. "I'm so, so sorry. I've done a terrible thing, a terrible thing."

I remained silent. It's difficult to explain, even to myself, but though I should've been crying and throwing dishes or packing my bags and calling the police, my love for him was expanding, deepening. He was feeding me what I was hungry for—himself.

"Can you forgive me?" he asked, his face smooth, glistening with moisture, even youthful.

"You kept this from me for twenty years," I said, wavering. "I don't know who you are."

He rubbed his fingers across his face, pushed his drink to the side, and lowered his forehead to the granite counter. "You do now," he said to its cold surface. "You know me now."

I walked around the island, took a deep breath, and placed my hand on his shoulder, which shuddered under my fingers, then slowly relaxed. However awful the truth, he'd been honest with me at last. He was no longer a goldfish in a bowl, gliding through the water, sealed off from me, but in my hand, wriggling and flopping, suffocating in the air, *my* air.

"What do I do?" he asked. "Wait for someone else to make the connection and drag it to the surface?"

I staved off the dread by massaging his shoulder. "We brace ourselves."

He lifted his forehead. "Does that mean you're sticking around?"

"Maybe no one will make the connection," I said, digging into his muscle tissue and pressing him back down to the stone. "But even if someone does—"

I let the pressure of my touch say the rest: I would stay.

Sgt. Pepper's Lonely Hearts Club Band

Released May 1967

"Sgt. Pepper's Lonely Hearts Club Band"
"With a Little Help From My Friends"
"Lucy in the Sky With Diamonds"
"Getting Better"
"Fixing a Hole"
"She's Leaving Home"
"Being For the Benefit of Mr. Kite!"
"Within You Without You"
"When I'm Sixty-Four"
"Lovely Rita"
"Good Morning Good Morning"
"Sgt. Pepper's Lonely Hearts Club Band (reprise)"
"A Day in the Life"

"Within You Without You" is by George Harrison.
All other songs are by John Lennon and Paul McCartney.

She's Leaving Home
Martin Edwards

Wednesday morning, crack of dawn

On any other day, Lucy would be fast asleep, dreaming of...well, she didn't quite like to admit what she dreamt of, even to herself. But today was different. Today was the first of June. Freedom Day.

By a quarter to five, she was dressed and ready, taking care not to make a sound. She mustn't wake her parents. That would ruin everything. Last night, she'd packed her pink suitcase and stowed it under the bed, in case Mother popped in to say night-night. She still did that sometimes. It made Lucy cringe, especially when Mother called her Baby. When would she realize her daughter wasn't a child anymore?

Maybe when she read the note.

Lucy had spent weeks composing it. There was a lot of stuff she wanted to get off her chest. But she wasn't good at expressing her feelings, certainly not in writing. Her spelling was hopeless. Whoever said schooldays were the best of your life must have been insane. The teachers who taught her weren't cool, and she'd begged her parents not to send her back there.

It hadn't been an easy time for Lucy. First, Granny had lost her marbles and died. And then Will Shears had come along. In the end, Lucy *was* allowed to stay home. The doctor was kind and sympathetic, and things hadn't been too bad for a while. Her parents kept saying how much they loved her, but life in Riversdale Road...how to describe it? Claustrophobic was a good word. Suffocating.

Finally, she couldn't take it any longer. It was time for her to spread her wings and fly away.

Her note had been scribbled on blue Basildon Bond stationery, taken from the sideboard in the sitting room. It was a poor effort, but it would have to do.

Peering through a chink in the curtains, she watched the sun rise. The Hendersons' house looked out over the cricket field and toward the gray expanse of the River Mersey. The weather forecaster had promised a nice day. Lucy had never paid attention to the weather before, and she'd fretted that her parents would be surprised when she sat with them to endure the national news that came before the forecast. Thankfully, they'd both fallen asleep and begun to snore. Since Granny died, they had been drinking more sherry in the evenings.

She sealed the note in an envelope and propped it against the mirror, checking her reflection one last time. She fiddled with her hair till it looked just right, then draped her new coat over her shoulders.

Her bedroom was a symphony in pink. Mother had decorated it herself, when Lucy was tiny. Lucy's contribution was photos of film stars snipped out of newspapers and magazines and stuck on a big cork board she'd hung on the back wall. Not Troy Donahue or Sean Connery or the other men adored by most girls her age, but Julie Christie, Susannah York, Jane Birkin—and of course Janet Leigh. Glamorous, independent women. She loved to read about the exotic lives they led.

A final check of her watch. She'd settled on five as her departure time, as soon as it was light outside. She didn't fancy walking down Aigburth Road in the dark. There were some funny blokes about. Mother was obsessed with them, warning her about strange men and what they were capable of.

The last time Lucy had her hair done, a bloke in the Kardomah café in Dale Street had told her she was lovelier than Rita Tushingham. Lucy agreed. No point in being modest. Rita had grown up down the road in Garston, and now she was a star.

At last her wristwatch showed five o'clock. The watch had been a birthday present from Father, who had a wholesale jewelry business and supplied posh shops like Boodle & Dunthorne. He'd told her to be careful where she wore it. *Thieves are all over the place*, he'd said. *They'll strip the clothes off your back, given half a chance.*

If her money ran short, she could pawn the watch or one of the brooches or rings he'd given her over the years. But surely there'd be no need. She'd taken thirteen pounds from Mother's handbag last night, while her parents were in the Land of Nod, and she had seventy pounds of her own, saved from her pocket money in preparation for her escape. How many girls her age could lay their hands on so much cash?

Silently closing the bedroom door, she felt tears pricking her eyes. She dabbed them with a lacy handkerchief, knowing they were tears not of sadness but of joy. This house had become a prison, and she was about to break out.

The handkerchief in her right hand and her case in her left, she tiptoed down the stairs. The Victorians had built this house, and its doors and walls were thick. *Excellent soundproofing*, Father liked to say. He was proud of the place, and often proclaimed that *an Englishman's home is his castle*. Well, she was a Scouse Rapunzel, fleeing from the tower.

Not that her parents thought of themselves as Scousers, despite being born and bred in Liverpool. Snobs, that's what they were. Hadn't the Beatles proved that nothing was sexier than a Scouse accent?

Stop daydreaming, she told herself. *You're not out of the woods just yet.*

Mother suffered from insomnia and, although she took pills,

complained that she still didn't get her eight hours of beauty sleep. Once upon a time, she really *was* a beauty, but now she was hollow-eyed and painfully thin. Forty-four, going on sixty-four. She had once admitted that she sometimes made herself sick deliberately, to stay as skinny as when she was Lucy's age. She'd sworn Lucy to secrecy, and keeping secrets was something Lucy enjoyed.

The front door creaked, so she headed for the back. She wasn't feeling peckish, but in the kitchen she stuffed a banana in her coat pocket for later.

For a fleeting moment, she remembered the long-ago night when Father had come into her room, stinking of beer and blundering around. After a few minutes that seemed like a life-time, he stumbled out, and it had never happened again.

Now why did that particular memory sneak into her head at the very moment she was making her getaway? Perhaps her subconscious was reminding her of all the reasons she wouldn't be sorry to see the back of this place.

Quietly, she turned the back-door key and stepped outside. There was a chill in the morning air, but she didn't mind.

She'd made it. At last she was free.

Riversdale Road was quiet. It was too early even for the groundsman at the cricket club to be lugging his heavy roller over the pitch. She walked briskly toward the main road, swinging her hips. Everything was going according to plan.

She passed the Murder House, a few doors from where—until a few moments ago—she'd lived. In the last century, a young American lady called Florence Maybrick had been sentenced to death for killing her husband, a randy cotton broker with a mistress and an assortment of bastard children. She had been accused of using arsenic to poison him, but it turned out to have all been a mistake. They released her, and she lived to a ripe old age.

Lucy loved a story with a happy ending.

At the end of the road, opposite the cricket ground, she came to a halt. At this time of day, there wasn't much traffic. It would take ages to walk all the way to Lime Street. She'd rather hitch a lift than make for Aigburth Station and wait for a train. A chap with a car was always interesting. Though, actually, a lot of them were boring or unpleasant or both; even with her limited experience of the world, she knew that.

Beneath the blue suburban sky, a VW Beetle pulled up ahead of her. Not exactly what she'd hoped for. Lucy believed you *could* judge a book by its cover, and the little car was a heap of rust. Its driver was a young man with spectacles, spots, and a serge suit.

Winding down the window, he said, "Hop in if you'd like a lift to the Pierhead."

A local lad, by the sound of him. He looked harmless enough.

She dazzled him with a smile. "Perfect."

"Let me give you a hand with that case."

They stopped at a traffic light, and the boy coughed before casting a furtive glance at her legs. She was wearing her best nylons.

"Did anyone ever tell you you look like that actress?"

"Cheeky," she said primly. "Go on, then. Which actress?"

"You know, from *The Knack* and them others. *Taste of Honey, Girl with Green Eyes.* What's her name? You're her spitting image."

She gave him a wide-eyed stare. "You really think so?"

"I do. Prettier, actually."

"I bet you say that to all the girls."

"No, honest, it's true."

A van behind them tooted its horn. Her chauffeur hadn't noticed that the light had changed.

At the Pierhead, the young man took a deep breath and asked if she'd like to meet up for a drink sometime. She said she'd see him at half past five outside the Grapes in Matthew Street and left him staring delightedly after her as she swung her case from side to side on her way toward Derby Square, where she ate her banana and watched the city wake up.

When the Kardomah on North John Street opened its doors, she was the first customer. There were several Kardomahs in the center, each with its own distinctive personality. This was her favorite, decorated in an exotic Turkish style with curved and pointed arches and colored tiles on the roof and walls.

For once, she didn't order a coffee. This was a special day, and to celebrate she treated herself to Russian tea, served in a tall glass in an ornamental metal cage with a curved handle. She added sugar but no milk. Who said Scousers didn't have a touch of class?

The waitress was an extrovert with dyed red hair. When she spotted the suitcase and asked if she was going on her holidays, Lucy said she was off to stay with her auntie in Blackburn. This would confuse anyone who tried to follow her trail, since she didn't have an auntie in Blackburn or anywhere else. In fact, she'd never set foot in Blackburn. She knew it was somewhere in Lancashire, though it wasn't a seaside resort like Blackpool.

Lucy lingered over her tea, and eventually a middle-aged man sat down at the next table and cast covert glances in her direction before deciding on his opening gambit.

"Eh, love, has anyone ever said you look like that Rita Tushingham?"

Lucy opened her eyes very wide.

"Who, me?"

"She's gone," Mother screamed, standing alone at the top of the stairs. "Daddy, our baby's gone!"

Father came out to the landing in the twill pajamas she'd bought him from George Henry Lee's last Christmas and rubbed the sleep from his eyes. "You what?"

She waved Lucy's note at him. "Read this!"

He peered at the message and swore. On any other occasion,

she'd have snapped, "Language!" But this was different. This was an absolute disaster.

She began to cry, and Father awkwardly put his arm around her. "There, there, Vera. There, there."

"How could she treat us so thoughtlessly?" Mother demanded. "I don't understand it."

"We'll find her, love."

"And how are we going to do that?"

"I'll call someone."

"Have you reported her missing, Mister Henderson?" Chuck Pepper asked.

Father shook his head. "She turned sixteen last month, so you know what they'll say." He put on an officious policeman's voice. "Happens all the time, sir. Girls nowadays reckon they know about the outside world because they watch saucy films and read a lot of trash in magazines. They don't have the faintest idea of what can happen to an innocent kid. But there's no reason to suspect a crime as yet, sir. Nothing we can do."

He and Mother were sitting in Pepper's cramped office on the third floor of a grimy building in Stanley Street. The door was emblazoned with gilt lettering: *Charles Pepper, Private Enquiries and Process Serving, Discretion Assured.*

At one time, Pepper had been the youngest sergeant at Mather Avenue, but he hated taking orders, so he quit the police department and got himself an office of his own. He was said to be the best private detective in the north of England, and he was certainly the most expensive—though you wouldn't know it from the fraying carpet and battered desk. Or the rumpled tweed suit and smelly Woodbines.

"I'll need a recent photograph," he said. "Plus details of her friends. Names, addresses, telephone—"

"She doesn't have any friends," Mother said.

"None at all? A girl of that age?"

"She's not been well," Mother said.

Pepper's eyes were small to begin with. When he narrowed them, they became almost invisible. "What do you mean?"

"It's her nerves," Father said quickly. "We had to take her out of school early. First her granny died, and then there was...an incident."

"An incident?"

"A boy. She said he—molested her. The police weren't interested, which is when I realized they're a bloody waste of time."

Mother couldn't keep quiet any longer. "Everyone tried to blame Lucy. They said she was a...well, they said she led the Shears boy on."

"An absolute disgrace," Father said. "She's such a beautiful kid. Just...not very grown up. Show him the picture, Vera."

Mother fumbled in her bag and produced a color photograph, taken in the back garden. Lucy was wearing a blue-and-white gingham frock with a Peter Pan collar, white socks, and sandals. Father had taken the photo on her birthday, just a few weeks ago, but the girl could have passed for twelve or thirteen.

"She looks young for her age," Mother said. "That's one of the reasons we're so worried. There are men out there who would—"

"What about boyfriends?"

Mother shook her head. "She's far too sensible. And we've taught her that boys are only interested in one thing. Once they get what they want, they leave you high and dry."

"Does she wear cosmetics?"

There was a pause. "She used to buy them, but I found out and told her not to. Children these days grow up too quickly. You need to enjoy your youth, I said, don't—"

"So she might look a bit more...sophisticated than she does here?"

Father nodded miserably.

* * *

"—and no gentleman callers," the landlady said. "This is a respectable house."

"And I'm a respectable person," Lucy retorted. "I'll thank you to keep a civil tongue in your head." She'd heard the line in a film.

The landlady blinked, and Lucy had guessed that no one had ever spoken to her like that before. She muttered something about the gas meter and made herself scarce.

Lucy's room smelled of mold and had fading wallpaper and a damp patch on the ceiling. Taking off her coat and shoes, she lay on the bed and stared up at the stain. It was shaped rather like Father's head. Even now, in a King's Cross boarding house, she hadn't quite managed to escape. She closed her eyes and let her thoughts run free.

So far, everything had gone like clockwork. But her parents were sure to come after her. They were obsessed with her—a shrink would have a field day if he got either of them on the couch.

She'd told the landlady her name was Marilyn Heron, and she'd paid a week's rent in advance. She'd stay here for one night and then vanish. *The girl who never was.* Even if Father and Mother got as far as this dump, they'd get no farther. Her trail would be stone cold.

"Why didn't you tell him?" Mother asked.

She'd spent the day in floods of tears. Father had been outside, doing the garden, digging the weeds, before nipping across the road for a pint with his chums. Even in the height of summer, everyone was talking about football. The World Cup wasn't far off, and tickets for the matches at Goodison were changing hands for big money. But he wasn't in the mood, and he'd come home without even standing his round.

"You know why," he said. "It's none of his business. We're paying him to find our daughter, not rake over the past."

"He doesn't look like much of a detective. That awful suit!"

"What do you expect? A trilby and pipe, like bloody Maigret?"

It didn't even cross her mind to rebuke him for swearing.

Riding through the London streets on the top deck of a red bus, Lucy went into a dream. She'd spent the morning shopping in Carnaby Street and then Oxford Street, buying a fur coat, a pair of kinky boots with high heels, and the red Samsonite suitcase that now contained her small pink case.

Next she'd treated herself to a hairdo at Leonard's in Mayfair. It cost more than she'd expected but was worth every penny. *Goodbye, Rita Tushingham.* Nobody would recognize her now. The assistant—also a film fan, thankfully—was amused when Lucy explained the style she was aiming for.

"You want to look like Marion Crane?" she asked. "Not on the run like her, are you?"

Lucy giggled and put a finger to her lips. "Not saying!"

"Are you sure? I mean, Marion was lovely, but what happened to her was awful, wasn't it?"

"Don't you worry," Lucy said. "Me, I was born lucky."

"Any news?" Father demanded. "It's been more than twenty-four hours. God knows what's happened to her."

Pepper frowned. He didn't care for clients who interfered, and Henderson was a pain. Frankly, he wasn't surprised the kid was desperate to see the back of him and her neurotic mamma. He pushed some sheets of paper across his desk.

Mother snatched them up and started reading. "So you think she's covering her tracks?"

"No question. She told one story to the lad who gave her a lift, another to the waitress in the Kardomah."

"Have you tried the other Kardomah branches? Perhaps

she—"

"Look at what the chap in the Lime Street ticket office said. There's no doubt in my mind—she's in London."

"We must go there. Right this minute."

"Too soon. London's a big city. It'd be like looking for a needle in a haystack. I want to make a few more enquiries locally."

"Not the police," Father said quickly.

"No, but I need to find someone who's seen her lately and get an idea of what was on her mind. Then I'll go to London. If I can find her, I'll see if I can persuade her to come home."

Mother folded her arms. "We must go ourselves."

"I really don't advise—"

"She's our only child!"

Pepper sighed. His enquiries had been more productive than he'd revealed, but not everything had gone into his report. From the first, he'd suspected the Hendersons of keeping back crucial information. Now he *knew* that they'd lied to him.

Marble Arch was only about three miles from King's Cross, but the hotel Lucy chose after getting her hair done couldn't have been more different from the grotty place where she'd spent her first night of freedom. A uniformed porter wrestled her new suitcase up to a spacious room on the third floor. Before leaving, he gave a discreet cough, and she guessed he expected a tip. Her parents would have been appalled, but she handed over half a crown with a casual nod worthy of a Rothschild.

Time for a bit of pampering. She ran a bath, eased into the warm water, closed her eyes—and thought about Dave Kite.

Dave had come into Lucy's life a few weeks ago. She'd advertised in the lonely-hearts columns of her favorite film magazines. Even though she hadn't actually written "no time wasters," the way people did in *Exchange and Mart*, she'd made it pretty clear that she was a north-of-England equivalent of An-ouk Aimée and looking for *la dolce vita.*

Of course, she'd had to be clever. The return address she listed in her ad was a shop in Cressington, run by Mr. Mustard, an old lecher who enjoyed looking down her blouse but asked no questions. She'd had a load of replies, most of them obviously from lads pretending to be grownups and boasting they were millionaires, despite the poor quality of their paper and envelopes. Quite a few made rude suggestions. In the end, she'd drawn up a shortlist of six. Dave was the best of the bunch by a country mile.

He was in the motor trade; Daimlers were his firm's specialty. He wasn't a salesman but worked on the finance side. At thirty, he was already hoping for promotion to the board of directors. He drove a Majestic Major with automatic transmission and power-assisted steering—which certainly put Father's Sunbeam Rapier in the shade.

They'd exchanged photographs. Father had taken a snap of Lucy one Saturday afternoon last summer, when Mother was out shopping. She was wearing a bikini, and Father had let her have a copy of the picture in return for her not saying anything to Mother.

Dave's photo looked like everything she was hoping for, a younger version of Laurence Harvey. He said he'd been too busy for romance until now. That probably wasn't true, but it didn't bother her. A man with experience was what she wanted. Not a fumbling kid like Will Shears.

Stepping out of the bath, she toweled herself dry. She was tingling with anticipation. Dave was coming back to London tonight from a business meeting with a dealer on the Continent. He'd booked a week off work, and they'd agreed to meet by Marble Arch at nine tomorrow morning.

She couldn't wait.

* * *

Chuck Pepper didn't bother with preliminaries. There was no time to waste.

"Lucy has made an appointment for tomorrow morning with a man called Dave."

Father stared at him. "How do you know?"

"I told you I'd be making further enquiries."

Pepper had no intention of disclosing his methods. It didn't take Fabian of the Yard to reason that a pretty girl who left home might search for romance, and Lucy seemed like the sort who might join a lonely hearts club. Shortly before leaving the force, Pepper had interviewed a creepy old fellow called Mustard who kept a shop not far from the kid's home. The place served as an accommodation address, and Mustard—who was in the habit of steaming open letters addressed to his customers in the hope of discovering whatever they were trying to hide—was suspected of blackmail. The case against him had fallen apart after the woman who'd reported him decided not to testify.

Pepper had decided to pay Mister Mustard a visit, and a combination of menace and bluff had worked wonders. Mustard admitted to glancing at a letter to Lucy from some bloke called Dave. The envelope hadn't been properly sealed, he said, and the letter had slipped out. It might, he thought, have said something about Bowling Green Lane in Clerkenwell.

"We must catch the earliest train to London," Mother said.

"No need," Pepper said. "Let me handle this, Missus Henderson."

"Don't you Missus Henderson me! We need to find her before we lose our baby forever."

Lucy didn't bother with breakfast. She was too busy trying on her new green minidress.

In her letters to Dave—written with much trial and error and recourse to Mother's old *Oxford English Dictionary*—she hadn't told lies, at least not many…though Dave *might* have gained the impression that she was nineteen and had been caring for a beloved grandmother, now sadly deceased, after the death of her parents in a plane crash.

Mainly, she'd focused on the future. What she wanted to do with her life, what she might get up to if she ever had the good luck to meet the right sort of fellow.

They got on like a house on fire, and Dave eventually invited her down to London and offered to put her up at his flat in Finsbury. He was careful to mention that there were two bedrooms.

By ten to nine, she was shimmying out the hotel's swing doors. The sun was shining. It was going to be a magical day.

"It's time for you to level with me," Pepper said.

He and the Hendersons were sitting on a bench in Clerkenwell. His plan was simple: he would knock on doors in and around Bowling Green Lane until someone gave him a lead. That would require patience and determination, but Chuck Pepper possessed those qualities in abundance.

"What do you mean?" Father demanded.

"For you to have any chance of getting Lucy back, you need to tell me the truth."

There was a silence. Mother stared at the ground, and her husband pursed his fleshy lips as if trying to frame a crushing retort.

"When I asked around in Liverpool, I found out the name Lucy likes to use. A sort of alias, but a peculiar choice."

Mother stared at him. "I don't understand."

"You told me she stole some cash, Missus Henderson."

"Borrowed, I meant."

"To find her," Pepper said, "we need to figure out what's going on inside her head."

Father's patience snapped. "We didn't hire you to have our ears bashed with armchair psychology."

"Take it easy," Pepper said, reverting to American cop mode. "Marilyn Heron is a simple variation on Marion Crane—a character in a film your daughter has surely seen. In the movie, Marion steals some money and heads off to meet up with her boyfriend."

"Romantic nonsense."

"*Psycho* is not a love story, Missus Henderson. The girl takes a shower in a motel and is stabbed to death by a maniac."

The Hendersons stared at him.

In the flesh, Dave really *did* look like Laurence Harvey. What he'd failed to mention in his letters was that he was short and skinny and had a bad stammer. He was full of apologies, explaining that the stammer was a nervous thing, always worse when he was excited. Lucy decided to take that as a compliment, and they had a lovely morning together, strolling hand in hand through Hyde Park and Kensington Gardens.

Dave was a perfect gentleman, and Lucy hadn't expected that. To be honest, she hadn't particularly cared. What she was looking for was a strong, handsome man with plenty of cash, someone she could feel proud to be with. Good manners didn't come into it.

Granny, on the other hand, had been obsessed with politeness and old-fashioned courtesy. *Manners maketh man.* She said it so many times she sounded like a scratched record. That was one of the many irritating things about her.

Dave's stammer was rather sweet, but she was already beginning to tire of it. Thankfully, he seemed quite tongue-tied, as if he couldn't believe his good luck to be squiring around a girl who looked like a film star.

Twitching with anxiety, he asked if she was ready to see his flat.

"That would be lovely," she said. Gazing soulfully into his eyes, she squeezed his hand.

* * *

"You're wasting time," Father said. "We need to find this fellow Dave."

Pepper gave his clients a third-degree stare. "You didn't tell me what happened with Will Shears."

Mother turned to her husband. "I—"

"Quiet!" Father rounded on her. "That boy was a pathetic specimen. Always mooning after her. He got her on her own one day and—"

"The way I heard it," Pepper said, "she led him on. Teased him for weeks, then promised to go round the back of the bike sheds with him."

"The teacher caught him with his pants down. Her dress was torn. What more evidence do you want? She was only a child."

"She still *is* a child," Mother said.

"One of the other girls said Lucy tore the dress herself. Before the...incident. And she scratched Will's face to pieces. Made a real mess of him."

"That was self-defense."

Pepper sighed. "He said, she said. The authorities—"

"They didn't believe Lucy. It was criminal, the way she was treated! As if *she* was to blame and not the boy."

"Lucy was terribly upset," Mother said. "No wonder she fell ill. Especially after losing her granny."

"And that's it?" Pepper glared. "Nothing else you want to tell me?"

"Nothing." Father took a breath. "Now let's get on with it before it's too late."

The sex was an absolute let-down.

No, worse than that. It was a disaster, the opposite of everything Lucy had hoped for. She was sure it had been Dave's first time.

Now he lay beside her, sound asleep, exhausted by his frantic and ultimately futile exertions. His snoring disgusted her. When he rolled over, the touch of his bony back made her recoil in horror.

She hadn't felt the faintest shiver of excitement, not even when he said that he adored her, that she was the perfect woman, that he would never let her go.

His clinginess appalled her. This was not what she had wanted, not even close.

She felt grubby and used and desperate to get away, her dreams of a fresh start crumbling into dust. Instead of escaping from prison, she'd fallen into a brand-new trap.

A terrible throbbing blotted out her thoughts. Another of her headaches coming on.

She hadn't felt this bad when Will Shears had fumbled around with her so inexpertly. Not even that time when Granny had caught her reading a naughty magazine she'd nicked from Mustard's when the shopkeeper wasn't looking. Until then, she hadn't realized that Granny *knew* such terrible words.

Actually, this was worse, because this time she'd truly believed she was free at last.

What to do?

She only knew one way to make herself feel better. It had worked before, at least for a while. Maybe it would work again.

Pepper went into a shop on Farringdon Road to enquire about local residents named Dave, leaving the Hendersons on the pavement outside.

Tears misted Mother's eyes. "He blames us. But what did we do that was wrong? We struggled so hard to take care of her. Never a thought for ourselves."

"We gave her everything," Father groaned. "Everything money could buy."

Mother dabbed at her eyes. "You should have told him what

she's really like."

"Oh? Should I have told him about your mother, too?"

"That was completely different."

He glared at her. "You *saw* Lucy bending over the bed with a pillow in her hand."

"She was trying to make her granny comfortable!"

"And five minutes later, the old girl was dead."

Mother sobbed. "Senility is a curse. She had no life worth speaking of. The truth is, it was a merciful release."

"Lucy hated her. We both know that."

"She didn't like being told off, that's all. Children don't."

After a while, Lucy released her grip on the pillow.

Dave looked quite peaceful. *Just like Granny*, she thought.

Her headache had gone, and waves of pleasure eddied through her.

This was what turned her on, gave her a sense of release, of freedom.

There was something inside Lucy, something she had always denied.

But she wasn't in denial any longer.

She began to laugh, and she was still laughing when Chuck Pepper knocked on the door.

Magical Mystery Tour
Released November 1967

"Magical Mystery Tour"
"The Fool on the Hill"
"Flying"
"Blue Jay Way"
"Your Mother Should Know"
"I Am the Walrus"
"Hello, Goodbye"
"Strawberry Fields Forever"
"Penny Lane"
"Baby, You're a Rich Man"
"All You Need Is Love"

"Flying" is by George Harrison, John Lennon,
Paul McCartney, and Richard Starkey.
"Blue Jay Way" is by George Harrison.
All other songs are by John Lennon and Paul McCartney.

Baby, You're a Rich Man
Joseph S. Walker

I was at a corner table in Bemelmans—the Carlyle Hotel bar—with Amaryllis Blunt and Mason Creel. Amaryllis was my boss. Creel was the guy she'd recently hired to be my second-in-command and, when I hit sixty-five in a few months, replacement. I tried not to hold it against him.

My name is Eddie Dillon. My business card reads "Edward M. Dillon, Security, Blunt Enterprises," because you can't put words like "fixer" and "bagman" on org charts. It confuses the people in HR.

"I resent this," Amaryllis said. "Paying hush money goes against everything the Blunt name stands for."

A big part of working for Amaryllis was keeping a straight face when she said things like that. I nodded and took a sip of my sparkling water. I never knew if she believed the shit she said or just enjoyed the sound of her own voice.

"I particularly resent doing so because of Lawrence."

That, I had no problem believing.

"You're likely to have to deal frequently with Miz Blunt's least-favorite nephew," I said to Creel. "You're getting a crash course today."

"He's the one the papers call Baby," he rasped. I spent a lot of time wishing Creel would clear his damn throat. He was right about Lawrence, though. The kid was fourteen when the

193

Post ran a front-page photo of him dancing at an afterhours rave, a spewing bottle of champagne in each hand and white powder caked around his nostrils. The headline read *Baby Blunt Paints the Town*, and his fate was sealed. Amaryllis was the only person who still called him Lawrence.

"He's no baby," she said. "He's a jackass. One stain on the Blunt name after another."

"There was a cheating thing at Columbia," I told Creel. "That wasn't cheap. For a while he wanted to be a UFC champ, so he promised money he didn't have to a couple of mid-card guys to throw fights. You can imagine how that went. Last year he grew a conscience and fell in with a bunch of ecoterrorists called the Beautiful People. They derailed a coal train in West Virginia. I was down there six weeks, spreading cash like it was fertilizer."

"He hasn't seen a dime of family money since," Amaryllis said. "I told him to start cleaning up his own messes."

"So why are we talking about him now?" Creel asked.

Amaryllis signaled the waiter for a refill. She didn't ask if we wanted anything. "He's made another fucking mess, of course. I should have known better than to think he'd change."

"The Bratva operates a high-stakes poker room uptown," I said, "and Baby got himself dealt in. He owes them two million, and their patience has run out. They're threatening to make a very public example of him."

Creel shifted his massive rump. Bemelmans wasn't built with him in mind. It's an elegant place, with pricy cocktails, muted lighting, and murals by the guy who did all the *Madeline* books for kids. The kind of classy the wealthy think impresses regular folks. Amaryllis met people there who didn't merit reception in her penthouse. "Not to talk out of line, but if the kid causes so many problems...."

"If it was just a matter of getting rid of him, I'd load the gun for you and hold him down," Amaryllis said. "But Clayton is running a law-and-order campaign for Senate next year."

Amaryllis's son was a state representative and looking to step up. "It's hard enough for a Republican to get elected in this woke hellhole. I can't have his cousin turning up dead and tied in with criminals."

"It may have already happened," I said. "Nobody's seen Baby in four days. I've got people looking. Maybe the Russians are holding him until they get paid. The immediate problem is, the only way he could get credit from them was by giving them collateral, and he owns only one thing that's worth two million bucks."

"Stock," Amaryllis said. "Every single share of Blunt Enterprises is in family hands. We answer to nobody. That's how Father wanted it. That's how *I* want it. Foreign mobsters holding Blunt stock would look even worse for Clayton."

"So you're paying," Creel said.

"We're paying," I confirmed. "I've been negotiating terms. At first, they insisted on a bank transfer through the Caymans."

"Out of the question," Amaryllis snapped. The bartender set her third martini in front of her, gentle as a butterfly fart, and faded back into nowhere. "There will be no record of this, no digital trail for the taxman to latch onto. This is what cold cash is for."

"I finally got them to accept an exchange in a public place." I looked at my watch. "In forty-five minutes, I'm supposed to be near the entrance to the Central Park Zoo. I'll have the money in a brown gym bag. I give it to a bald man wearing a shirt with black and orange stripes. I come alone, he comes alone, no guns."

"They'll have somebody nearby," Creel said.

"So will I. You." I patted the empty bag on the fourth chair, looking at Amaryllis. "I've got the bag. You have the money?"

"In the trunk of the car," she said. Amaryllis always likes handling actual money when she has the chance.

"Follow me, but hang back," I said to Creel. "Try to spot the Russian's backup and make sure they keep their distance.

After the handoff, follow the money if you can."

"Why bother?" Amaryllis asked.

"Never hurts to know something we didn't know before. If they're holding Baby, we might even find out where."

She waved this away. "Handle it however you want. Just don't let me down."

"Have I ever, Lissy?"

Outside, Amaryllis got into the back seat of her Rolls. I stood at the trunk and put the payoff in my bag, shielded from view by Creel and Norbert, Amaryllis's ancient chauffeur. He looks like a stiff breeze would blow him over, but he carries an automatic under each arm and has a very smooth draw.

Creel's eyes kept sliding to the banded stacks of green paper. I forget sometimes that most people go their whole lives without seeing that much cash.

Loaded up, I slung the bag over my shoulder and walked west. I didn't look back. If Creel was any good at his job, I wouldn't see him anyway.

New York was having a warm spring, but there was enough bite in the air for people to wear light jackets. It was a pleasure to be walking. I spend too much of my time in offices and cars. Too much time on phones. Too much time dealing with people who are always hustling.

I entered the park across from 76th Street. I could have just walked down Fifth Avenue until I was closer to the zoo, but it wouldn't take much more time to go past the Alice in Wonderland statue just north of the Model Boat Pond. That statue used to be my wife Maya's favorite thing about the city. Sometimes she sat near it for hours, reading.

Half a dozen screaming toddlers clambered around the statue under the sharp eyes of women with strollers and snack bags. I let my hand brush the March Hare's ear but kept moving. Even if I wasn't on the clock, you never want to be an adult male hanging around a bunch of kids. The last thing I needed was a cop asking what I had in the bag. I adjusted the strap, wondering what Creel made of my little detour.

The zoo takes up a cramped chunk of land in the southeast corner of the park, alongside a broad walking path lined with food carts and souvenir booths. By Manhattan standards, there weren't many people around. I spotted my man from seventy yards away. His striped shirt was made of some synthetic fiber that shimmered in the sunlight. He sat alone on a bench, arms stretched along the back, radiating energy that would discourage anyone from sitting next to him.

I didn't look for his backup. That was Creel's job. My attention was fixed on the Russian—too fixed, because it took me a split second more than it should have to register the footsteps coming up behind me, a little too fast and a little too close to be a jogger. I started to turn, but something slammed into the base of my skull. I stumbled forward, falling to one knee. Somebody yanked at the bag. I made an instinctive grab at my right hip, forgetting I wasn't armed, then clutched at the strap as it moved down my arm. The thing—some kind of metal rod—hit me hard on my left shoulder, and then there was a blurred impression of something red moving away fast and the ground coming up at me faster.

I don't think I actually passed out, though I had a few moments when the world was a blur. By the time it slipped back into focus, I was on my hands and knees, supported by two women kneeling on either side of me. A few other people stood at the other edge of the path, filming the scene with their phones in case it turned out to be important. Everybody else ignored us. New York.

I let the women help me to a bench. The younger of the two was quiet. The older one hadn't stopped talking since I'd become aware of her, but I wasn't really registering what she was saying. Something about her phone. Something about policemen.

I couldn't see Creel or the man in the striped shirt. The younger woman gave me a water bottle. I nodded and took a swig.

"Don't bother with the cops," I said. "Way too late for that."

"You've been robbed! You have to fill out a report."

"It was just my laundry," I said. "Now I've got an excuse to buy new clothes."

I explored the bad spots gingerly. I was mostly numb. Pain would come later. The first blow had hit me just where the big shoulder muscles bunch close to the spine. Another couple of inches higher would have meant a nasty concussion at best, maybe a pine box. The shoulder blow was making it tough to do much with my left arm. Nothing felt broken, but I'd see interesting colors in the mirror tomorrow morning.

Sensing that I wasn't going to die or say anything racist, the people with phones drifted off. The younger woman took my chin in her hand and turned me to face her. She peered closely at my eyes, patted my hand, and walked away.

The older woman was still processing the idea that there wasn't going to be a report. She looked both directions on the path, clearly hoping for a badge. "I really think it's our duty to tell the police, don't you? It might help keep him from robbing somebody else."

"Ma'am, I'm fine. Thank you for your help, but I can take it from here."

She took out her phone. "I have a civic duty to report this."

I grabbed the hem of her shirt. "You're trying to retraumatize me, aren't you?"

She jerked back, her eyes widening. "I'm what?"

"You want to make me live it over and over." I let my eyes roll back in my head. Drooling would probably be a little over the top. "The room with the needles. You're one of *them*. Admit it!"

Creel appeared at the southern end of the path, coming my way. His hands were on his hips, and his head was thrown back to take in air.

I clutched her arm. "I'm not hiding anything," I hissed. "Neither is my monkey." She jerked away, looked around for potential witnesses and, finding none, hustled off, backing up for the first thirty paces.

Creel plopped down beside me, still breathing heavily. "You hurt?"

"I'll live," I said. "I'm noticing a distinct lack of recovered gym bag."

He growled.

"There's no way you come out of this looking dumber than me," I said. "Just tell me."

He ran both hands over his face. "The asshole who hit you was wearing jeans and a red sweatshirt with the hood pulled up. Skinny son of a bitch. Fast. I kept him in sight, though. I think the bag slowed him down."

"It would. Thing weighed about forty pounds."

"Then he got to the statue down there, at the corner of the park?" He waved south.

"Sherman."

"Whatever, yeah. There was a whole crowd, a couple dozen at least, all clustered together, every single damn one of them wearing a red hoodie and jeans, every single damn one carrying a brown gym bag. Our guy runs right into the middle, and they all take off in different directions. A couple duck into the subway, one goes into the Apple store, all of them running east, south, west. It was like watching a fucking pool rack break." He lifted his hands, let them drop in his lap. "No hope of figuring out which one was ours."

"It may be the head injury talking," I said, "but I've got a feeling this was not a random mugging."

"No shit. I figure the Russians are aiming to get paid twice. Snatch the first payment, then, hey, not our fault you got robbed, you still owe us."

"Most likely. Though it's not completely impossible somebody on their end talked, and a third party dealt themselves in."

"Or our end? We need to be thinking about fixing a hole?"

"I came up with this plan about two hours ago, Creel. I told you and Amaryllis Blunt and no one else."

"I don't suppose she'd steal from herself."

"Lissy? From orphans and widows, sure. From herself, no."

"So what now?"

"I'm guessing you get your name on my door a lot sooner than expected." I stood up. "Go back to the office. Write up everything you saw, in detail. Look into surveillance footage. Maybe we'll see a face we know."

"What are you going to do?"

My phone rang. I looked at the screen. "Talk to the Russians," I said. "Then I'll have to break the news to Amaryllis. We'll work it out. Get moving."

I waited until he was twenty feet away before I answered the call. "Eddie Dillon."

"That was quite a performance." The voice had no accent. "The red hoodies and everything. You should move it a few blocks west, try it out on Broadway."

I started walking deeper into the park. "That's funny. I was going to say pretty much the same to you."

An edge of anger. "This was a silly ploy, feigning payment without actually giving us anything. I doubt you even bothered putting money in the bag. You're playing for time, probably for the same reason you wouldn't just transfer the funds days ago. I'm adding ten percent to Baby Blunt's debt. Call it an inconvenience fee."

"What's ten percent of zero? Far as I'm concerned, the guy who hit me works for you. We're paid up."

"You're making me nostalgic, Mister Dillon. Back in the USSR days, I had all kinds of ways to deal with defiant behavior."

"Yeah, I get misty-eyed over car batteries and needle-nose pliers, myself."

"You have twenty-four hours from this moment to execute

payment in full to our Caymans account. No excuses, no negotiations. You know what Baby Blunt gave us, Dillon. If I look tomorrow and the money isn't there, I'm using it."

I walked past the Bethesda Fountain. "I think you're bluffing."

"I think you should convey our terms to your boss."

"I've known Amaryllis Blunt thirty years, Boris. I'll give her your message, but I know what she'll say. Fuck you."

The silence was so prolonged that I looked to be sure the call was still active. "Hello?"

"Goodbye, Mister Dillon."

I took my time walking the long, winding path around the southern shore of the lake, lingering on Cherry Hill. The blossoms were out. I hoped the chillier air wouldn't hurt them. Every year, Maya used to pick exactly one of them to press in an old dictionary. People talk a lot about the cherry blossoms around the Mall down in Washington. I've seen them, and I'll take New York's.

A dozen people sat scattered on the benches around the "Imagine" mosaic in Strawberry Fields. Two guys with guitars played soft folk music, trading vocals. Across from them, a man ate a bagel from a Russ and Daughters bag. He had a mohawk haircut and a goatee, both dyed jet black. I sat next to him.

"Either the Beautiful People truly suck at following directions, or I am very deeply annoyed with you," I said. "They were supposed to grab the money *after* I gave it to the Russian."

Baby Blunt ate the last piece of his bagel before he answered. "I got to thinking," he said, "and decided it would be better if we took it from you, so you'd be surprised. I figured the plan would work better if you'd act naturally."

"Who said *you* could decide anything about my plan?"

"Emil did good, huh? Ran track at Rutgers."

"He came within a couple inches of crippling me."

"So that makes you the walking wounded and beyond suspicion, right? You're welcome. The important thing is, we got it. Enough to fund the Beautiful People's next disruption and then some." He grinned. "You're going to love it, Eddie. We're—"

"Shut up," I said.

Baby looked shocked. Other than Amaryllis, not many people talked to him this way.

"You're about to tell me to watch for headlines from Texas or keep an eye on Zimbabwe or some damn thing," I said, "and I don't want to know. And keep in mind: anything you don't tell me is a thing I can't testify about."

"Anybody ever tell you you're paranoid?"

"Nobody who wasn't out to get me. You know, the Russians really *are* looking for you. They won't care you did all this just to trick Amaryllis into funding your little band of merry men."

"Why do you think I got the mohawk and grew the goatee? All anybody sees now is the hair. Anyway, in a couple of days I'll be in—someplace I guess I shouldn't tell you. Far away."

"Until the next time you need money and have to come up with some new scheme for prying it out of your aunt. I don't know why you don't just sell your stock. That ought to be enough for even you."

"No chance," Baby said. "That's my leverage, man, my connection. As long as I've got those shares, Aunt Lissy has to deal with me, one way or another."

"Deal with you. Jesus. You ever hear how I met your dear Aunt Lissy? She and your grandfather sent me to meet a guy she was in law school with who had her on a sex tape. He thought he could trade it for a million bucks and a lifetime gig as Blunt Enterprise's house counsel. I made him a counteroffer."

"What was that?"

"Not spending the rest of his life blind and in a wheelchair. Amaryllis intimidates you, Baby? She ought to scare the hell out of you. Sooner or later, she might deal with you permanently. She's more than capable of it."

"Always the dark note, Eddie." Baby slapped my knee. "Be happy, man. Your first successful job with the Beautiful People. How's it feel to be one of us?"

"I'm not one of you. I didn't do this to save the wetlands or whatever you're trying to accomplish."

He frowned. "So why did you?"

"You want to know a secret? Thirty years I've been working for your family, keeping you silly, self-important assholes out of jail, making sure the road is nice and smooth for you. You know how many times I've been to your aunt's penthouse? None. Grand total of—let's check the board—zero."

"That's it? You're what, upset we don't invite you to Thanksgiving dinner?"

"No, that's not it." I looked at my hands, hanging down between my knees. "My wife died last year."

"Oh, yeah." Baby scratched his cheek and looked at the guitar players. "I think somebody told me. I'm sorry for your loss."

"Don't worry about it," I said. "The Blunt family sent an enormous wreath to the service. No actual people, but a fantastic wreath. Nice note, too. *We are profoundly saddened by the loss of your precious May.*"

"That's something."

"My wife's name was Maya."

"Oh." I watched him try to think of an excuse that wouldn't make it worse.

"I stood between her casket and that fucking wreath thinking how Maya never knew what I really did for a living. She was *proud* of me, if you can believe it. She thought I did good out in the world." I was quiet for a moment. "I couldn't stop thinking about it, and I finally figured out who I was and who I wanted to be."

So I began compiling a set of private files on a thumb drive. Offshore bank accounts utterly unknown to the U.S. government. Recovered blackmail material going all the way back to

Amaryllis's sex tape, implicating various Blunts in crimes ranging from embezzlement to sexual assault and involuntary manslaughter. Evidence of bribes paid to everyone from county zoning officials to sitting senators. Proof that the family's primary business was laundering money for hostile governments and criminal cartels.

I built a bomb, designed specifically to blow up Blunt Enterprises, and then I made a copy of the thumb drive for Baby and told him exactly how to use it. But the dumb schmuck thought it just implicated his cousin Clayton in a minor real-estate swindle, and it never even occurred to him to look more closely before handing it over to the Russians so they would let him play cards.

"I'm sorry for your loss," Baby repeated, in exactly the same tone and cadence as before. "I'm sorry the family does bad things. But that's not as important as what the Beautiful People are doing." He put on a pair of sunglasses and got to his feet. "I'll be in touch."

"That stock you're sitting on, Baby. Might be a good idea to sell it. Soon."

He shook his head and left.

From where I sat, I couldn't see the building downtown, the one with the big ugly B on every side. I couldn't see Lissy Blunt, in her penthouse in the sky with the gaudy, diamond-encrusted golden faucets. But I could feel the cracks in the foundations, even if they didn't yet show.

The Blunt empire was about to burn, and watching the flames would make me feel like the richest man in the world.

The Beatles ("The White Album")

Released November 1968

"Back in the U.S.S.R."
"Dear Prudence"
"Glass Onion"
"Ob-La-Di, Ob-La-Da"
"Wild Honey Pie"
"The Continuing Story of Bungalow Bill"
"While My Guitar Gently Weeps"
"Happiness Is a Warm Gun"
"Martha My Dear"
"I'm So Tired"
"Blackbird"
"Piggies"
"Rocky Raccoon"
"Don't Pass Me By"
"Why Don't We Do It in the Road?"
"I Will"
"Julia"
"Birthday"
"Yer Blues"
"Mother Nature's Son"

"Everybody's Got Something to Hide
Except Me and My Monkey"
"Sexy Sadie"
"Helter Skelter"
"Long, Long, Long"
"Revolution 1"
"Honey Pie"
"Savoy Truffle"
"Cry Baby Cry"
"Revolution 9"

"While My Guitar Gently Weeps,"
"Piggies," "Long, Long, Long,"
and "Savoy Truffle" are by George Harrison.
"Don't Pass Me By" is by Richard Starkey.
All other songs are by John Lennon and Paul McCartney.

Happiness Is a Warm Gun
Kate Ellis

Liverpool, December 1967

There were bound to be questions. *Who is Miss Howlett? Where does she live? Who else is going? Why on earth would a teacher, a grown woman, invite a group of sixteen-year-old pupils to her flat to celebrate her birthday? Surely she sees enough of you at school?*

Julia knew Mum would stop her from going, which meant another evening in the bungalow with Bill slumped in his favorite chair like a sly, watchful lizard, so she lied and said she was going to Prudence's house to study for exams. She added that Prudence's dad had offered to bring her home—which was true, because Prudence had also been invited to what Miss Howlett called her *soirée*.

Julia had bought a bright yellow dress with the money she'd earned from her Saturday job selling truffles and cherry creams from Des Barrow's stall in the market. According to Mum, the dress was far too short, but Bill told her it suited her. The way he said it had made her shudder, but she was still determined to wear it for the *soirée*, along with the grown-up velvet gloves she'd found at a vintage stall. She wanted to look her best.

Miss Howlett wasn't like the other teachers at St. Martha's. She wore long skirts, lots of cheesecloth and flowing scarves, and the nuns regarded her disapprovingly—which, to her teen-age pupils, gave her an aura of glamor. Julia and Prudence often wondered what Mother Superior thought of Miss Howlett, and whether she regretted employing her as their new art teacher.

Miss Howlett lived in a flat on Princes Road, which the girls considered terribly modern. Julia lived in a bungalow, the height of suburban dullness, although the place had acquired an edge of danger since Bill moved in.

On the evening of the *soirée*, Julia walked to Prudence's house around the corner to change into the yellow dress. At school the girls wore navy-blue uniforms, but that evening the dull caterpillars would be transformed into butterflies, and they wondered if Miss Howlett would recognize them in their finery. And whether any boys would be at the *soirée*.

As the girls headed toward the city in the back of Prudence's dad's Rover, Julia's palms tingled with excitement. The *soirée* would be a taste of the adult world outside home and school. As they neared their destination, that world seemed full of promise.

There was a row of bell pushes next to the shabby front door of the tall Victorian house, and Prudence pushed the one labelled *Sadie Howlett*. They'd never heard their art teacher's first name before, but "Sadie" seemed to fit her.

"Sexy Sadie," Prudence whispered as they waited for the door to open. Julia giggled. "Sexy" was the ideal word to describe Miss Howlett.

"You're the first. Come up," their teacher greeted them. She wore a long, brightly colored dress, and her wavy auburn hair fell around her shoulders, glossy and untamed. Julia thought she looked magnificent.

The flat was what Julia's mum would have described as bohemian, filled with old oriental rugs and stripped pine furniture with a large Mucha mirror above the marble fireplace and stained glass decorating the windowpanes. There were three doors at the far end of the spacious room—one leading to a tiny kitchen, one to a bathroom, and the third to Sadie's bedroom, where they left their coats on a big double bed covered in a patterned Indian bedspread. The scent of patchouli hung in the air, and on the bedside table a thin ribbon of smoke rose from a burning joss stick protruding from something that resembled a glass onion.

"Drink?" Sadie asked, when they returned to the living room.

The girls nodded eagerly, feeling very grown up. Sadie poured cider into a pair of cloudy glasses, and Julia regarded hers nervously as their hostess placed *Sgt. Pepper's Lonely Hearts Club Band* on the turntable. As soon as the record's first track started, the doorbell rang. When Sadie left the room, Julia saw Prudence wrinkle her nose as she took her first sip of cider. It was rough and acidic. No doubt it was an acquired taste—but one Julia was determined to master.

After a while, Sadie reappeared with an attractive boy. Attending an all-girls convent school, Prudence and Julia's unfamiliarity with the opposite sex made any reasonable looking boy as alluring as a pop star. Julia stifled a giggle. Her two mouthfuls of cider had begun to take effect.

"Girls, this is Richard, my nephew."

"Rocky," the boy said, with a confidence Julia couldn't help admiring. He didn't have a Liverpool accent, which added to his air of mystery.

"Pleased to meet you," said Prudence with a giggle.

But Rocky's eyes were fixed on Julia, who took another sip of cider for courage.

The doorbell rang again, and Sadie disappeared, leaving the girls and Rocky standing in awkward silence until she returned with three more girls from their art class at school. Like Julia and Prudence, they'd dressed up for the occasion, vying with each other to see who could wear the shortest skirt.

Their classmates were followed by a trio of boys, friends of Rocky's. But unlike Rocky, the spotty newcomers took no interest in Julia. As the party got going, Sadie dimmed lights and refilled glasses. After a while, one of the girls felt sick and locked herself in the bathroom.

Sadie watched the proceedings with a beatific smile and glazed eyes. The cigarette she was smoking smelled strange, but the girls thought nothing of it at the time.

When Julia allowed Rocky to lead her into Sadie's bedroom, she knew that if Mother Superior ever found out about this, Sadie Howlett would be in huge trouble. But she trusted there would be a pact of silence among the girls who were there. It would be a big secret...unless someone was tempted to boast about it at school.

Julia let Rocky kiss her, and she was beginning to enjoy the experience when he pulled away. "You live with Bill Harrison."

The mention of Bill's name shocked her. "How did you know?"

There was a long silence before he answered. "I went to your house once and saw you come out, but I wasn't brave enough to knock on the door. When I passed my driving test, my dad said that I'd have to pay for it myself if I wanted a car. I was told that Bill Harrison lent people money, so I borrowed some from him. But he kept upping the interest, and in the end, I couldn't pay him back. He called me a stupid rich kid and said I had to pay up three times what he'd lent me. I had to confess what I'd done to my dad. He's a solicitor, and he threatened Bill with legal action."

Julia's heart was beating fast, fearing that her mother's appalling choice of boyfriend was going to put an abrupt end to any budding romance before it even started.

"Bill made threats of his own," Rocky continued, "and they weren't the legal kind. My dad backed off, because he didn't want to put me in danger. Bill said he knew some very nasty people."

Julia understood. Some of those nasty people had visited the bungalow, and they had scared her.

"I can't stand Bill." Her words came out in a rush. "Mum was lonely after Dad died, and Bill can be charming when he wants to be. I keep telling her that he gives me the creeps, but she won't listen. I wish he'd move out." It felt good to meet someone who felt the same about Bill as she did. Prudence, with her nice respectable family, had never really understood.

"Can I trust you?" Rocky said solemnly.

"Of course."

"I've got something to hide. Will you look after it for me?"

She nodded again, breathless with cider and infatuation.

He opened the bottom drawer of a large pine chest in the corner of the room and brought out an object wrapped in patterned cloth. "Promise you won't scream?"

Julia suddenly felt nervous. "What is it?"

He handed it to her. Whatever it was, it was heavy and hard, like a piece of machinery, like the wrenches Bill used to work on his motor bike. "Take it home and hide it somewhere safe. I don't want to keep it at mine, because my people are too nosy. Put it in your bag and don't tell a soul. I'll let you know when I need it." When he kissed her again, it felt like sealing a vow.

She would never betray him. Even when she unwrapped the package and saw the revolver, she said nothing. It was her secret, hers and Rocky's. And it meant that she'd see him again soon.

Julia hid the gun under the sweaters in her bottom drawer, and every time she looked at it, she felt a warm glow of excitement because it reminded her of Rocky, who was in the sixth form at the local private school. Rocky lived in a big house on Menlove Avenue, and his dad was the pinnacle of respectability, so she had no idea where the gun had come from. When she'd asked him, he'd said the less she knew, the better.

She wished her dad were still alive to advise her. But he was dead, and Bill had replaced him in her mum's affections. Since meeting Rocky, though, she'd begun to feel safer in the bungalow—especially when she took the gun from its hiding place and hooked her finger around its trigger.

To Julia's delight, Rocky started meeting her after school, although they always parted at the end of her road because he didn't want Bill to see him, which she thought was wise. The only cloud on her horizon was Prudence's unexpected jealousy. Since the evening of Miss Howlett's *soirée*, her best friend had barely spoken to her. But at least this meant Julia wasn't tempted to betray Rocky's secret.

As the days went by, she managed to convince herself that the gun was just a convincing replica, an expensive toy. A boy like Rocky would never possess a real gun. That sort of thing was confined to criminals—and people like Bill.

Rocky hadn't mentioned the gun since the night he gave it to her, but a couple of weeks after Miss Howlett's *soirée* he took Julia to the cinema to see *The Graduate*. Someone at school had heard from an older brother that it was good, but Julia's mum said there was sex in it, not realizing that, to a teenage girl, this was a recommendation. As she was walking home from the cinema with Rocky by her side, Julia felt an unfamiliar surge of happiness and knew she was in love. Then Rocky stopped suddenly and took her face in his hands.

"You know that thing I gave you? I need it back. Where is it?"

"It's safe. I put it in my drawer."

She thought he was about to kiss her, but instead he looked angry. "I told you to hide it."

"I did. Nobody except me ever looks in that drawer."

"How can you be sure of that with Bill Harrison about?"

"I'd never let Bill in my room." She wrinkled her nose in disgust.

"What about when you're at school?"

"Well, anyway, it's just a toy—isn't it?"

There was a long silence before Rocky replied. "'Course it is. But it cost a lot of money."

Something about this answer didn't ring true. "Where did you get it?"

He hesitated. "I lied. It's not a replica. My dad brought it back from the war and hid it in the attic. He doesn't know I took it, and I want it to stay that way, okay?"

"Why did you give it to me?"

His eyes were cold, and she suddenly regretted her curiosity.

"I took it to Auntie Sadie's party to show my mates, because they didn't believe I had it. But then I saw you and"—he looked embarrassed—"maybe I wanted to impress you. Look, I'll meet you on the corner of your road tomorrow after tea, and you can return it to me then."

"Why do you need it?"

"Best if you don't know."

He was no longer holding her hand, and they walked on in silence. Julia sensed a change in him, and she knew his mind was on the gun.

As soon as they reached the corner of her street, Rocky walked off without their usual passionate kiss. She couldn't find her door key, so she had to ring the bell. As soon as Mum opened the door, she rushed straight to her room, opened the bottom drawer, and delved beneath the sweaters. But she couldn't feel the hard gun amongst the soft wool.

Julia didn't sleep that night. The gun that had once brought her such happiness—the secret bond between her and Rocky—had been taken. And she knew so little about firearms that she wasn't even sure if it was loaded and lethal.

There was only one explanation: Bill must have been looking through her things. The thought made her sick. Bill with the slicked-back hair, sharp suits and permanent smile; Bill who rested his hand on her shoulder just a little too long for comfort; Bill who called her "Honey Pie," which she hated, and whose most innocent remarks were full of innuendoes she didn't quite understand—Bill had been rifling through her most intimate possessions. She hated him, and she was sure he made her mother unhappy. She'd heard him shouting at her. She'd heard Mum gently weeping in her room when Bill was out. And she'd seen the bruises on her mother's arms.

She lay awake, trying not to think about him but only too aware that he was lying in the adjoining room in his pajamas, sharing her mother's bed.

At two that morning, she heard her door open and sprang out of bed.

What followed was confusing. There was the sound of breaking glass and the deafening noise of a shot. A minute later, her mother started screaming. Then the police cars arrived.

Later, the police concluded that an intruder had broken into the bungalow and one fatality had resulted.

The intruder, according to the fat police inspector who dealt with the case, must have gained access by smashing a pane of glass in the back door. Some people would never learn about security, a uniformed officer added with a sigh. The police hadn't found the weapon that killed Bill, but the inspector said guns were easy enough to obtain, if you knew who to ask. Nothing was missing from the bungalow, so they were working on the theory that Bill's death was connected to his dubious business dealings. It appeared that he had made a lot of enemies over the years.

Julia's mum was in a state of shock, and after breakfast Julia left her in the care of a neighbor and walked to the phone box to telephone Rocky. When she broke the news, there was a long silence before he said, "Where's that thing I gave you to look after?"

"It's missing. Did you sneak in and take it?"

He didn't answer the question. "Don't call me again," he said, and ended the call. His words were brutal, and Julia felt as though she'd been struck.

After that, Julia had no further contact with Rocky—but she

reconciled with Prudence, who slipped easily back into the role of Best Friend. Other things changed, too: Sadie Howlett left her teaching post in the middle of term, and word had it that Mother Superior had somehow found out about the *soirée*, though Sadie's arrest for possession of cannabis might have had more to do with her dismissal. Julia's brush with bohemian life was over, just like her relationship with Rocky.

Liverpool, March 1975

A business associate of Bill's had been charged with his murder—a man with a long record of violence who'd accused Bill of double-crossing him and had sworn revenge. At the trial, he was acquitted due to lack of evidence, and no one else was ever arrested.

Julia and her mother tried their best to put that part of their life behind them. For the two years following Bill's death, they lived quietly in the bungalow. Then, after A levels, Julia moved to London to study English at university before returning to Liverpool to take up a teaching post at her old school. She rented a flat in Penny Lane, because the bungalow held too many bad memories. Bill was dead, but his spirit seemed to linger there, and she still had nightmares about that terrible night. The breaking glass, the shots, her mother's screams. Some things stay with you for life.

But at weekends Julia felt obliged to visit her mother in the Bungalow of Bad Memories and stay for dinner. One Saturday in March, she arrived at three o'clock as usual and heard voices when she opened the front door. Mum had a visitor. When she entered the living room, she was amazed to recognize the woman sitting in the armchair that had once been Bill's favorite.

Sadie Howlett had changed in the years that had passed since their last meeting. Her hair was shorter, and she looked older and more careworn, as though life hadn't been kind to her.

"Julia, I hoped I might find you here. Would you mind if we spoke in private?" She glanced anxiously at Mum, who took the hint and left the room, claiming she had things to do. Julia knew this was a lie. She'd be out in the hall with her ear pressed to the door.

After a long silence, Sadie spoke.

"I believe you were once given something of mine."

"I don't think so."

"My nephew Rocky...borrowed it from me. He's only just told me that he gave it to you for safekeeping because he didn't want his parents to find it."

Julia leaned forward, surprised. "Keep your voice down. Are you talking about the gun? He told me it was his father's. He said he found it in the attic."

"That was a lie. It was mine, and now he's admitted that he stole it on the night of that...party. I honestly thought someone else had taken it, a man I'd been seeing. I used to know some dodgy people in those days," she added with an embarrassed smile. "I never suspected Rocky for one minute, but he said he took it to impress his friends." She smiled sadly. "Isn't that just like an adolescent boy? He's all grown up now, of course, and working in his dad's law firm. Anyway, last week he owned up about the gun. He said it had been on his conscience, and he needed to come clean."

Julia said nothing. Sadie's words made sense. Rocky had taken the gun from his aunt to impress his friends, then lost his nerve and got rid of it by giving it to her. He probably asked for it back because he intended to replace it, only to be told that it was missing. Then she'd accused him of stealing it from her room. No wonder he'd been angry with her.

"I used to know Bill Harrison," Sadie said, almost in a whisper.

The sudden change of subject took Julia by surprise.

"I met him at a party. He tried to pick me up and told me he lived with a woman who had a pretty daughter who went to St. Martha's."

Julia looked away.

"I felt awful, because I put Rocky onto him when he wanted to borrow some money to buy a car. Big mistake. When Rocky confessed, his father told him how stupid he'd been and tried to help by threatening legal action. But Bill frightened him into backing off. My brother-in-law's not used to dealing with that sort of people. In the end, he advised Rocky to put it down to experience. But I suspect Rocky's pride was hurt."

"You think Rocky went out with me to get at Bill?"

Sadie said nothing, but the answer hung in the air. It *was* possible that Rocky had been using her. But that was a long time ago.

"Julia, could Rocky have taken the gun from wherever you'd hidden it?"

Julia closed her eyes and thought back. "I suppose there's a chance he crept into the house while Mum and Bill were out— and then blamed me for losing it."

"What better way to cover his tracks?"

"You don't think *Rocky* killed Bill, do you?"

Sadie didn't reply, and in the long silence that followed Julia could hear a blackbird singing on the tree outside the bungalow. Its carefree noise jarred with her thoughts. Sadie had almost accused her of aiding a killer, of allowing Rocky to exploit her infatuation and take deadly revenge on Bill.

"Should we tell the police?"

Sadie shook her head. "Rocky's doing well in his career, and he's just got engaged. The last thing I want is to ruin his life. Besides, I'd get in trouble for having the gun in the first place. I lost my teaching job, and now I'm struggling to sell my art. I don't need the police on my back, as well." She hesitated. "They never did find the weapon that killed Bill, did they?"

"I believe not. You can't really think Rocky did it."

Sadie Howlett gave a secretive smile. "I think we should let it be. My new partner's asked me to move to Devon with him, so perhaps you and I won't meet again. Good luck, Julia. I hope your teaching career's more successful than mine was."

At that moment, Mum bustled in with tea and biscuits, and when Sadie Howlett said she had to go, Julia saw disappointment on her mother's face.

After Sadie left, Julia made for her old room and squatted down to fold back a corner of the carpet, careful not to make a sound. She lifted the loose floorboard where she'd once hidden her childhood treasures from prying eyes and took the gun out carefully, stroking the hard metal, remembering how warm it had felt after she'd fired it and the relief and elation she'd experienced when Bill fell to the floor.

When he'd come to her room that night, drunk as a sailor, his intentions had been clear, and he had shown her the gun he'd stolen from her sweater drawer to compel her to give herself to him—but he backed off when she wrestled the weapon from his clumsy hands. She had followed him into the kitchen and fired, then smashed the glass in the door to make it look like a break-in before hurrying back to her room to hide the gun. It hadn't been difficult to convince Rocky that the horrible thing had been stolen. And he would never have betrayed her to the police, since he should never have had an unlicensed gun in the first place.

She'd only been sixteen at the time, but committing murder had been surprisingly easy—and now she needed to dispose of the one piece of evidence that could lead the police to her in the unlikely event that Sadie Howlett had an attack of conscience and told the truth. She put the gun in her handbag, said goodnight to Mum, and threw it into the churning gray waters of the River Mersey.

When she returned to her flat in Penny Lane, she put the Beatles' *White Album* on the turntable. When "Happiness is a Warm Gun" began to play, she poured herself a glass of wine and smiled.

Yellow Submarine
Released January 1969

"Yellow Submarine"
"Only a Northern Song"
"All Together Now"
"Hey Bulldog"
"It's All Too Much"
"All You Need is Love"
"Pepperland"
"Sea of Time"
"Sea of Holes"
"Sea of Monsters"
"March of the Meanies"
"Pepperland Laid Waste"
"Yellow Submarine in Pepperland"

"Only a Northern Song" and "It's All Too Much"
are by George Harrison.
"Pepperland," "Sea of Time," "Sea of Holes,"
"Sea of Monsters," "March of the Meanies," and
"Pepperland Laid Waste" are by George Martin.
All other songs are by John Lennon and Paul McCartney.

Hey Bulldog
Anjili Babbar

When she started in the Honors English program at Brentworth College, Serene Jacques had no illusions about becoming a tenure-track professor at some grand R1 school. Those jobs were cherries that went to people of a different class and color, academics with the connections and participation trophies to make their actual *merit* irrelevant.

Serene suspected that the other students in the program didn't think she belonged. The mean girls certainly didn't invite her to their parties, and she once overheard one of them whisper "diversity candidate" as she entered the Renaissance Lit classroom. They had broad synthetic smiles, asses that announced they had time after class to devote to the gym instead of slinging burgers, and daddies with grad-school besties on the college board. Never mind that the mean girls' papers were slogging rehashes of tropes handed down by decades of tired old white men. They were all but guaranteed to wind up teaching the next generation of students to be as brutally average as themselves.

Serene began to hope for a better future on the day that Mackenzie Russell, the English Department chair, tapped her shoulder outside Stuart Hall and said, "Come talk to me."

When they got to her office, Russell slipped into her desk chair with practiced ease, despite her signature tight skirt and stilettos. "I was impressed by your paper at the Honors Conference. *Ulysses* was a bold choice for an undergraduate. What are your plans after Brentworth?"

"Plans? Like, for a job?"

The chair laughed, but not unkindly. "For graduate school. You'll be a senior in the fall, right? You need to start thinking about where you're going to apply."

"I can't afford grad school. Not—not right now, anyway."

"No one with your talent *pays* for a Ph.D, Serene. I can help, if you like. We can review your work together, maybe even get you published in an undergraduate journal."

"You'd do that for me? I mean, *thank* you."

"You'll need to be careful, though," the chair went on. "Don't affiliate yourself with hostile people on the margins. Nobody likes a troublemaker—and whatever they pretend, nobody likes woke-talk or self-victimization."

Serene assumed Russell was referring to Maddie Corbin, the only professor of color in the department, the only person—until now—who had really made time to discuss *ideas* with her. But Corbin was fish-cold, all woke ideas and no emotion. It wasn't strange that she rubbed people the wrong way.

"And let's do something to get you looking more…professional," Russell added, eyeing Serene's Doc Martens. "Looks shouldn't matter, but it's a man's world, isn't it? Trying to be pretty won't kill you."

The light of her iPhone was a beacon in Maddie Corbin's dim apartment. There was little warmth in the brick walls, antique steel barn door, and candelabras collected from a dozen countries, all arranged like feathers in a nest, building blocks in anticipation of a life well spent. But a show apartment was of little use without anyone to show it to. The smell of sauteed garlic and mirepoix and the clatter of dishes punctuated by laughter from the apartment next door made Maddie's solitude torture.

Any woman in academia—but particularly a childless woman of color—could expect to be taken advantage of. Her students deluged her with emails, cataloguing their anxieties in multi-paragraph monologues and telling her what she *would* do: "You will give me an extension on my paper," they demanded. And her colleagues were no different: "You will join this additional committee, because Noah and Jenna and James are too busy driving their kids to soccer practice." And any objection from her, any expression of emotion, would see her labelled angry or hysterical.

She checked her phone's screen and saw she had a text from Alex Wolf.

I'm sorry you had to cover classes for Jenna and James this week.

As she read the words, a follow-up pinged in.

No, "I'm sorry" doesn't cut it. You're always the one expected to pick up the slack.

And another.

For what it's worth, I think it's unfair and discriminatory. You deserve to have a life. I'm going to bring it up at the meeting tomorrow.

And another.

Coffee?

They had coffee on campus before the department meeting, and he listened to her catalog the constant encroachments on her time—the first time she had felt safe saying such things out loud. Then, in the meeting, he advocated for her as promised.

And when her afternoon class ended, he waited for the students to leave, slid into the room and closed the door behind him—and pushed her against the wall, hard enough to make her head bounce.

* * *

She fled to Mackenzie Russell's office, expecting a scolding for her unprofessional tears, but the chair looked genuinely concerned.

"It's about Alex Wolf," Maddie began, unsure how much she was willing to tell. But there was something in the earnestness with which Mackenzie leaned toward her that urged her on.

After she finished her story, the chair held eye contact for several seconds, and for a moment Maddie wondered if she had zoned out completely, had only been pretending to listen, like the girls who lolled in the back of her classroom, applying sticky pink lip gloss during lectures.

Then Mackenzie did something unexpected: she laughed. More childlike than malicious, it created an awkward dissonance with the coiffed bottle-blond hair and spiky heels that spoke to a very adult life outside of teaching.

"Men, my God," she finally said. "Even a doctorate can't make professionals out of them." She picked a stray hair from Maddie's sweater, a strangely intimate gesture. "You never hear about women behaving like that. But with men, ugh, it's all the time—and it happens to us all, eventually. *All* of us."

Maddie nodded but fixed her eyes on a patch of stained carpet near the door. She didn't know what she had expected, but there was something off about this speech. An insinuation that Alex's behavior was nothing more than an occupational hazard.

Still, the chair had believed her. That was the important thing.

"I'll take care of this," Mackenzie said. "I promise. And in the meantime, don't stress too much about it. Alex is just a dumb bulldog. He barks and howls like all of them—but not all dogs bite."

Professor Wolf looked exactly like Commander Putnam from *The Handmaid's Tale*: more lemur than wolf, more petulant than commanding. His affect in class—the efforts to sound casual with twenty-year-old slang, the hovering over certain girls during lectures—suggested that he considered himself thirst-worthy, though he was older than most of his students' parents. Now, in his office on the third floor of Stuart Hall, his attempts to puff out his chest were undermined by poor posture.

"If there's something you want to tell me about this paper, Miss Jacques, now is the time."

Serene stared at his shoes. Nothing she had heard about the man was good. Just last week, she'd overheard the mean girls whispering that Maddie Corbin had filed a harassment complaint against him, and that she wasn't the first. She considered admitting to plagiarism she hadn't committed, just to avoid stoking his animosity.

Then she remembered she had an ally.

"If you have questions about my paper, Professor, I think you should talk to Doctor Russell. She watched my process and gave me feedback on my first draft."

Wolf's narrow nostrils flamed. But where Serene expected to see at least a flicker of insolent humiliation, there was only smugness.

"I *did* talk to Mack," he said. "That's how I know you stole her ideas."

There was no point in asking Russell about it. Wolf's claim was startling, but in hindsight it rang true to Serene. The chair had made her thoughts about hostile people on the margins clear; she had just neglected to mention her own role in *making* them hostile and marginalized.

Maddie watched student aides wheel boxes of her books and papers to a dusty former storage closet at the far end of the corridor. The chair called the move an "interim solution," putting distance between Maddie and Alex while her complaint was investigated—but Mackenzie's idea of an "investigation" boiled down to asking Alex if he had done it and then grumbling about how challenging it was to "arrive at the truth."

"Alex describes the incident very differently," she reported. "He claims he was trying to give you advice about your teaching style, and you became belligerent and violent."

In other words, she was an angry, hysterical woman of color. Academia would embrace that trope every time to avoid looking itself in the eye.

Stretching to pull thumbtacks from the last poster remaining on the wall—a picture of Edgar Allan Poe with his quote about "long intervals of horrible sanity"—Maddie considered dropping the matter altogether. She would be denied justice for the way Wolf had treated her, but backing down would be safer than playing David to the Goliath of his privilege.

"Um, Doctor Corbin?"

A student stood in her doorway, puffy-faced, arms trembling, and she dragged herself back into prof mode.

"It's been a minute, Serene. Can I help you with something?" The girl, once a regular in her office, hadn't come around for quite a while. Maddie knew she shouldn't have emotional expectations of someone so young, but she had missed their discussions. The only real reward for teaching was the rare student whose enthusiasm gave you a glimpse of the spark that got you into the profession in the first place.

The girl wobbled on her Doc Martens, as if unsure whether to enter the office or run. Then the boots stopped rocking and the wide brown eyes steeled.

"You're the only one"—she trailed off, then tried again—"no one else will understand."

Maddie listened with shock—but perfect credulity—to the story, which jounced out of the girl like pachinko balls.

"Mackenzie Russell is exactly the sort of person who *would* back that vulturine Alex Wolf," she spat, registering the surprise on Serene's face, but tired of holding back. "*Especially* in a false accusation of plagiarism against a student of color." She wanted to be relieved that it hadn't been more than that, given what she knew of Alex, but all she felt was a deep flush of guilt. Presuming that *she* had been Alex's only victim was a kind of willful blindness. He had probably been damaging lives for years—enabled by the chair, who gathered intel for him by feigning sympathy for his victims.

"I've seen how two-faced she can be," she explained. "Maybe this is inappropriate, Serene, but I want you to understand that it isn't just *you* who's had run-ins with Professor Wolf."

After Maddie recounted her own experiences with Alex and the chair, Serene said, "She's disgusting. They're *both* disgusting. We need to *do* something."

"Yes," Maddie agreed, "we do."

Maddie was glad that Serene's bravery had brought her to her senses and gladder still when the girl left her office. She needed to confront Mackenzie while the bile was tangible, before it faded into fear or, worse, apathy.

The door to the chair's office was partly open, and Maddie could see Mackenzie leaning toward Alex, the top of her low-cut blouse level with his chin, the form-fitting suit forcing her into an awkward angle on her power heels. A bullfrog half-stuffed into a sausage casing, thumbtacks stuck to its bulbous feet.

Maddie's stomach pitched. Her hands felt sweaty in a way they had not since the third-grade playground. Mackenzie and Alex hadn't noticed her, and the chair spoke in low whispers, laughing uncomfortably, as if afraid of being overheard.

She couldn't see Mackenzie's face when Alex muttered the words "diversity hire," but the chair's laughter told her all she needed to know.

* * *

At midsemester, the plagiarism investigation was still underway, and only Maddie Corbin had taken Serene's side at the hearing. Mackenzie Russell sent a sealed letter to the Student Conduct committee but was otherwise conspicuously absent. Serene could only imagine what atrocities the chair's letter contained.

To avoid the gossiping mean girls, Serene spent her breaks in a bathroom in the Stuart Hall basement. There were no classrooms in the basement, and the lights fizzed and belched. On Wednesday morning, with one exam finished and two still to be endured, she sought sanctuary there. It was just after ten, and she had more than an hour to kill.

From inside the left-most of the three stalls, she heard a faint murmuring—so low at first that she barely noticed it, though the voice was familiar, like background music that doesn't quite hit the consciousness. She peeked through the crack between the stall door and its frame and saw Maddie Corbin with an iPhone pressed to her ear.

Later in the day, Serene considered how fitting it would be if a bathroom turned out to be the image by which Brentworth was remembered. Mackenzie Russell, who had been so willing to flush Serene's future down the toilet, had been discovered by the eleven o'clock custodial staff in Stuart Hall's basement bathroom, dead.

Sobs arose from gathered students and faculty as officers carried the chair's body from the building, zipped into a black bag. Serene wondered if she too might have mourned Russell's passing if she hadn't gotten to know her.

She tried to catch Maddie Corbin's eye, but the professor was huddled under an awning, engrossed in her iPhone, as casually as if she were waiting out a routine fire drill. Serene felt a tickle of admiration at this insouciance—especially since, given Corbin's anger at Russell and her presence in the bathroom that morning, she was sure it was Corbin who had murdered the chair.

* * *

Maddie watched as the chair's body was unceremoniously hauled out of Stuart Hall.

She shuddered at the idea of the body as not just a body but as someone she *knew*—then shook off the thought. She checked her phone, avoiding eye contact with the girl who, until recently, she had merely thought of as a favorite student.

Still, she couldn't resist stealing a glance. All Doc Martens and ironic pigtails, the sight of Serene almost made Maddie smile. And then reality returned, and she remembered seeing Serene in the basement bathroom, not an hour before the chair had been found there. The girl hadn't used the toilet, hadn't made a call, had only come in and looked around. In retrospect, it seemed obvious Serene had been looking for Mackenzie Russell—and that she had ultimately found her.

Maddie had always wondered to what lengths she would go to protect her students. Would she be one of those profs who used her own body to shield them from an active shooter? Or would her lizard brain kick in and tell her to save herself instead?

She had imagined the scenario many times, though always— *always*—she was protecting them from a killer, not covering for them after they themselves had killed. But when a big man in uniform approached her, notebook in hand, her answers to his questions came surprisingly naturally.

"Can you tell me your whereabouts between, say, ten and eleven, ma'am?"

Maddie's spine spiked at that "ma'am." Fury at petty things was the best avenue for dissociation, from grief and fear alike.

"I snuck out to my car for a cigarette between proctoring exams."

She instantly regretted the lie—not the lying, but *that* lie. Were there cameras in the parking lot near Stuart Hall? She had never bothered to look. She persuaded herself that it didn't matter, since there were surely no cameras in the neglected Stuart Hall basement—no cameras that could prove Serene had been there, or that she had seen the student staking out her prey.

You might not have friends you can count on to bury a body, Serene, she thought wryly. *But you can count on me.*

When it was her turn to speak to the police, Serene made up her mind to protect her only ally. She had listened to enough true crime podcasts to know that displacing herself from the scene of the crime was the only way to avoid being grilled as a witness.

"I was in the library studying from ten until eleven," she said. It came out mucousy, like a thing from the ugliest part of her insides.

Maddie was astonished when the police brought Alex Wolf out of the building in handcuffs, slouched like a comma. She suppressed an untimely smirk, wondering if he had kicked up a fuss when they arrested him.

A reporter startled her out of her reverie. "Are you a professor here?"

She nodded curtly, noting that Serene had edged away, fading into a group of her classmates.

"Do you have any thoughts about today's events?"

Did she have any *thoughts*? Sure, she had plenty of thoughts.

"I guess all dogs really do bite," she said.

The mean girls were ablaze with theories about Wolf and the chair. The snippets of info they had received from their connected daddies blossomed in a thousand improbable directions, highlighting their roles in this great moment of justice.

"Apparently she was already dead before he stabbed her," one of them said, shaking her glossy hair in exaggerated disbelief. "He shoved her lipstick down her throat, blocking her airway. The stabbing was just patriarchal overkill."

"Her lipstick? Huh, I guess trying to be pretty *can* kill you," Serene blurted. She was glad that the mean girls, already engaged in mythologizing elsewhere, didn't seem to hear her.

Serene bumped into Maddie Corbin as the professor was heading for her car.

"It's good they made an arrest," she said tentatively. "Brentworth will be safer with Alex Wolf behind bars." She hoped the reminder that Corbin's crime would result in a greater good would help the professor sleep at night.

Maddie was ready to return home to her thoughts and a very hot bath when Serene stopped her in the parking lot. She had considered the girl brave, if woefully misguided, but now she wondered whether she was too young and innocent—no, not *innocent*, but naïve—to understand the gravity of her actions. Even if a charge against Alex Wolf stuck, Serene would carry the murder on her shoulders for the rest of her life.

"I wonder what they think they have on Alex," Maddie said, pulling her phone from a pocket and scrolling to a local news livestream. The move was designed to end the conversation, but Serene just edged closer. Together, they leaned into the blue light of the iPhone.

Multiple witnesses saw Wolf and Russell arguing early this morning, with Wolf accusing Russell of damaging his reputation and Russell accusing Wolf of harassing female colleagues and students. A search warrant led to the discovery of a jackknife—believed to be the murder weapon—in a filing cabinet in Wolf's office. Russell's friends describe her as old-fashioned, sheltered, and not particularly worldly, suggesting she was unlikely to be aware of the danger posed by Wolf.

It would have sounded convincing to Maddie if she hadn't been privy to a broader context. Briefly, she wondered how the knife had made its way to Alex's office, then decided she didn't want to know.

"They make Russell sound like she was only guilty of being ignorant," Serene scoffed. "Like she was his victim as much as"—she lowered her voice—"as *we* were."

Maddie nodded but kept her eyes fixed on the screen, where a reporter asked Alex's next-door neighbor if he had noticed violent tendencies in Alex—anything that suggested he might be capable of murder.

The neighbor hung his head as he replied. "You think you know someone," he said, "but you only know that little part of them you can see. In the end, you don't really have a clue."

Abbey Road
Released September 1969

"Come Together"
"Something"
"Maxwell's Silver Hammer"
"Oh! Darling"
"Octopus's Garden"
"I Want You (She's So Heavy)"
"Here Comes the Sun"
"Because"
"You Never Give Me Your Money"
"Sun King"
"Mean Mr. Mustard"
"Polythene Pam"
"She Came in Through the Bathroom Window"
"Golden Slumbers"
"Carry That Weight"
"The End"
"Her Majesty"

"Something" and "Here Comes the Sun"
are by George Harrison.
"Octopus's Garden" is by Richard Starkey.
All other songs are by John Lennon and Paul McCartney.

Maxwell's Silver Hammer
David Dean

Chief Inspector Fergus Dalrymple yawned and stretched beneath the Bahamian sun, his flaccid body glistening with oil. "By gad," he murmured, "what a welcome change from England in November!"

"I'm sorry?" a distinctly non-English voice responded.

Startled, Fergus opened his eyes to find a clean-cut, muscular young man with dark hair standing over him.

"Do you mind?" Fergus asked, indicating with a flicking motion that the new arrival was blocking his sun.

Taking the chaise lounge next to Fergus—though dozens of unoccupied ones were available—the newcomer replied, "Didn't mean to startle you, but one of the fellas from your group pointed you out, said you're from Liverpool."

Dalrymple's group was the U.K contingent at the International Convention of Police Investigators, which was being hosted by the British Colonial Hotel.

"Did they?" he responded to the American—for that is what he took him to be. "Why were you enquiring, if I might ask?"

"Well, you know, *Liverpool*, home of the Beatles. I thought you might have seen them, maybe even worked security for them."

"Here comes the bloody sun," Fergus muttered, rising up onto his elbows and looking about in desperation for a waiter.

"No, I never met the musical mop-tops, and I'd have had a few choice words for them if I had."

Eyes rounded, the American blurted, "But one of your people said you had some connection to them. I'm sorry if I misunderstood." He rose to go.

Fergus sat up, placing the white snap-brimmed hat he'd picked up at the Straw Market on his balding head. "Hold your horses, young man. Michael Kraken put you onto me, didn't he? Always one for the jokes, our Michael. I take it you must be an American police officer."

"Richmond P.D.," he answered. "That's in Virginia. I was promoted to detective sergeant in '78," he added with a touch of pride.

"Just last year, was it? Well," Fergus relented, "I *might* have had a tenuous connection to the Fab Four, but it'll cost you a drink to hear it. Would that set international relations aright for you, Sergeant—?"

"—Paxton," the American responded, smiling now. "Josh Paxton. Call me Josh."

"Call me Fergus, Josh, and fetch me a G and T, would you? There's a good lad."

Josh frowned his incomprehension.

"Gin and tonic," the Englishman explained. "Twist of lime, if you don't mind."

"Wait a minute." Josh hesitated, eyes narrowing. "I'm not springing for drinks without knowing what I'm paying for."

"Good man," Fergus congratulated him. "You've the makings of a chief inspector, you have." He paused for effect, then asked, "Heard of Maxwell and his little silver hammer, have you?"

"Sure," Josh replied, "who hasn't? *Abbey Road*. Great album. So?"

"So were you aware that the song was based on an actual case of multiple murder?"

"You're joking."

Removing his sunglasses, Fergus answered, "No, I'm not. I am—or rather *was*—Police Constable Thirty-one. Now do I get that G and T or not?"

It took a moment for the coin to drop. "PC Thirty-one," Josh breathed, and was off like a shot for the cabana bar.

Ten minutes later, they were settling in with their drinks— Fergus with a sweating glass of gin, Josh with a bottle of Kalik, the local beer. Pulling on his flower-patterned shirt to cover his pinking belly, Fergus took a long sip of his drink and lit a cigarette. "Shall we begin?"

"All ears," Josh replied, sitting on the edge of his seat.

"You already know how I came into the story, thanks to that bloody song."

"You caught a dirty one."

"So I did, but the song is just that, mind you—a song. The *facts* in the case of Maxwell Edison were another thing altogether. The murders happened in '67, and the bloody song didn't come out until '69. After that, the constabulary had to retire my number—thanks to your Beatles. Every call I responded to, I was greeted with, 'Oh, look, it's PC Thirty-one! Have you caught a dirty one, Thirty-one?'" Fergus blew out a stream of smoke worthy of a dragon. "They had to assign me to desk duty until they got permission to issue me a new shield number. But I'm getting ahead of myself."

"There really *was* a Maxwell Edison?" said Josh in a daze.

"Oh, he was real enough, him and his little hammer," Fergus assured him, stubbing out his cigarette....

The hilarious Michael Kraken and I were on patrol, Dalrymple began, *when the first body was discovered—a bludgeoning victim—and off we went, as fast as our little clunker would take us, blue light whirling, klaxon wailing. We were often called out to the university to quash the antics of the more boisterous of the hippies and bolshies that stank it up, and our arrival was heralded with the usual jeers and obscene gestures from the student body. The greeting from the chancellor, who appeared a trifle pale and unsteady, was no more cheering.*

"There's been murder done!" he cried. "Professor Clayborne's been battered to death! Oh, poor Tessie...poor, poor girl. Come quickly! The provost and the custodian who found her are guarding her classroom's doorway."

Michael—who you may've noticed is the size of a Cumbrian bull and about as intelligent—forged a path through the curious and unwashed students, as the chancellor directed the way to the art room, where the deceased lay in situ.

"Wait," Josh interrupted. "Wasn't Maxwell a medical student?"

Dalrymple shook his head ponderously. "You can't believe every lyric that makes it into the Top Ten, my friend. Maxwell Edison was about as bright as my partner—he wouldn't have known a shin bone from a thigh bone—though he did demonstrate a fondness for skulls."

Josh deflated a little.

"There, there," the older officer murmured, "we've hardly begun, have we?" He took another sip of his gin....

The victim had been attacked from behind, and her head was a bloody mess. There was no obvious weapon left at the scene— though it being an art studio, there were various instruments and objects about that could've done the job.

Scrawled on the chalkboard in blood were the words "Mum did it."

Michael and meself were securing the scene for the chief inspector when a young woman approached us, wishing to give a statement.

Stacy Forrester, an art student, had attended the deceased in-structor's last class and, prior to dismissal, had witnessed some-thing of a scene.

"It was one of the other students, Maxwell Edison," she ex-plained. "Normally, he's a quiet lad—good looking, too. Tall, with blond hair and blue eyes—summer sky blue, I'd say, al-most robin's-egg blue...."

"Blue, yes, I see. But what happened?*"*

"Well, Professor Clayborne stopped to look at something Maxwell was drawing," she continued. "I heard her gasp and looked up in time to see her go quite pale. Before I could regis-ter what was happening, Max was balling up the sketch and looking as if he might cry. He seemed so young, like a child. 'Don't look at me!' he cried, and Professor Clayborne asked him to stay after class to discuss the matter."

I looked about the room, thinking Mister Edison might have discarded the drawing, but found nothing.

"What was the lad wearing?" I asked.

"He didn't dress like the rest of us," she replied, smiling down at her pin-striped bell bottoms and fringed vest. "He wore heavy-looking black shoes and woolen trousers with a jacket to match. He even had on a tie with a collared shirt—rather frayed, I think."

"Did he have an overcoat or mackintosh?" I was thinking of all that blood.

"Yes, he always hangs up a mac as he comes into class. It must've been white once, but it's rather gray and stained now."

I glanced at the empty coat pegs to the right of the classroom door.

About then, DCI John Patterson and his people swept in, and I informed him of Miss Forrester's statement and the de-scription of a possible—nay, likely—suspect. Granting me a job well done, he had me telephone the description in for broadcast.

He wasn't long about his business, and as his sergeant had called in sick with flu that day, he seconded me to drive him to

Edison's last known address—which I'd obtained from the school's bursar while the DCI conferred with the medical officer.

With Michael stuffed into the back seat of the Rover, we trundled along to a neighborhood of moldering pre-war bungalows. The address in question was a two-story affair with a low brick wall surrounding it, crowded round by untended fruit trees. Rotted apples buzzing with late-season hornets littered the lawn. I sent the stalwart Michael to the back, in case our quarry bolted in that direction.

DCI Patterson led the way to the front door. Old school, he was. Bowler hat, military mustache, driving gloves. Must've been six foot six in his stocking feet. He directed me to ring the bell, which I did—several times. The door finally opened.

"Yes?" this old biddy snaps at us. "What do you want?"

Gray as the weather, she was, looked to be in her sixties, wearing a high-collared dress, a pearl necklace, her hair gathered into a bun.

Unfazed, DCI Patterson tugged at the brim of his hat and, holding up his warrant card, introduced us. "Are you perchance Missus Edison?"

"I am not," she replied. "My name is Esme Pennyworth. I am not married, nor have I ever been."

Mulling this unhelpful tidbit over, the guv'nor replied, "Does a Maxwell Edison reside here with you, Miss Pennyworth?"

The starch went out of her, and she sagged a bit, the hard line of her mouth going soft, her eyes fearful. "Why? Why do you ask?"

"Is he in?" Patterson went on. "We'd like to speak with him about an incident at the university."

"What's he supposed to have done?" She clutched the doorframe as if to support herself. "He's not come home. Has he been hurt?"

"Not that we're aware of, Miss Pennyworth," Patterson answered. "Let's take this inside, shall we? Perhaps you can help us locate the boy? You do want him found, don't you?"

As she led us into the house, the guv'nor gave me a nod, so I peeled off to search the premises, which were as dark and musty as the outside. Our head-bashing suspect was nowhere to be found, but I noticed a tablet with scribblings and drawings on it as I passed the phone. In the center of this ad hoc art was a name: Joan. I also noted a framed photograph of a woman and a boy beside the phone. The woman wasn't Miss Pennyworth, though there was a slight resemblance. The picture reminded me more of someone I'd recently seen.

Tearing off the page and taking the photo, I proceeded into the parlor, where DCI Patterson was having a natter with the lady of the house. As I walked in, she was dabbing at her eyes with a piece of lace that must've once been a kerchief. He glanced at me, and I shook my head.

"He's my sister's boy," she was explaining. "She died, so I took him in after—after his confinement. This was about two years ago, and he's never been any trouble—so quiet and polite. He's like a child, Chief Inspector."

"Yet you were fearful when you met us at the door. What were you expecting?"

"I—I was afraid he might've done something like, like—he was just a little boy, and my sister's husband was a nasty brute of a man and abusive of her and the lad. From a child's point of view, it's almost understandable what occurred. He couldn't have comprehended the result of his actions—he was only ten years old!"

"What had he done?" Patterson asked.

"I thought you must know," she resumed. "He killed his father as he was upholstering a chair in the garden shed. Nigel—my sister's husband—was kneeling to examine some detail when Maxwell seized the tack hammer from the workbench and struck him several blows to the back of the head."

"I recall the case now, Madam," Patterson responded without turning a hair. "Not one I worked, and I'd forgotten the lad's name. His mother discovered the body and phoned the police, is that correct?"

"Not exactly. She only became aware of what had happened when she heard two girls from the neighboring houses screaming their heads off. They'd come over to play with Maxwell and discovered the horror in the shed. Lavinia—that's my late sister's name—told me all this afterward."

"Is this her?" I interrupted, holding out the photo. She nodded, and I showed it to DCI Patterson.

"That's your nephew, I take it, next to her?" he asked.

"Yes. He was packed off to Newsham Park's psychiatric wing after the legal formalities were completed. Since my sister had removed herself to Spain, it was left to me to visit Maxwell regularly. When it was finally decided that he could be released, I brought him home here." She took a deep breath and, squaring her shoulders, said, "Now please tell me what you think he's done. I must know."

"It's necessary that we rule him out as a suspect in a murder, I'm afraid. Can you tell us where he might be found? Is there anyone he would turn to besides yourself?"

The old girl turned even grayer at this news. "Dear God," she breathed, "he's been such a lamb. Even those five years in Newsham, never a complaint from the staff—the nurses adored him."

"Madam?" the guv'nor persisted.

I held out the page with the name and number. "Someone named Joan, perhaps?"

"That girl," she responded. "He speaks of her often. I've never met her, don't even know her last name. Poor boy met her at the university and has taken quite a fancy to her. I suspect she's led him on as a bit of fun—she must know Maxwell's...simple, inexperienced in such matters."

"Do you know her address, Miss Pennyworth?"

Even as she shook her head, I was ringing up the exchange to match the number with a full name and address.

After rescuing Michael, who was being chased about by hornets in the back garden, we were on our way to the flat of a Miss Joan Scattergood.

"Good work there, Constable Dalrymple—that phone-pad bit," DCI Patterson murmured as we beetled along through the wet congested streets.

"Glad to be of service, Guv'nor."

As if matters weren't grim enough, the morning's mist had turned into a lashing rain. We were soaked by the time we dashed from the car to the council flat Miss Scattergood resided in. Her place was on the third floor, with an exposed walkway, leaking gutters, cracked and stained concrete. The residents had done their bit by decorating the place with discarded crisp packets, cigarette ends, and lager cans.

As we approached the flat, the door next to it opened a crack, and a spidery-looking bloke stuck his head out. "You lads here for the ruckus next door?"

"What kind of ruckus?" I asked.

"Some fella was shouting and cursing to beat the band, and then there was a crash and all went quiet. A young woman—I wouldn't call her a lady—lives there, and I never heard a peep out of her."

"Has anyone come or gone since?"

"How would I know? I'm not a bloody curtain twitcher."

"I'll take that as a no," I said, and we moved on to Joan's door.

Finding it unlocked, I directed Michael to throw it open. The girl appeared almost peaceful: she lay on the sofa, one arm thrown back, a syringe lying next to the other—which was bruised by previous injections. The coroner would later determine she had died of what the junkies call a hot shot—an accidental overdose.

Her pusher lay on the shabby carpet, in the same position as the murdered art teacher, his head coshed in. Beside his body stood Maxwell Edison, shoulders slumped, looking sad and lost. "He hurt our Joan," he said softly.

He was just as described—a good-looking boy, if one disregarded the blood and gore splattered across his face and mac. It appeared that he'd arrived on the scene just in time to witness

Joan's drug-dealing friend administer the lethal dose.

Taking the hammer from him without the least resistance, I asked, "Where did you acquire this, Maxwell?"

As Michael cuffed him up, the boy replied, "It's from art class—a tack hammer like Pa used for his upholstery work. We use it for nailing canvas, you see. I was going to return it, once I'd given it a wash-up." Butter wouldn't melt.

Searching the young murderer's pockets, I retrieved a wadded piece of paper and, unfolding it, discovered the drawing that had presumably led to the slaying of the art teacher. The subject matter, though unquestionably violent, was puzzling. Even so, our case was rock-solid. So with our killer in hand and the chief inspector beaming like the sun revealed, off we went to HQ to book our catch.

The following morning, we were scheduled to appear for magistrate's court, the Right Honorable Judge Barbara Guffman presiding. Insofar as I was concerned, this would be a typical hearing to determine whether the accused should be bound over for trial.

Liverpool's first female magistrate was not known to suffer fools gladly, so I was surprised to find the upper galleries filled with unruly students. Such proceedings are sparsely attended, as a rule, but we had failed to take into account the interest the arrest of a student might have for these would-be scholars. It was the 'Sixties, of course—peace, love, and beer bottles hurled at coppers.

When Her Righteousness was announced, however, her bewigged and black-gowned presence served to silence the murmurings of unrest.

Settling herself in, she nodded that the hearing should begin, and I was called to testify as to the facts in the case of M. Edison. Taking my place in the witness box at the judge's right hand, I was duly sworn in by the bailiff and began my narrative. As I was describing the lurid scene we had found at the university, two young women began to shout from the upper gallery that Maxwell had been wrongly accused. Within mo-

ments, the other students joined in, and the court descended into chaos.

Demanding order be restored, Judge Guffman sent the bailiff to quell the uprising. Seizing the moment and surprising his guard, Maxwell leapt lightly as a panther from his position in the accused's box. With a second bound, he was atop the Crown Prosecutor's table, scattering lawbooks and papers and clambering up to the judge's bench.

Snatching up a legal tome that must've weighed a stone, he hoisted it over his head and was in the act of bringing it down on hers when I finally broke out of my shock and acted. Diving over the cowering judge, I caught Maxwell at thigh-level— rugby style—and bore him backward into the arms of several court officers, the book flying from his fingers and the lot of us ending up in a scrum.

The courtroom was cleared, and Maxwell was sent to a cell. Michael, meanwhile, had bagged the two birds—Rose Hutchings and Valerie Sherbow—but the rest of their chums had fled the scene.

What a sight they made: Rose in her quilted Mao jacket and red-starred cap, dear little Valerie wearing a black beret like bloody Che Whatever-His-Name-Was.

The guv'nor gave me the nod to do the interviews and make out the charges. With Michael taking notes, I began by saying, "Well, you two have certainly stepped in it. Care to explain?"

"Maxwell's not responsible," Rose declared, staring me down through her tinted granny glasses. "You don't have to be Sigmund Freud to see that."

"I'm not required to be Sigmund Freud, Miss Hutchings—I'll leave that to the medical set. It's only necessary that I establish there's enough evidence of a crime to make an arrest, and I can assure you there's ample evidence in this case. So, besides rabble-rousing, what's your interest here?"

"Maxwell's done his time," Valerie piped up. "Whatever he's done now is a result of the injustice in the system! He's innocent!"

"And how the devil would you know?"

"We know Maxwell, have done all his life—until he was sent to Newsham Psychiatric," Rose jumped back in. *"We tried to tell the police what happened, but no one would listen to two little girls, would they? They told us to run along home and not talk nonsense. Male chauvinist pigs, the lot of them!"*

It dawned on me then that I must be speaking with Maxwell's childhood playmates.

"Was it you two who chanced upon the scene of the elder Mister Edison's murder?" I asked, leaning onto my elbows.

"Too right we are," Valerie replied, *"for all the good it did poor Maxwell."*

I thought of the perplexing drawing that had led to the death of Professor Clayborne, and of her resemblance to Maxwell's mother, and of the cryptic words scrawled on the chalkboard.

"What did you see that day?"

They looked one to the other, then Rose spoke for them both. *"We'd often play dolls with Maxwell, as he enjoyed being father and was ever so gentle. Much like his own father, it seemed to us. Mister Edison was a kindly and soft-spoken man, with all the patience in the world for Maxwell despite his...slowness. In fact, he was teaching him the upholstery trade, and Maxwell quite enjoyed it. Whenever the shed wasn't in use, however, we were allowed to play there with our dolls, it being almost like a proper little house to us."*

"You never saw any evidence of Mister Edison abusing the boy or his mother? Never heard him shouting, being belligerent, threatening?"

"Never," Rose insisted. *"They kept to themselves—perhaps because of Maxwell—but Mister Edison was gentle as a lamb. It was the missus did all the shouting. We once saw her slap Mister Edison's face, cursing him a blue streak. She didn't know we were watching from the shed. He often had bruises and black eyes, which he chalked up to carelessness."*

"She always smelled funny, too," Valerie chimed in. *"We didn't realize what it was at the time, of course, but she reeked*

of alcohol. I suspect that may've had something to do with Maxwell's condition."

"What exactly did you see that day?"

Valerie took up the narrative. "Rose and I met in the lane that ran behind the houses and went into the Edison garden by the back gate. Hearing some commotion in the shed, we peeked in its little window just in time to see Missus Edison standing over the body of her husband. She was wearing his old mac, her face red and shiny with sweat, the silver tack hammer clutched in one crimsoned fist. Fortunately for us, she didn't look up. Instead, she turned to Maxwell, who was standing in the shadows, his face pale and blank, tears in his eyes."

Valerie put a fist to her mouth and sobbed, and Rose continued the story: "We saw Missus Edison take Maxwell's hand and place the hammer in it. She said something we couldn't hear, and then did something to his face that we were blocked from seeing by her body. As she turned away, we ducked down so as not to be seen, and the next thing we knew she came flying out of the shed and into the house, stripping off the bloody mackintosh as she went."

Rose took a steadying breath. "Once she'd gone, we went in to Maxwell—and that's when we started screaming. It wasn't because of what we'd seen, as I don't think we properly understood what had happened—it was because Maxwell's little face was smeared with blood. We thought she'd hurt him. As we screamed, Missus Edison returned, drying her hands with a dishcloth. Hissing at us to be quiet, she told us not to touch anything and to get out of the shed at once, as the police had been called. We did as she bid, of course, thinking we could tell the police everything we'd seen. Well, you know how that turned out."

Taking the drawing from my pocket, I placed it before them. It was a workmanlike sketch depicting the very scene they'd just described from the perspective of a ten-year-old boy. Now I understood: Professor Clayborne had been an unfortunate substitute for Maxwell's mother, and the drug dealer who'd killed Joan Scattergood—well, I guess Maxwell wasn't going to let

David Dean

another *injustice go unavenged, now, was he? As for his at-
tempt on the magistrate, she'd directed her ire at the only two
friends he'd ever had. In for a penny, in for a pound, I reckon.*

*After briefing DSI Patterson on the matter, I asked that we
delay charging the Gallery Gals—as they might be useful in further enquiries—and re-interviewed Miss Pennyworth. In light of
the surprising disclosures of the day, I thought it worthwhile to
ask exactly how Missus Edison had died and where. And the
answers to those questions—along with my saving of Judge
Guffman from a bashing—were the making of me.*

*The only evidence Miss Pennyworth could produce of Lavin-
ia Edison's death was a letter from some acquaintance of her
sister's here in the Bahamas. She'd kept a copy and allowed me
to read it. It was clearly in a man's handwriting and offered little more than that Lavinia—much beloved in the short time
she'd been allowed amongst her expat friends—had succumbed
to a heart attack, no doubt brought on by the loss and suffering
she'd endured prior to her arrival. Her final wish was to be in-
terred in the last place she'd known some little happiness. No
death certificate was included, nor so much as a local obituary
clipping.*

*With Miss Pennyworth's permission, I had a copy made of
the photo I'd noted on my previous visit and sent it along to our
embassy here, along with a request that a death certificate for
Missus Edison be located and produced.*

*No such certificate could be found. What was located, how-
ever, was Lavinia herself, alive and well and soaking up the
Caribbean sun with her new husband, the same scoundrel who'd
written Esme Pennyworth the news of her sister's demise.*

*Lavinia Edison had received a tidy sum from an insurance
policy she'd taken out on her first husband's life and left her
only child to bear the brunt of her actions. As Mister Edison's
death had appeared to be such an open-and-shut affair, she had
been paid off without much fuss. The faking of her own death
was simply to avoid any further scrutiny. It was a pleasure to
engineer her extradition and see her face judge and jury.*

Though we had no direct evidence of Lavinia's guilt, we did have sufficient circumstantial evidence to make a case: the recent insurance policy, and Rose and Valerie having seen her place the bloodied hammer in Maxwell's hand. The faking of her death also invited speculation.

Lastly, but not unimportantly, there was Maxwell's drawing, as well as his scribbled "Mum did it" on the chalkboard in the art classroom. He may have had the mind of a child, but juries believe children, you see, and they believed Maxwell and the girls.

Sadly, hanging had been suspended just a few years before, so the jurors were left only the pleasure of meting out a life sentence for our murderess. Within a month of being lodged in Her Majesty's Prison, though, Lavinia managed to do herself in.

"And what happened to Maxwell?" asked Josh Paxton.

"Back to the asylum, I'm afraid. He'd killed two people the day of his arrest—that was indisputable. Even so"—Fergus finished his drink—"I can't help but pity the lad."

Perking up, he added, "The affair put me into the detective division and onto the fast track for promotion. I made detective chief inspector in record time, even got to meet the queen."

"You met the Queen of England?"

"A command performance, old son! The year after the Edison case, I was placed on the Honors List for Her Majesty's Police Medal, which she duly pinned on my narrow chest."

"What was she like?"

"Well, as I was one of a hundred chosen for honors that year, she'd only a moment for me. 'Good work, PC Thirty-one,' says she. 'Well done, you.'

"I must say," he concluded, grinning widely, "she seemed like a pretty nice girl."

Let It Be
Released May 1970

"Two of Us"
"Dig a Pony"
"Across the Universe"
"I Me Mine"
"Dig It"
"Let It Be"
"Maggie May"
"I've Got a Feeling"
"One After 909"
"The Long and Winding Road"
"For You Blue"
"Get Back"

"I Me Mine" and "For You Blue" are by George Harrison.
"Dig It" is by John Lennon, Paul McCartney,
George Harrison, and Richard Starkey.
"Maggie Mae" is traditional.
All other songs are by John Lennon and Paul McCartney.

The Long and Winding Road
Marilyn Todd

Millie's earliest memories were of dolls: rocking them, dressing them, feeding them tiny cups of pretend tea and miniature plastic cakes.

But dolls weren't the real deal. What she *wanted* was a little brother she could teach to read and swim. Someone to skate with, blow bubbles in the park with.

Oh, and sisters. Lots and *lots* of sisters, who she could cover with glitter, and go to ballet lessons with, and paint their nails like you see on television.

Not that Millie fancied ballet lessons in *any* shape or form. She simply wanted some living, breathing troops to take care of. She would hug them—oh, how she'd hug them!—and hide Easter eggs for them to find in the garden, and make real tea and cakes for them, and build them the most amazing dreams.

Sadly, her own dream never came true.

At five years of age, Millie didn't understand the concept of black ice. Of a car skidding out of control and crushing two pedestrians against a wall.

All she knew was that Daddy was never coming home, and that Mummy would be in a wheelchair for a long, long, long, long time.

And that any hope of siblings had burst, like those imaginary bubbles in the park.

* * *

Time passed, though Millie's maternal instinct remained. Right through school, through university, she leaned into pushchairs, tickled babies' cheeks, complimented mothers on how lucky they were.

And now, at long last, here she was on a wild and windy night, with Mac clutching the ultrasound beside her on the passenger seat and her stomach churning with excitement.

"Can't wait to see Mum's face when she finds out she's going to be a gran!" she said, for at least the tenth time during the hour they'd been driving.

Mac was the love of Millie's life, and Mum adored him, too. And the icing on the cake was that he craved kids every bit as much as she did. Oh, what a family they'd have! The fun that lay ahead!

Windscreen wipers going nineteen to the dozen, Millie turned into the estate—to see flashing blue lights and police tape blocking their way forward.

"What's all this, then?" she said.

"You been speeding on your crutches, Mum?" teased Mac. "Playing Thin Lizzy too loud for the neighbors?"

"Cops catch you smoking weed?" Millie giggled, joining in the game of speculation.

They were still grinning when a tight-faced officer waved them over and told them they weren't allowed any farther.

Millie's smile dropped. She'd been down this road before, a long, long time ago. Was history repeating itself, this time without the black ice?

Ahead, they saw scenes-of-crime officers traipsing in and out of Mum's front door.

There's never an easy way to break bad news—though God knows DCI Caldwell was used to it by now. All the same, the sight of this young woman on her knees, clutching her stomach to protect her unborn child, almost broke his heart.

"How—?" The husband had his arms wrapped around her and looked up at Caldwell dazedly. "How did she—?"

"Too soon to tell," the DCI replied. That was a lie, but a well-intended one. They'd find out soon enough that Deborah Ann Edwards, known locally as Debs, had been attacked from behind and strangled. He thought it was best to let the shock settle before notifying them that Debs' death hadn't been any-where close to instantaneous.

"Who found her?" the daughter managed to gasp through her sobs.

"The couple upstairs."

"Paul and Linda?"

"The McGears, that's right."

"Ohmygod, they'll be distraught, poor things."

Amazing, Caldwell thought. *Her mum's dead, and she's wor-ried about the impact on the neighbors.*

"Can I see her? *Please?*"

That *please* would stay with Caldwell for the rest of his life.

"Why?" Millie wailed, when her mother's body had been taken to the morgue and, at Caldwell's request, she'd done an inven-tory of the flat. "It wasn't robbery: there's cash in the kitchen drawer, her bank card's in her purse, and her rings are in the jewelry box in the bedroom."

"Her pain meds are missing," Caldwell said.

"God, how did I miss that?"

"Debs always keeps them close at hand," Mac said, then re-phrased the verb tense. "Kept."

"Given that she was well-liked and doesn't seem to have had any enemies or been in debt to anyone, we assume an addict saw her coming out of the pharmacy and followed her home. There's no sign of forced entry, so—"

"She always leaves the front door unlocked, except at night."

"If Forensics can find prints," the DCI said, "we're hopeful they'll be in the system."

While patrolmen knocked door-to-door and Forensics sifted through wheelie bins and dumpsters in search of discarded packaging to print, Caldwell went upstairs to interview the couple who'd found the body. Another sodding awful job.

"Who is it?" a male voice responded to his knock.

"Detective Chief Inspector Caldwell, sir. Armsgrove Police."

"Can I see some identification?"

Why on Earth, Caldwell thought, *would anyone be impersonating a police officer at a time like this? But there was a killer in their building, so they've got every right to be scared.*

He held up his warrant card to the peephole.

"How do I know that's not fake?"

"I'm with PC Farr, who took your details earlier."

It had been PC Farr who'd responded to the call and found Linda McGear, ashen and shaking, kneeling beside the body in prayer while the husband performed CPR. And now Caldwell was about to ask them to rake over the trauma.

"Mister McGear, I—"

"Paul. Call me Paul. This is my wife Linda."

The first thing he noticed when the door swung open was how young they were. He'd expected a middle-aged couple, but the McGears were in their early twenties. The second thing he noticed was the many pictures of Jesus on their living-room walls.

"I'm sorry to have to ask you this," he began, "but—"

"She was just lying there on the floor!" the woman interrupted.

"We thought she might still be alive," her husband added.

"We couldn't untie the cord around her—her neck in time to save her."

"It was the Lord's will," Paul McGear murmured, hands clasped in prayer.

Caldwell reassured the couple that it was highly unlikely the killer would return, but their swollen red eyes and jumpy nerves told him their faith was fading, despite all their "I am the resurrection and the life."

An hour later, Caldwell left—even more depressed than when he'd first knocked. The McGears hadn't seen anyone who didn't belong in the neighborhood. No strangers, no kids hanging about, nothing out of the ordinary or out of place.

Bugger.

Though she hadn't been confined to a wheelchair, Debs Edwards *had* been mostly housebound, except for her brief excursions to the shops and the pharmacy. While many women in their forties would have wallowed in self-pity, she wasn't one of them. She loved her cozy ground-floor apartment in a quiet corner of the estate, had set up a feeder outside the lounge window so she could watch the constant blizzard of finches and the antics of the gray squirrels that scampered around.

Unfortunately, finches and squirrels don't talk, so they couldn't give Caldwell any more information than he'd gotten from the McGears.

His examination of Debs' body had revealed no defensive injuries. Did that mean she'd known her killer? Did he know her habits? Had he been watching her, waiting for an opportunity to strike?

Strangulation is no simple matter. It takes strength—and, more importantly, it takes *time*. There was no suggestion that the McGears had interrupted the murderer's work, so why leave behind the money, the bank card, and the rings? Was he so exhausted—or so repulsed—by the act of murder that he merely grabbed the pills he'd come for and scarpered, without searching the house?

The callousness of the crime made Caldwell sick to his stomach, but at least the possibility that Debs had been stalked was a lead to follow up on, and for that he was grateful.

You can talk all you want about abnormal numbers of chromosomes or embryos that don't develop properly.

But when you come right down to it, her mother's murder was the reason Millie lost the baby.

Paul and Linda would have undoubtedly told her, had she asked, that her miscarriage was God's will. But Millie knew better. She was an unfit daughter, and that would have made her an equally unfit mother.

If she'd been a better daughter, she'd have insisted Mum keep her door locked at all times, because not everyone was as honest as she was.

If she'd been a better daughter, she'd have bought Mum a smart phone to make opening and locking the damn door easier. And one of those doorbell cameras, too, so Mum could check who was there before she let them in.

Mac held her, night after night, mopping up her pools of tears.

"This wasn't your fault," he whispered, over and over. "Not your mum, and not the baby."

Oh, but it was, it was, it was....

Time passed, but there was no news about the investigation. Weeks drifted by, and Millie was desperate for answers.

"We're going through the neighborhood's CCTV footage again," DCI Caldwell told her when she phoned. "I'm hoping fresh eyes might pick up on someone who may have followed your mother home. We're canvassing house-to-house again, too. People sometimes remember things they didn't think of when they were first interviewed."

He remained hopeful, he said.

* * *

A month after finding their friend's body, Paul and Linda McGear moved away. Whether or not they'd found their faith again was uncertain.

They weren't the only residents unsettled by the senseless act of violence in their community. The whole area erupted in protests and pickets, some ugly, all demanding better security from the Council in the form of more CCTV, higher fences, and a faster response from the police when things went sideways. In their minds, Debs' murder was proof that petty theft and vandalism were the thin end of the wedge. Someone ought to *do* something about the use of drugs on the estate....

Millie's phone calls to the DCI slipped to once a month. Mac talked her into seeing a therapist—and, to her surprise, that helped. For one thing, it put an end to her blaming herself for her mother's death. It also allowed her to grieve for the baby she'd lost.

A year passed, and then another, with no news, no leads, no nothing.

Eventually, DCI Caldwell retired. His replacement was no less enthusiastic about the investigation, but like her predecessor she had nothing to work on.

No one said out loud that the case would never be solved, but deep in their hearts, everyone knew it.

No matter how hard Millie and Mac tried—and you'll never know the many ways they tried!—she simply couldn't get pregnant again. But they had each other, that was the main thing, and they slowly came to terms with being childless.

Work kept them occupied. Mac rose to become the youngest-ever CEO of his firm at thirty-five, and Millie was appointed commercial director of *her* company, responsible for overseeing the management of offices, retail spaces and storage facilities nationwide.

They sold the house where they'd decorated a nursery for the child they'd lost and moved to a nicer, larger home.

"We're going to New York," Millie announced.

Her PA jerked up from his notes. "I can be packed in five minutes."

"You wish! Mac's fortieth birthday is coming up, and I thought I'd surprise him with a bite of the Big Apple. Can you book two tickets?"

"Just two? Because you'll be needing a tour guide—"

"Out!"

"—an eager beaver to chauffeur you around, carry your bags—"

"Out, out, out!"

She was still laughing when the phone rang.

"Millie? It's Bryan Caldwell."

"Who?" But then the penny dropped. "How's the quiet life suiting you, Bryan? Must be, what, five years since you retired?"

"Six. I took a job working security at the docks, so no, not that quiet. Look"—his tone changed—"I'm obviously no longer officially involved, but I wanted it to be me who—"

"You've found him? You found the bastard?"

"Not me, but yes. The police finally know who murdered your mother." He paused. "You might want to sit down for this."

"What kind of monster kills for no other reason than the enjoyment of watching other people suffer?" Millie demanded.

"And how could it have taken *sixteen* years to track down the sadistic piece of fill-in-the-blank?"

"Serial killers are notoriously hard to catch," ex-DCI Caldwell explained. "Especially if they keep on the move."

Millie had watched a lot of true-crime documentaries over the years, had listened to a lot of podcasts, and she was well aware of the complexity of tracking such villains.

"How many women has he killed?"

"Honest answer? We have no idea. Probably never will know for sure." He cleared his throat. "The thing is, Millie, it wasn't just women, and the victims were chosen randomly—in London, the Home Counties...anywhere, really. Men, women, young, old, drug addicts, prostitutes—there was no common denominator, other than the fact that they were people whose absence wouldn't raise eyebrows. And to complicate matters, the method wasn't consistent. Sometimes a hammer, sometimes a garrot, sometimes a knife."

"But Mum—"

"I know, and that's what threw us. Your mother didn't fit the pattern. She wasn't homeless and didn't live on the edge of society. She was well-known, well-liked—loved, even—and she would most definitely be missed. But—and I'm sorry, Millie, I know this is hard—but that's exactly why she was chosen. Killing strangers was no longer enough of a thrill for them. They needed more, and—"

Millie barely heard the torrent of words that followed.

Them? What did he mean, *them?* All along, the police had been convinced that Debs' murderer was himself a junkie, *one* man working alone and after her pain meds.

"Sorry, I—I didn't catch that. Could you repeat it?"

"I was saying that there was no link between any of the murders. But cold-case investigators test for DNA regularly, and your mother's murderers—well, they finally got sloppy."

Murderers. And *they* again.

Plural.

"I wanted you to hear it from me first," Caldwell said. "It's been a long and winding road to bring these killers to justice, Millie, but the nightmare is finally over."

Momentous news is not something you want to share over the phone. Mac was at a conference in Manchester when Bryan Caldwell dropped his bombshell and not due home until that evening, but Millie had waited sixteen years for this moment, so what was another six hours?

And while she waited, she received another piece of welcome news.

"The worst part," she said, when she was once again safe in her husband's arms, "was that no one ever even *suspected* Paul and Linda."

Those monsters in sheep's clothing had hidden in plain sight, adopting mild-mannered church-going personas and befriending a defenseless disabled woman. Sitting at her mother's table, drinking coffee and eating the cakes she'd baked, playing cards with her while the birds and squirrels frolicked outside her window. From anyone else, all that would have counted as kindness.

For those two, though, it had been foreplay.

Yes, their eyes had been red and swollen—from laughing about what they'd done. Yes, they'd been jumpy with nerves—at the prospect of being caught.

"But I have something else to tell you," Millie said, and now the waterworks were flowing again—only this time they were tears of happiness. "I'm pregnant, Mac! We're going to have a baby!"

His face lit up. "Yeah?"

"Yeah."

"*Yeah?*"

"*Yeah!*"

ACKNOWLEDGMENTS

My thanks to the authors who enthusiastically contributed stories, to Eric Campbell and Lance Wright at Down and Out Books for greenlighting my sixth "inspired by" anthology, to my wife Laurie Pachter and daughter Rebecca Jones as always and for always...and, most of all, to John, Paul, George, and Ringo, the Fab Four, whose words and music have traveled with me (and often guided me) down the long and winding road of my life...

ABOUT THE CONTRIBUTORS

ANJILI BABBAR is a writer, professor, and scholar. Her new book—*Finders: Justice, Faith, and Identity in Irish Crime Fiction*—is an extensive survey of Irish crime writers and the ways in which they subvert literary traditions and genre conventions. With "Hey Bulldog," she turns her attention from nonfiction to fiction.

MICHAEL BRACKEN is the Edgar- and Shamus-nominated, Derringer-winning author of some twelve hundred short stories, several of which have been selected for inclusion in both *The Best American Mystery Stories* and *The Best Mystery Stories of the Year*. He is also the editor of *Black Cat Mystery Magazine* and numerous anthologies, including the Anthony-nominated *The Eyes of Texas*. He lives and works in Texas. *CrimeFictionWriter.com*

PAUL CHARLES, born and raised in the Northern Irish countryside, is the author of eleven books in the Detective Inspector Christy Kennedy series, most recently *Departing Shadows*. Charles may be unique in that, not only was he *around* for the 1960s, but he also *remembers* the decade vividly, as seen in his latest publication, *The Essential Beatles Book*. He is currently working on *The Return of the James Gang*, a new DI Kennedy mystery. *PaulCharlesBooks.com*

JOHN COPENHAVER's historical crime novel *Dodging and Burning* won the 2019 Macavity Award for Best First Mystery, and his second novel, *The Savage Kind*, won the 2021 Lambda Literary Award for Best LGBTQ Mystery. He cohosts the *House of Mystery Radio Show* and for years wrote a crime-fiction review column for Lambda Literary. He's a founding member and vice president of Queer Crime Writers, a faculty mentor in the University of Nebraska's Low-Residency MFA program, and he teaches at VCU in Richmond, VA. *Hall of Mirrors*, a sequel to *The Savage Kind*, is forthcoming. *JohnCopenhaver.com*

DAVID DEAN is a prolific author of short crime fiction. His stories have been finalists for the Shamus, Barry, Derringer, and Edgar Awards, have received *Ellery Queen's Mystery Magazine*'s Readers Award twice, and have been included in *The Best American Mystery Stories*. Genius Books recently published three Dean collections—*Tomorrow's Dead and Other Stories of Crime and* Suspense, *The Wisdom of Serpents and Other Stories of Tragic Misunderstandings*, and *Her Terrible Beauty and Other Tales of Terror and the Supernatural*—and a fourth volume is forthcoming.

MARTIN EDWARDS is the author of twenty-two crime novels, including the Harry Devlin, Lake District, and Rachel Savernake series. He has written many short stories for EQMM and anthologies. His non-fiction books include *The Golden Age of Murder* and *The Life of Crime: Detecting the History of Mysteries and Their Creators*, a history of the genre. He is a former chair of the CWA, consultant to the British Library's Crime Classics, and current president of the Detection Club. He has received the CWA Diamond Dagger, Short Story Dagger, and Dagger in the Library awards, plus other honors including an Edgar, an Agatha, and two Macavitys. *MartinEdwardsBooks.com*

KATE ELLIS is the author of twenty-six novels featuring archaeology graduate DI Wesley Peterson, five supernatural crime novels featuring DI Joe Plantagenet, and a trilogy set in the aftermath of the First World War featuring Scotland Yard detective DI Albert Lincoln. She has twice been shortlisted for the Crime Writers Association's Dagger Award for best short story, and in 2019 she received the CWA's Dagger in the Library Award.
KateEllis.co.uk

JOHN M. FLOYD has contributed more than a thousand short stories to EQMM, *Alfred Hitchcock's Mystery Magazine*, *Strand Magazine*, *The Saturday Evening Post*, four year's-best anthologies, and many other publications. A former Air Force captain and IBM systems engineer, he is an Edgar finalist, a Shamus Award winner, a five-time Derringer Award winner, a three-time Pushcart Prize nominee, and the author of nine collections. In 2018, he received the Short Mystery Fiction Society's Golden Derringer for Lifetime Achievement.
JohnMFloyd.com

VASEEM KHAN is the author of two award-winning crime series set in India. His debut, *The Unexpected Inheritance of Inspector Chopra*, was selected by the *Sunday Times* as one of the forty best crime novels published between 2015 and 2020. In 2021, *Midnight at Malabar House*, set in 1950s Bombay, won the CWA's Historical Dagger. His latest novel is *Death of a Lesser God*. Born in England, Khan spent a decade working in India.
VaseemKhan.com

ROBERT LOPRESTI is a retired librarian who lives in the Pacific Northwest. More than ninety of his short stories have appeared in leading mystery magazines (and four anthologies edited by Josh Pachter). He has won the Black Orchid Novella Award and three Derringer Awards. His most recent novel,

Greenfellas, is a comic caper about the Mafia trying to save the environment.
RobLopresti.com

DRU ANN LOVE is the proprietor of the blog *dru's book musings,* which includes not only reviews of crime fiction but also the popular "A Day in My Life," "Get to Know You," and "A Word With the Author" features. She has been a Fan Guest of Honor at the Malice Domestic, Left Coast Crime, and Bouchercon conferences, and a two-time finalist for Bouchercon's Anthony Award. In 2017, the Mystery Writers of America honored her with its Raven Award for outstanding achievement in the mystery field outside the realm of creative writing. "Ticket to Ride" is her first venture *inside* the realm of creative writing.
DrusBookMusing.com

TOM MEAD is a UK author whose work has appeared in EQMM, AHMM, and numerous other places; his story "Heatwave" was included in *The Best Mystery Stories of the Year 2021,* edited by Lee Child. He is a member of the CWA and the International Thriller Writers. *Death and the Conjuror,* his debut novel, was an international bestseller and was named one of the best mysteries of 2022 by *Publishers Weekly.* The sequel, *The Murder Wheel,* was published by Mysterious Press (US) and Head of Zeus (UK) in 2023.
TomMeadAuthor.com

JOSH PACHTER was the 2020 recipient of the SMFS's Golden Derringer for Lifetime Achievement. His stories appear in EQMM, AHMM, BCMM, *Mystery Magazine, Mystery Tribune,* and elsewhere. He edits anthologies (including Anthony Award finalists *The Beat of Black Wings: Crime Fiction Inspired by the Songs of Joni Mitchell* and *Paranoia Blues: Crime* Fiction Inspired by the Songs of Paul Simon) and translates

fiction and nonfiction from multiple languages—mainly Dutch—into English.
JoshPachter.com

CHRISTINE POULSON, after a career as an academic with a Ph.D. in art history, turned to crime writing. She is the author of three Cassandra James mysteries set in Cambridge and three thrillers featuring medical researcher Katie Flanagan, most recently *An Air That Kills*. Her short stories have been published in EQMM, *The Mammoth Book of Best British Mysteries* and elsewhere, and have been short-listed for various awards, including the Margery Allingham Prize, the CWA Short Story Dagger, and the SMFS's Derringer Award.
ChristinePoulson.co.uk

KAL SMAGH is the author of *Larceny in Liverpool, Mayhem for Her Majesty*, and three more titles in the Cozy Beatles Mystery series, which follows Helen Spencer as she rises from Beatles Fan Club helper to amateur sleuth and all-around fixer for the Fab Four. Raised in Colorado, he now makes his home in Atlanta.

MARILYN TODD was born in London but now lives on a French hilltop, surrounded by vineyards, châteaux and woods. She is the award-winning author of twenty historical thrillers, more than a hundred short stories (many of which have appeared in EQMM), and three story collections (most recently *Burning Desire*, published by Untreed Reads). A fourth collection, *Desperate House Wines*, is forthcoming.
MarilynTodd.com

JOSEPH S. WALKER lives in Indiana and teaches college literature and composition courses. His short fiction has appeared in AHMM, EQMM, *Mystery Weekly, Guilty Crime Story Magazine, Tough, Mystery Tribune*, and other magazines and

anthologies, including *The Mysterious Bookshop Presents the Best Mystery Stories of the Year*. He has been nominated for the Edgar and Derringer awards and has won the Bill Crider Prize for Short Fiction. He also won the Al Blanchard Award in 2019 and 2021.
JSWalkerAuthor.com

KRISTOPHER ZGORSKI is the founder of and sole reviewer at the *BOLO Books* blog. In 2018, he received the MWA's Raven Award for "outstanding achievement in the mystery field outside the realm of creative writing" and his blog was nominated for the Anthony Award. He writes a regular column on digital crime-fiction resources for EQMM and has served on the board of directors for Malice Domestic. "Ticket to Ride" is his first published fiction.
BoloBooks.com

On the following pages are a few
more great titles from the
Down & Out Books publishing family.

For a complete list of books and to
sign up for our newsletter,
go to DownAndOutBooks.com.

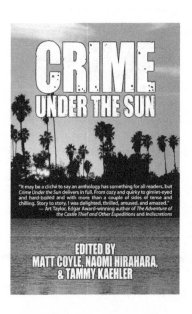

Crime Under the Sun
A Sisters in Crime Anthology
Edited by Matt Coyle, Naomi Hirahara
and Tammy Kaehler

Down & Out Books
July 2023
978-1-64396-322-8

In *Crime Under the Sun*, the second anthology offered by Partners in Crime, the San Diego chapter of Sisters in Crime, fifteen stories capture the hopes and dreams of characters trying to live the idyllic SoCal life. Instead, they bump up against greed, treachery, corruption, and murder.

These stories will thrill readers with unexpected twists and turns and surprise endings.

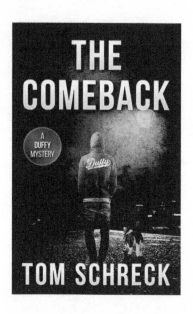

The Comeback
A Duffy Mystery
Tom Schreck

Down & Out Books
August 2023
978-1-64396-326-6

After almost a decade, our social-working, pro-boxing, Schlitz-drinking, basset hound-loving, bleeding heart tough guy, Duffy, has no idea what he's in for. His world literally blows up with a new gig, a career shift, another hound and, though he's still spending most of the time in AJ's, now it is from the other side of the bar.

On the trail to get even for a friend, he's up against the Chicago Mob, the city's toughest street gang and a crooked doctor preying on the addicted.

Killin' Time in San Diego
Bouchercon Anthology 2023
Holly West, Editor

Down & Out Books
August 2023
978-1-64396-328-0

Welcome to San Diego, where the perpetual sunshine blurs the line between good and evil, and sin and redemption are two sides of the same golden coin.

Killin' Time in San Diego is a gripping anthology featuring twenty of today's best crime and mystery writers and published in conjunction with Bouchercon 2023.

From the haunted hallways of the Hotel del Coronado to the tranquil gardens of Balboa Park, from the opulent estates of La Jolla to the bustling Gaslamp Quarter, *Killin' Time in San Diego* is your ticket to the hidden side of "America's Finest City."

Prohibition Peepers
Private Eyes During the Noble Experiment
Michael Bracken, Editor

Down & Out Books
September 2023
978-1-64396-337-2

The 18th Amendment created prohibition, which banned manufacture, transportation, and sale of intoxicating liquors and gave rise to bootlegging and gang violence. During the 1920s and early 1930s, private investigators were there working both sides of the law.

The hardboiled and fast-paced tales in *Prohibition Peepers*—written by today's hottest crime fiction writers—will have you reaching for your own highball glass of bathtub gin.